Will
Rew

By Colin Childs

CRUCIAN PUBLISHING
2024

© Colin Childs 2024

All rights reserved. No part of this publication may be reproduced, stored in a retrieval system, or transmitted, in any form or by any means without the prior written permission of the publisher, nor be otherwise circulated in any form of binding or cover other than that in which it is published and without a similar condition including this condition being imposed on the subsequent purchaser.

Published in Great Britain by Crucian Publishing.
Set in Palatino Linotype 10.5 point
Cover image by Fabio Sanna
ISBN: 9798338476499

For Enikő

Chapter One

Itching To Get Out

The mole, wrapped warmly in an ancestral moleskin pelt, was slumped in his armchair and dreaming of hot pursuit. His whiskers twitched as he saw the rump end of his quarry escape from view again. How long had he chased her at the tail end of the season, to no avail? He began to stir, his eyelids flickered then opened, closed, and reopened. A shaft of sunlight flooded the earthen floor of his den, warming his feet –

'Half-past April' he muttered, in surprised disbelief.
Just as spring's sunlight had awoken his father, his grandfather, and all his ancestors right back to the illustrious Mole of lore, whose pelt he bore, spring, so very long in its arrival, always came as a surprise. On one day only did the sun's rays penetrate the long passageway to his inner sanctum.

The mole shifted in his seat, yawned, stretched, blinked in the brightness, and promptly grimaced. His paw went to his groin and although he knew better than to scratch, he couldn't help himself. 'Oh, not again' he hissed through gritted teeth.

Fishing in his pocket, he brought out his spectacles, spectacles that were his best yet and fashioned from fragments of glass, the bottom of bottles he had chanced upon during the mating season. Barbed wire encircled the glass with the barbs acting to anchor the spectacles in the deep fur of his head. Warily, he turned his attention upon his smarting todger and sighed heavily at the sight. It resembled a poisonous mushroom, bright red with white spots – 'Fly Amanita, that its name', he recollected, bitterly.

He thumped the arm of his armchair with his free paw, but then brightened as he reflected 'what does it matter now? Season's over in any case.' With that reassuring thought, he made his way up, up, upward, toward the light of day.

It was always a little discombobulating initially, being wholly above ground for the first time in months. There was the brightness of course and the sun's heat to contend with, not forgetting his mother's warning – 'Moles that don't look up, quickly go down.' The mole now scanned the sky; what a boon these spectacles are, he considered; he was the only mole he knew of with ingenuity to make them. Hawks didn't stand an earthly.

His attentions now turned to his field, his patch, and he marvelled not only at the number of mounds created, but at the plethora of ridges that zigzagged crazily as far as his eyes could see.

'No wonder I'm shagged out', he mouthed. He bent to examine a mound – 'one of mine'– he declared, noting with pride his trademark swirl at the mound's peak.   'Hello, hello, who's this then?' Bending down to sniff a molehill, not of his own, he was met with the fragrance he had been chasing for weeks.

'Next year my girl, next year.' He muttered, determinedly. Still, the mole savoured the scent and breathed it in deeply and, for an instant, the heady perfume made his head swim. This was of an order he had not encountered before. Exotic was the word that sprang to mind.

Straightening with difficulty, for his back was playing him up, his smarting todger then insisted that a balm be found. Skirting the hedgerows, he went in search of stinging nettles for, nearby, dock leaves were sure to be found. Having found a couple of leaves, he was now in search of a sapling Willow to strip; the bark would act as a tie. The mole reckoned the riverside to be his best bet and, as he rounded the end of the hedgerow, a panorama opened before him.

The valley lay below with its little braid of silver threading through it, the river. Memories of that river, his own recent adventures, and the stories passed down generations, flooded back.

And so, it was with renewed vigour that the mole scurried downhill toward its banks. Now was he filled with the joys of spring, aches, and pains were forgotten, and his nose, his most reliable organ, took in the blackthorn, honeysuckle and the, oh, so delicate, primrose.

He found his sapling willow, stripped off the bark and sat by the river's edge to bandage his less-than-fragrant todger. The coolness of the dock leaf, still wet from the morning dew, provided an instant balm. The mole sighed with relief and looked up dreamily at billowing, white clouds sailing by. Turning his gaze back on the river he started, his back stiffened rigid and adrenalin coursed through him. He couldn't move, he was petrified. At the river's edge, two wet, black eyes held him transfixed. The head, of whatever animal this was, poked above the water's surface. The animal's nostrils flared as it sniffed audibly.

'Fuck me, you don't half pong mate! said the animal, jocularly.

The mole, less than reassured, remained silent.

'Mixture of fear, mole… and yes if I'm not mistaken, gone off fungus. Yuk!'

Still, the mole had not the courage to speak, although he felt his back relax a little.

'I ain't interested in you, am I? Bleedin 'ell, I'd rather starve.'

Hesitantly, the mole made to speak, but the animal beat him to it, yet not before belching loudly-

'Fer fuck's sake that bream just won't go down – slimy bastard...you was about to say something?'

Stutteringly the mole asked 'What...are you? I mean what kind of...?

The animal looked offended. 'Not you un all'. It turned to look ruefully downstream.

'What is it around 'ere? Anybody would fink I dropped in from the sky fer Pan's sake.'

'I didn't mean to offend, far from it...it's just that I've never seen...never seen a you.'

The animal rolled its eyes.

'Well, you ain't no river-banker I suppose. I sunshine, I am an otter.'

'Well, I'm very pleased to meet you Mr. Otter'. The mole replied, ingratiatingly, not quite having conquered his fear. The animal laughed.

'Mr. Otter? I've got me whole family in 'ere. What you gonna call em? Listen, call me Reg.'

The mole looked baffled, all the animals he knew were simply known as Rat, Badger, Fox, Hare and so forth.

'Wot they call you then?'

The mole looked puzzled.

'Yer name mush?' Reg, the otter, pressed. 'Look, you ain't the only mole about 'ere are yer?'

As no answer was forthcoming, Reg fished up a name. 'Brian, I'll call yer Brian. You've gotta 'ave a moniker, incha?'

The mole, anxious to please, agreed to the name, even though he'd never heard of it.

The pair then fell into a conversation, although this was a little one-sided as the mole's description of his territory, where he had lived his whole life, was quickly exhausted.

Reg made the running, and it was immediately apparent that he was unhappy with his current situation.

'Fuckers dumped me in 'ere didn't they? Not so much as a by-your-leave. Me and the missus, we was unceremoniously dumped. Then wot 'appens? She gets up the duff and we're stuck.'

The mole, unsure who *they* could be, simply punctuated Reg's diatribe with – 'reallys' and 'oh dears' as Reg, well into his stride, carried on.

'I mean to fink that we once dined on salmon, trout, crayfish, and the like. If push came to shove, we had grayling at least, but in 'ere? Chub? Rubbery, bony fuckers-Roach? You need dozens to feed a family and as for bream…' Reg belched again and went on.

'And don't get me started on the turds; when it rains they all shit in the water, it's a fuckin' disgrace that's wot it is.' Reg angled his head, cocked it to one side to listen.

'That's the missus. Listen Brian, I'll catch you around.' With that Reg slipped beneath the surface with barely a ripple and was gone.

The mole sat in bemused silence for a while, he wondered if all otters were as coarse as Reg. The last time he had heard such vulgarity was when he was in the woods with the badger. 'Ignore them Mole, they don't know any better'. The mole's attention was then caught by a Heron on the opposing bank.

'We don't talk with him,' the bird said imperiously, indicating downstream with her long beak. 'Greed is so unbecoming in an animal. One simply takes what one needs and leaves the rest for others. Barely a fish left in the river since *his* arrival…and his rabble,' the heron concluded disdainfully. She fixed the mole with a stare, and then took to the wing.

Some animals seem to have got out of bed on the wrong side, thought the mole. Such a beautiful spring day and all I hear are gripes and groans. It wasn't like this last year...or was it? He was unsure of the answer. Memory plays tricks.

A nudge in the shoulder had him spin about in alarm, but oh, how quickly it fell away, for his nostrils filled with the very fragrance he had been chasing for weeks. Coming now into focus, was the object of his dreams.

'Hey you. Catch you at last,' said the newcomer with an impish grin. Mole, once again tongue-tied, felt a crimson flush invade his cheeks.

'*Ooh la la*! You chase me all the season, and now you have nothing to say?'

The mole's first impression of Taupe, for she was a French mole, was that she was uncommonly attractive, not beautiful in the classical sense, but glamorous. His second, that she had the strangest accent he had ever heard. Next, that her ancestral coat was a vivid green, suffused with perfume. There reigned an aura of mystery about her. The mole, in two seconds flat, was smitten.

'Brian,' said Mole, extending his large paw formally.

'*Quoi?*' shot the disbelieving response. '*Mais, ce n'est pas possible!*' What? But that's not possible.

An uncomprehending Brian simply hunched his shoulders in response and was quite taken aback when two paws clamped him firmly and kisses were planted either side of his muzzle.

'Taupe, they call me Taupe, zat is French for Mole. Brian? Your mother call you that? It mean king of course, which is quite nice I suppose, *mais*...'

'No, no, Reg just named me that. Really? It means king?' Replied Brian, encouraged.

'Reg? Who is zis Reg?'

'Oh, just an otter, you know,' Brian replied nonchalantly, hoping to sound worldly.

The pair fell into an easy conversation and Brian found himself quite at ease as he expanded on the virtues of spectacles and their manufacture. He let Taupe try them on. He was too much of a gentleman to comment on how his beer-bottle lens occluded Taupe's eyes. He was all too conscious of his own; he was sure that one of his eyeballs was circulating clockwise whilst the other orbited in the opposing direction. Certainly, Taupe was in raptures with the spectacles.

'*C'est incroyable* – I can see the other side!' She shouted excitedly as she stared across the river. 'Oh Brian…yes, I will call you this, for only a king mole can be clever enough to make these *lunettes*, they are *formidable*!'

Brian, puffed-up with pride, then went on to make an utter arse of himself on several occasions during the ensuing conversation. Yet it didn't appear to matter one jot, save for a few quizzical looks from Taupe that went unnoticed by him. Taupe's green pelt turned out to be not just a fashion accessory, as Brian had thought, but an essential piece of survival kit.

She threw herself on the ground and in a coquettish voice said 'Moley, oh Moley, if you find me, I have somesing for you!'

Without his glasses, Taupe still wore them, Brian felt an idiot in not locating her quicker than he did. She had rolled into the long, grass, pulled the pelt coat over her head and drawn her legs up into it. It was only when Brian fell over her, something he did deliberately as he had spotted her outline when close, that he received his little something, another kiss.

'You see, in my country, we have some very big birds. Zis is called camouflage. *C'est bon, n'est pas?'*

Lying next to this heavenly vision, and looking upward at the scudding clouds, Brian's one regret was that it was half-past April. Taupe then rested her head upon his chest and Brian truly felt like a king. Somewhat less so however when Taupe began to sniff audibly.

'Hmnn...Moley, is there somesing you need to tell me?' she asked, pointedly.

If Brian's face had flooded crimson when Taupe first kissed him, then it turned scarlet now. Obfuscation, his initial recourse, proved hopeless and he was powerless to prevent Taupe from getting to the root cause. As she removed his dock-leaf bandaging, he was buoyed by two thoughts, firstly that she was concerned– 'need to tell me'– surely this hinted that sex, at some point in the future, was a possibility; secondly that due to the malady, his todger had swelled to twice its usual size.

Chamomile in conjunction with sage was Taupe's prescription and she returned with both in a matter of minutes. She then tended expertly to, a still mightily embarrassed, Brian. Her jocular, bedside manner put him at ease and, if it were possible, she endeared herself even more to her love-struck patient.

'Bloody-fucking glad I tunnel faster than you, ' she joked. And that was it, this was spring, this was love and new beginnings. Brian was in raptures.

He walked the banks in a daze. She had gone as quickly as she had come and yet he knew he would see her again, if only to reclaim his spectacles.

Some minutes later, Brian chanced upon a small raft of Mallard ducks. The group of females referred to the male as Rear-Admiral Canard and the name seemed apt as they were evidently dragooned by him. Brian sat unnoticed as the females chatted. He smiled because, whenever the Rear-Admiral plunged his head to eat, the women would make barbed comments at his expense.

Brian caught himself ruminating on the inequities of the mating game. Here he was out of action and with almost a year to wait for his chance with Taupe, whereas ducks always seemed to be at it every ten minutes. This puzzled him greatly and, if anyone could shed light on the matter, then it had to be the Rear-Admiral. Brian coughed to draw his attention.

'I say, Rear-Admiral, why is that we moles have only a moment to mate, while you lucky ducks are at it all summer long?'

The females broke into uproarious laughter at the question, whilst the Rear-Admiral took umbrage.

'Silence in the ranks!' he commanded. He then rose in the water and flapped his wings and for one horrible moment, Brian thought he would fly at him.

'Never, in all my days, have I been asked such an impertinent question! Here is your answer.' To his fleet, he quacked loudly 'come about!' All ducks turned about. 'Present...wait for it, wait for it...present arses!'

In unison, the flotilla went tail-upward and one arse, that of the Rear-Admiral, waved and waggled at Brian for all it was worth.

Affronted, he didn't regard his innocent question as having been impertinent, Brian sauntered further upstream. The late morning sun was beginning to bake the black fur of his head and he made a mental note to fashion a new twig hat that evening. Through the still-growing reeds, he glimpsed a hat he knew well. A straw-boater drifted past accompanied by the sound of oars in rowlocks. Excitedly, Brian rushed to a gap in the reeds to peer, as best he could, (how he now longed for his spectacles) at a rowing boat gliding past. At the oars, he was certain he could distinguish the form of the Rat. But what on earth was that awful smell?

'Rat, Ratty, it's me the mole!' he cried.

There followed a long pause. The rowing had ceased, but no reply came.

'Ratty, is that you? I can't make you out, it's me the mole...you know, the mole, we picnic every year.'

The boat came a little closer and Brian could indeed make out the rat who now took a long drag on what looked to be an outsized cigarette, tipped up his snub snout and exhaled. Once more, Brian was greeted with a waft that he found objectionable.

'Rum days mole. Bad vibes on this river. Got to keep rollicking on my friend,' came the plaintive reply and with that, the rat took up the sculls and went on his way.

Brian walked slowly back to his abode with a strange melange of emotion coursing through him. At one moment a wave of exultation as Taupe passed before his eyes, the next an emptiness in the pit of his stomach at being neglected by his best, his only, riverbank companion. He sighed and hunched his shoulders. Everything will be fine tomorrow, you've just been underground too long, every animal is mad up here, he told himself.

A spray of fry caught Brian's attention as they scattered manically on the river's surface. Old Esox, the pike, hunting his lunch again, he thought, but two brown backs arching from the surface suggested otherwise. Otters, he recognised them now. Old Esox won't be happy about that, he imagined.

He was close to his abode when it happened. Deep in thought, he wandered a few metres out from the hedgerow. A black shadow appeared suddenly at his feet and Brian froze in abject terror. The very next thing he knew was being pulled violently by the arm and falling to the ground, banging his head on the trunk of a tree as he fell. He caught sight of the bird as it batted its powerful wings and ascended, and he gulped at its enormous talons, just before they retracted. He then caught the rough edge of someone's tongue.

'What you do?' screamed Taupe. 'Bloody-fucking idiot! He nearly have you!'

Brian looked up at a face, incandescent with rage.

'I should have let him, you such a cretin. What you think, I am your mother? I can't be here all the time.'

It was some time and some tears later, first shed by Brian and then by Taupe, before the pair made their way tentatively to Brian's abode. It was only after several reviving drams of Brian's distilled root hooch, which Taupe declared *degueulasse* – disgusting – that peace prevailed once more.

Taupe, unused to root-hooch, had drifted into sleep in Brian's old armchair. Brian's heart had grown too large for his ribcage, she had saved his life. And yes, he was indeed a bloody-fucking cretin, a *plouc* – a hick-country-boy – an idiot, and every other insult he could no longer recall, all merited, all warranted, he considered.

Before she had fallen asleep, she had told him that she was pregnant. Only twenty days to go before she gave birth. Brian had offered his spacious caverns to her, they were larger than her own apparently, and the children would all be gone before the summer's end in any case, he estimated.

He was left wondering who the father was, yet as he had no idea of how many children he had sired, he didn't think it his place to enquire.

She had arrived in the 'root ball of a garden tree.' That's all he knew about the mysterious, sleeping beauty before him. Gently, so very gently, he lifted his spectacles from her. He took out his workbox and by the time she awoke, she had a pair of her own. How she delighted in them, and how she had laughed when Brian mentioned distractedly 'Actually, we're all a bit short-sighted in my family.'

'*Tu es un vrai cretin Brian*!' – You are a real cretin, Brian!

Chapter Two

High as a Kite

As was so often the case with Brian, olfaction brought him from his slumber. His twitching whiskers and hunting nose had detected an aroma and he followed it, bleary-eyed, from his bed chamber, down a narrow tunnel, to the kitchen. He was used to the scent of wild garlic, but unused to it playing any part in his cuisine. Standing at the hollowed-out stone filled with embers of charcoal stood Taupe, skillet in paw, as she expertly tossed her morning staple, *Lumbricina a l'ail* - earthworms in garlic - with an accoutrement of *larves de guêpes* - wasp grubs.

Mole quickly formed a mound of earth to sit upon, having ceded his chair to Taupe at his table for one. This was a novelty for an animal used to his own company and he did his best to overcome his habitual morning reticence. Certainly, Taupe had flash-fried the worms to perfection. They were still writhing, yet had not the wherewithal to escape the plate. The pungency of wild garlic took some getting used to. However, he was pleasantly surprised by the taste, it was not as he had imagined.

Breakfast over, Brian planted a tender kiss upon his newfound love's muzzle. They had slept the night together and enjoyed the warmth of each other's bodies. He had had trouble getting off to sleep. As a confirmed bachelor, he had never shared a bed before. Taupe, seemingly more accustomed to the arrangement, had drifted off in an instant. She smiled at him now and then indicated his still bandaged todger.

'I keep some garlic leaves for your *zizi*. We must change today.'

It was a blissful, if not slightly embarrassed, Brian who reclined in his armchair as his personal doctor attended to him. Blissful, as he liked being made a fuss of, embarrassed because the chamomile and sage had worked their magic and reduced the swelling considerably. The wild garlic leaves smarted causing him to cry out in pain and his eyes watered profusely. Taupe looked up in satisfaction.

'*Bon, ca marche bien alors*' - Good, that's working well then.

There then followed a discussion about the laying-in. Taupe stated that she would have to return to her tunnels, as childbirth needs must be a solitary affair. After all, this was Brian's abode, and she didn't feel comfortable in excluding him from his own home. In a surge of gallantry, Brian said he wouldn't hear of it and declared he would spend the next month or so with his old friend the water-rat.

It was decided upon, and Brian swelled with pride as he was hugged at his tunnel entrance with the teasing suggestion that, next year, it might be him who would be first choice in the mating game. Taupe tapped him firmly on the chest and reminded him:

'*Faites attention toi, n'oubliez-pas a regarder le ciel.*'- Be careful you, don't forget to look at the sky.

Brian made a solemn promise to be more careful and to underline the point, he now scanned the skies. Looking up he was taken aback, whatever was that? Drifting high above the treeline was an enormous round object, beneath which hung what looked to be a basket.

'What in Pan's name is that?' he asked, incredulously.
Taupe scurried off to fetch her newly made spectacles.

'Ah, c'est une Montgolfière,' she declared, and for a moment or two seemed lost in her own thoughts. Brian was none the wiser and had to press further.

'But what is it, this golfee...whatsits name?'

'Vraiment, t'es nul Brian'- Really, you are rubbish Brian.

The explanation that it was a balloon held aloft with hot air both puzzled and fascinated Brian. However, not wishing to be accused of being a parochial country boy again, he replied. 'Oh, of course, I knew that...just forgotten that's all,' he said airily.

Taupe watched him go shaking her head and smiling as he went. She returned to the inner sanctum cursing her spontaneity, once again she had acted on impulse, and once more had she failed to think things through. This muddies the waters, she told herself. Still, he's an adorable little chap, clever too, in his own way. He hadn't asked what the symbols on the balloon meant, she supposed him to be illiterate.

'Wild World - A Better Life for All'. Above the slogan a huge letter M was emblazoned and picked out in green.

Taupe sat in Brian's old armchair and thought back on yesterday's near miss with the Red Kite. She surprised herself by praying that her little mole would now be a sensible boy.

Brian was indeed cautious that morning as he made his way down to the river. He had to cross some open ground at the end of the hedgerow, and he was not about to do so while a large hawk wheeled high above ground. Ordinarily he would make a smart dash for it, after all the bird was so high that he'd have time, yet the thought of the preceding day brought him out in palpitations. How close had he come to meeting his maker? In all his six years he had never had such a close scrape, not even when a fox had poked his head into his tunnel. That fox had received a powerful blow on his snout from his cast-iron skillet and thought better of returning.

A skylark twittered high above ground as Brian made his way, skirting the river edge close by the reeds, toward the water-rat's abode. The song of the lark, a full belly, and the thought of new-found love, all cheered him immensely. Life, although at times precarious, was bountiful.

It was then with some alarm that he heard his friend ranting and cursing like a rat possessed. He peered through the reeds to see the water-rat in a transport of rage, dancing about his landing and waving his fist in the air. The object of his ire was splashing and thrashing along the river making quite a commotion. Brian had chanced upon this animal before and knew to take cover.

It was what animals referred to as an Upright. Invariably they spelt trouble. He was surprised and alarmed that the water-rat had not taken cover too. As the Upright splashed off upstream in a graceless panic to remain buoyant, Brian hailed his friend from the opposing bank.

'Rat, I say rat old friend, it's me, the mole. Ahoy there!'

Brian cried out at the top of his voice, pleased with himself that he had remembered the nautical term rat had taught him. But, just as the day before, the water-rat seemed to ignore him. He went back inside his abode and reappeared with a bucket and tipped water into the river. This process he repeated as many as fifteen times cursing and muttering. The water-rat was given to outbursts, so Brian decided to wait until he had calmed down.

As he lay on his back in the still gloriously damp grass, his attention focused on a few white-lipped snails making their way slowly up a reed. He licked his lips and then thought better of it, his belly was full and his mother's parting words on the day he was left to his own devices, resonated: 'Only kill to eat your fill.'

So, he turned his attention to the damsel flies flitting this way and that. A Beautiful Demoiselle of an iridescent blue hovered above him, just as it had done when he lay on the bank with Taupe. A *Libellule,* she had called it and he mouthed the word now, luxuriating in the soft and delicate sound of the word.

A pungent waft broke him from his reverie. There it was again. No need for his acute sense of smell, evidently it came from across the river.

The water-rat took a heavy toke on his joint and paced his still-wet floor, occasioned by the idiot of a swimmer. He was in no mood for company, any animals' company. Nevertheless he did feel a pang of guilt. The little fellow on the opposing bank was a goodly soul and at the very least merited an explanation. Maybe he would finish his joint first, and then scull over.

He propped himself up against the front wall of his cabin and watched the river flow. A breeze had lifted, blowing against the current, raising wavelets that lapped gently on the hull of his boat. This peaceful sound, coupled with the effects of his joint, settled him. Presently, he called out.

'Mole old chap, are you still there?'

The predictable, enthusiastic reply caused the rat to sigh and look down at his feet, he'd rather hoped for no answer. With his joint clenched between his teeth, he threw off the painter, took up the oars, and made his way over.

'Oh, Rat old friend, what a joy to see you again. How long has it been, six months? Yes, it must be all of that. Spring and the summer before us, shall we picnic again this year? So much to catch up on, long days drifting downstream...'

Brian stopped. Evidently, his enthusiasm was not reciprocated. It was a tendency of those who lived solitary lives below ground to gush when an opportunity presented itself and conscious of it, he ceased talking. His friend seemed out of sorts and Brian's look of concern did not go unnoticed.

They reached the landing and clambered out in silence. A cursory wave of the water-rat's paw indicated a chair and Brian sat down with his brawny forearms resting in his lap.

Brian found the ensuing silence excruciating. Not a sound save for the wind in the reeds and the lapping of water. The water-rat sat in a gloomy corner dragging on his reefer, tipping his head back and expelling billows of smoke toward the ceiling. Things were certainly out of joint, thought Brian, dismayed, had it not been for Taupe, then he might just as well have spent the spring below ground. He had waited patiently for the rat to break the monotonous silence, but he could wait no longer.

'Rat, clearly something is bothering you. It's not me, is it?'

The water-rat stubbed the remnant of his joint in a green mussel shell, he had smoked it down to his claws.

'So much has changed Mole, I barely know where to begin,' he replied, dolefully.

Brian made to speak, but the water-rat's raised paw stayed him. The water-rat then took a deep breath and began.

'It would have been at the end of autumn, you'd already gone below by then, when I struck up a friendship with a vole upstream. He lived a good morning's row from here, we met halfway by chance. Turned out that he and I were cut from the same hide, he'd always lived by himself as had I. He had never felt the urge to…engage in the season, nor had I.'

The water-rat looked up to gauge the mole's reaction and finding him showing no surprise, continued.

'Long and short of it was that we developed an affinity, more than that in fact, much more. For a glorious two months before the winter truly set in, we became inseparable, we went everywhere together.'

The water-rat's voice began to catch with emotion and Brian sat forward in his seat with a look of concern.

'Oh, my dear friend...' began Brian. But the rat again stayed him. He swallowed hard and went on.

'It would have been two days before mid-winter. I'd made him a duck-feather blanket and I was going to surprise him with it, but he had gone.'

The rat cleared his throat loudly. 'Everything was upturned in his abode as if there had been a rumpus. His boat was holed and sunk. There was not a trace of him anywhere. It was then that I heard them, laughing, squealing and screeching. I went outside to look and when they caught sight of me, they came running for me. There must have been six of them, they were savage and it was all I could do to jump in my boat and pull for all I was worth. They followed me along the bank shouting. "You're next vole! We'll have you! We'll do for you..." Something like that anyway.'

Brian was perplexed, he couldn't imagine what type of river-banker would behave in such a brutish manner. The water-rat had begun to roll up another joint and was preoccupied, so Brian sat in silence and waited. Joint rolled and lit, the water-rat, who was in evident need to unburden, carried on.

'Mink Mole, ever heard of them?'

 Brian shook his head dumbly.

'They have it in for us voles. I don't understand why, they just do,' he concluded, bitterly.

A confused Brian stated assuredly, 'but you're a rat old friend, a swimming-rat...'

The water-rat blew a cloud of acrid smoke in the mole's direction-

'That Mole is what I thought too, once. I learned so much from my friend, he was worldlier than I.' He sat forward in his chair, adding 'from now on I want you to call me Vole, I am a water-vole...I never was a rat.'

Brian, somewhat surprised, simply hunched his shoulders. 'Ok ratt...I mean vole...err...would Voley do?'

'I hate that!' snapped the vole, sharply.

This angry rebuke stung. Never before had the vole raised his voice with him. Brian was quite sure that his old friend had got it all wrong in any case, voles were annoying little buggers who tried to pinch your winter stores when you were asleep. He sighed and looked to his lap.

'Look, if you must name me, then call me Trevor,' the water-vole said tersely, adding 'that's what the otter calls me anyway. Bloody silly name, but I'm getting used to it.'

Brian brightened. 'You mean Reg? He calls me Brian.'

For the first time that day, there came the trace of a smile on the water-vole's countenance.

'Pleased to meet you, Brian. What do you make of it, the name?' the water-vole replied, trying to suppress a snigger.

'Taupe says it means king. Oh, by the way, she's my new girlfriend...' Brian tailed off, berating himself for being untactful.

The water vole's gloom descended once more, yet he did manage 'I'm pleased for you Brian,' hoping not to sound too disingenuous.

The pair sat in awkward silence and to Brian's unwelcome surprise, he found himself wishing he hadn't come. The highlight of his springtime was to reconnect with his old friend, but here he was being pushed down with sad news and what was more, he had begun to feel light-headed. Not only that but ravenous too.

'I say, voll – Trevor, you don't happen to have any of those excellent potted shrimps, do you?'

His friend of old had always been a gourmet, and Brian's suggestion was intended to cheer him up.

'I'm a vegan' the water-vole replied, offhandedly.

Now, this was all becoming a little too much for Brian, first he's a vole, now he's a *vegan* – whatever one of those is.

'Oh, I see, of course. Well, I'll go and see what I can dig up,' replied Brian abruptly, rising from his seat. No sooner had he done so than he promptly sat back down again with a bump; for some reason he couldn't fathom, his head was swimming.

'You don't understand Brian, do you? Why pretend?' Trevor issued, harshly.

Brian shook his head. Words now failed him, why was his head spinning like this? His brain and mouth were no longer connecting.

'I no longer eat animal. I only eat plant. It has been a revelation to me. I no longer sit for hours trying to digest my food. I don't spend my days belching...and farting as I once did. My friend explained it all. I have always been a water-vole, and I should always have been a vegan.'

Brian had made his excuses but had not got far. Unsteady on his pins, he had made it to the landing stage of the vole's boat, fallen into a chair, and nodded off.

A keen easterly awoke him, and a shiver ran through him. But how could this be? It was dawn and he must have slept the afternoon, evening and night. He was a good sleeper, one of the best, yet over twelve hours was a record, even for him. He had a duck-feather blanket about his shoulders.

From within the water vole's cabin, he could hear the clanging of pots on the stove. Breakfast beckoned, only it didn't. One look at the mushrooms the vole was frying was enough. Those little bell-shaped chappies, Brian had been taught from a young age to steer clear of. Distracted, the vole was tipping a bag full into his pan.

The frown that then knitted Brian's brow was not occasioned by the mushrooms, however, rather it was due to bald patches in his friend's fur. His back was festooned with small, oval bald patches and his pinkish skin made these more apparent. Brian crept back out to the landing, sat down again, and wrapped the blanket around himself.

The sun went in. The wind's gusts bent the reeds, and a sharp April shower had Brian feigning loud yawns. He got up, stamped about the landing to signal that he was abroad, and when he entered, the vole was wearing his dressing gown.

'Care for breakfast, Brian?'

'Err, I'd rather not,' replied Brian casting a glance at the mushrooms and trying to cook up an excuse. 'They err…don't agree with me.'

The water vole hunched his shoulders- 'Suit yourself, I find they help me through the day,' he declared, and added, 'stroke of luck, I found some garlic leaves out back, normally have to scour the hedgerows for those, they'll go well with mushrooms.'

The vole, preoccupied with his breakfast, did not notice Brian's face redden for he had earlier relieved himself of his todger cladding and bursting bladder behind the cabin.

'Err, vol…Trevor, bit awkward, I've been meaning to ask if I might spend a few nights here.'

The vole looked up from his plate. 'Go on.'

'Oh, it's just that I may have acted in haste. I've given my place over to my girlfriend. She's pregnant you see, and we chaps aren't welcome until all is done and dusted. I'd make myself scarce during the daytime of course,' Brian concluded hurriedly, noting the vole's unease.

There followed a moment's silence, which made Brian feel wretched in asking. Presently, the vole looked up from his plate, his eyes had lost their focus.

'Yeah, whatever. If you must.'

Chapter Three

A Mere Truffle

A stout cudgel came to earth and had Jack the Stoat not made a sharp retreat into his den, it would have flattened his nose. His cry of 'cantankerous old twat!' brought down another blow and caused a landslide.

'Oh, thank you!' Jack shouted, sarcastically.

'Who put the lights out? What's going on up there Jack?' came Jill Stoat's shout from further down.

'Guess who's got a crab on...again.' Jack replied, wearily.

The badger was furious and had already accused any animal he encountered of rooting about in his truffle grounds. Not only was the badger inordinately fond of truffles himself but formerly they had served as an aphrodisiac to potential mates. He still presented them every year in small boxes woven from reed with the delicacies seated upon a cushion of the greenest moss. The mind was still willing even if now, his ageing body let him down.

Any animal who had witnessed his jaw hanging slack as he gazed in disbelief at the rooted-up earth about the oaks, would have been well advised to dive for cover.

Dressed in his habitual garb of waxed cotton jacket and brown boots, he was striding about the wood with a face like fury. The woodland animals, save for a few brave, reckless individuals, were all scared of him.

One such brave soul was Fergal Fenian the fox, whose keen nose now sniffed the air. He and his wife Molly were seated at their kitchen table plucking chickens, the spoils of Fergal's sortie the previous evening.

'Can you smell that Moll?'

Molly, whose nose was keener still, sniffed and pulled a face.

'Badger,' she declared, categorically. 'If he's tunnelling about here again,' – Molly drew the poker from her range – 'he'll get this sharp up his exit, so he will.'

There was only one woodland animal Fergal was frightened of, and she was sitting in front of him. Mollifying Molly was no easy task.

'Let's not be hasty dear,' calmed Fergal, standing. 'I'll go and look. He's probably just passing by sure. Smelly old fecker that he is.'

Essential apparatus though it be, a keen snout has its drawbacks. Fear has a peculiar pungency not dissimilar to putrid meat, and every fox instinct is to clamp jaws down hard to put the culprit out of its misery. Confronted, as he was now, with Badger's substantial rump blocking his porchway, Fergal was sorely tempted to clamp down but then thought better of it. This hulk of a creature before him was shaking, and bejabbers, wouldn't this be a story to tell? That at least was Fergal's initial reaction.

Badger, transfixed as he was, did not hear the fox's approach so when Fergal spoke, he practically jumped out of his skin.

'Fox!' – Badger never used first names – 'it's you...I umm...I was just sheltering from the rain.'

'Well, seems 'tis stopped,' said Fergal sniffing the air. 'Out you go now.'

'Just a minute more. Err...black clouds threatening… have to wait,' stuttered Badger.

"Twill be more than black clouds in a minute,' replied Fergal looking anxiously over his shoulder.

'Are you rid of that great lump of lard yet or am I coming to do it?' Molly yelled.

Molly's hearing was as sharp as her tongue.

'He's away soon dear. Just a little business.'

'What business?' Molly replied, suspiciously.

'Away with you now Badger, 'tis my arse that'll get it first,' hissed Fergal under his breath.

'I can't Fer...Fox,' the badger stammered. 'They're after me.'

'Who are?'

As no sensible answer was forthcoming, other than a hint that the danger lay outside, the fox and badger with great difficulty, attempted to squeeze past one another within the narrow confines of the porchway.

'Great hulking feller such as yourself...' Fergal said, trying to hold his breath as he squeezed past. 'Never heard the like of it. It's not Uprights, is it?'

Fergal's eyes bulged and his jaw hung slack. Moments passed before he exclaimed 'feck me fourways! What in the name of savagery is that?'

'You tell me,' the badger replied tremulously. 'I heard them on the other side of the great holly. Knew some animal...something, was at my truffles...thought it was a dog, so I charged through the bush and came face to face...' Badger shuddered at the memory. 'Great horns sprouting from its mouth, horrible, horrible!'

Badger's smell, as much as his tremoring body, disarmed an irate Molly who had arrived with a poker, the tip of which was glowing red. It hissed when she plunged it into the damp earth, albeit perilously close to the badger's exit.

'Tis a pig, ' Molly declared, assuredly.

'I've been about a fair few farmyards Moll and that…oh bejabbers there's another one look!' Fergal began, before being unceremoniously bundled aside by his wife.

'Let me get a better look, get out of my way, useless article that you are,' declared Molly, in no mood for this nonsense which was holding up her cooking.

'For the love of Pan, look at the teeth on the feller…and would you look at the goolies on him too, fair scraping the ground!'

It was agreed that the badger could make his getaway by the bolt tunnel, seldom used but, under the circumstances, the right thing to do. The tunnel led off the kitchen and would be a tight squeeze for the corpulent badger. Molly was not inclined to offer him refreshment however and she ignored Fergal's motions that she should. This was not because she was a hard-hearted animal, far from it, but when it came to the badger, she made an exception.

It was with a deal of huffing, puffing, and panting that Badger made his exit leaving Molly to curse the mess of earth tumbling down behind him onto her kitchen floor. If the gift of refreshment was not on offer, then Badger left his own parting gift, that of a sonorous, rancid fart. Fergal may have imagined it, suffering as he was from its heady affects, yet he later maintained that the fire flared two feet above the cooking range.

Badger's diet, of more or less anything he could scavenge, coupled with copious quantities of home brewed ale was a potent mix. Molly insisted on leaving their front and back doors open for two days despite the cruel easterly wind that whistled through.

In the days that followed, nothing was seen of Badger, and who was it that let on that the old bully was trembling like an infant? Neither Fergal nor Molly would own to it.

Many sightings were made of the newcomers and opinion was divided. A jay complained bitterly that the out-sized, hairy pigs had unearthed her acorn stores. Squirrels were in turmoil due to the arrival of red squirrels – redheads, as they termed them. Some wanted to fight them, others to befriend them; next to the redheads, the Boar's arrival was a secondary issue to tree dwellers. As for those in lairs, burrows, and dens, those small and fleet of foot knew their place in the pecking order. Therefore the arrival of those who could take Badger down a peg or two was to be welcomed.

On day three, the badger awoke on the floor of his sett with a thumping head. Strewn about him were empty beer bottles, picked bones, pips, and the spent shells of eggs and nuts. He had been on a bender. Not since his failed attempt at wooing the widow in the three-league wood had he resorted to such a binge. Greying about the gills, overweight and with a propensity to wind, what chance did he now have with the ladies'– sans truffles?

He tidied himself up as best he could, scrubbing at egg stains on his tweed trousers with a fir cone and combing his fir with a rib cage. He looked himself in the mirror and saw a pale reflection of the woodland king he had once considered himself to be. To cap it all, a chesty cough was now sapping his strength.

Donning his waxed cotton jacket and selecting his two stoutest cudgels, he made for the door. He drained the dregs of a beer bottle for courage and set forth. Fresh air was the thing and to be seen abroad and not cowering in his sett, was more important still. He was all too aware of woodland gossip and given that he only ever held this in check by menace, he was certain that in his absence, he had been the butt of tittle-tattle and jibes.

Yes, he heard sniggers and barbed remarks emanating from burrows in the earthen banks, yes, he was tempted to give them what for, however, today he held himself in check. He had decided to pay the water-rat a visit. Of course, this restraint only served to fuel the rumours circulating that Badger was a quashed force. He was cognisant of it so, as he made his way downward between the narrow, tall earthen banks, he contented himself with expelling a deadly brew of gas that had been fermenting all morning.

If Badger had a friend, and this was questionable, then it was the water-rat. He respected the rat, for he was the only animal he could converse with who possessed a modicum of intelligence. Fox, undoubtedly smart as he was, resented his elevated position in the woodland hierarchy, so no point in talking with him and even less with Madame.

Badger was unsure as to the point of his visit, yet he felt an uncommon need to talk to someone. A maelstrom of emotions clouded his reasoning. Usually, he felt content in his own company, he chose solitude, and indeed revelled in it, it was his natural state. For the past few days however, as he binged his way through every bottle he had, he felt lonely. Whilst other animals would, at a push, exchange a few words in passing, they expressed no warmth toward him.

This, he supposed, was what the term loneliness meant – to be amongst others yet alone. To compound it all he felt a simmering anger. He disliked newcomers, he disliked anything that upset the given order. Wariness was part and parcel of an animal's existence and occasionally there were moments of fear. But a life cannot be lived with an enduring sense of fear, he concluded, and this dread emotion now dogged him.

As he left the wood behind, Badger felt a huge relief sweep over him. Why didn't he visit the open ground more often? He posed this question each time he was under the blue canopy and felt the sun on his back. This was a different country, an open expanse not hemmed in by earthen banks, sullen shade, and tangled briar. Here were heady aromas of a different order. Already he could sense the river and he quickened his step.

Some way on he encountered a mole who, to his surprise, greeted him.

'*Bonjour*, how is it going?'

Badger made to reply but was beaten to it-

'Lovely day *n'est pas*? Suppose I must talk about the weather.'

The mole was the most curious mole Badger had ever encountered, dressed as she was in a green pelt that hugged her figure. Dotted in the fur on her head were primroses, yellow-starred celandine, and purple violets. Upon her snout sat a pair of thick-glassed spectacles. A curious animal indeed and one who now fired a succession of questions in rapid order upon an unsuspecting, taciturn, badger.

'So, what you doing eh, lost? How's it going up there in the wood, it works? Everybody happy? Seen anybody new, eh?'

The badger was at a loss and a little irritated in being quizzed so abruptly. He took a deep breath in preparation to reply, but was again beaten to it.

'*Alors*, I don't 'ave all day,' she said curtly, and promptly moved on.

Badger, now miffed, called out to the departing mole in a derisory tone.

'Your accent madam, where are you from?'

The mole turned in her tracks.

'*La belle France, blaireau*, don't suppose you know where that is?'

Believing that *blaireau* might have constituted an insult, and not merely his name in French, Badger sneered.

'Oh, dear...not your fault I suppose.'

'*Caisse-toi, petit con,*' – fuck-off you little jerk – was entirely lost upon the badger, although the tone of its delivery was not.

'You'd be advised to keep a civil tongue with me madam,' the badger shouted, raising one of his cudgels with menace. The mole turned; she was a good distance off now.

'*Eh oui, blaireau typique*. You are all bully. Even hit the women no doubt.'

And with that, she scurried along only turning once to check that she was not being followed.

'Well, this is a pretty pass,' the badger grumbled. 'Whatever is this place coming to?'

He walked out to the middle of a field from where he could survey the valley below. He leaned on his cudgel, raised his snout in the air, and took a deep breath.

'Ah, England,' he said aloud. He then looked back up the hill to the wood, his home and the home of his ancestors stretching back, for all he knew, to the dawn of history.

The kernel of a plan began to form in his mind and with renewed vigour and spring in his step, he strode down the hill toward the river.

Chapter Four

Mushroom Soup

Reg, the otter, swam out to take a look. He heaved himself up the gunwales and poked his head over the side, and glanced into the bottom of the water vole's boat.

'It ain't no use mate, it really ain't. No use going on like that Trev.'

Reg swam back to the bank to where Trace, his mate, and the two adolescent boys Clamp and Nipper, were sunning themselves. Feeding the boys as babies hadn't always been an enjoyable experience for Trace, hence their names.

'Ain't you gonna bring her in then Reg? The boys will give yer a hand.'

'No point,' Reg replied, matter-of-factly.

'But that's Trevor's boat innit? 'Trace pressed. 'He'll be lost without it.'

'Lost in it more like,' Reg said, resignedly.

Reg went on to explain that Trev was lying in the bottom of his boat, burbling nonsense at the sky.

'Well go and get him then!' Trace said, crossly. 'He's got a fever or somefink.'

'He, my love, ain't got no fever. He's stoned, narcotized, bombed, buzzed, flying fried, smashed, spaced-out, turned-on, turned-off, in short, totally wankered!'

'Oh, I see,' Trace replied, shushing the boys into the water. 'Such a shame, he's a lovely animal. Whatever's up with 'im?'

'Beats me. Got it all he has, lovely gaff, good boat.'

Trace considered for a moment. 'I know we ain't been 'ere long, but you ever see him with a partner? I mean, when's his season then?'

Reg hunched his shoulders. He'd never stopped to give it any thought.

**

The water vole burbled nonsense for many hours, as his boat drifted downstream until it wedged itself, prow first, between the roots of a weeping willow. The gnarled roots, exposed by winter's torrents, reached down from a small island into the water. Riverbankers knew this place as Esox Isle after its most notorious aquatic resident, *Esox Lucius* – the Pike. Old as the river, Esox was the devil incarnate or, a necessary evil, depending on who you spoke with. Those of modest size who had to ply their trade on, or below water, tended toward the former.

Concealed in the depths among the roots and weed, old Esox now inclined his head upward, his mouth opened slightly to display an array of fearsome, backward slanting teeth. A mouth of barbs from which no stranger returns.

He sensed vibrations coming from the shadow above, which told him all he needed to know. Just one slip and the three metres separating him from the surface would be traversed in a split second. Esox was hungry, he had never been hungrier, not since the otters' arrival had he resorted to ducklings and the occasional rat who was foolish enough to take a shortcut across the river. This was a vole, two gulps at best but enough to tide him over for a couple of days. He settled his long, green, yellow-spotted, torpedo-shaped body down to wait. Waiting was all.

The water vole fell silent as night came on, the vivid colours dancing before his eyes intensified due to his magic mushroom binge. In his hallucinogenic state, all connection to reality had evaporated. He fancied he could hear music, discordant music, that repeated the same phrase over and over until he writhed, squirmed, and thrashed his legs.

Three metres down, Esox stirred.

Next, was he speeding through a vortex of spiralling colours, and he twisted his body around and around laughing maniacally. Faces appeared, leered, laughed, and dissipated. Then, the sound began again except this was not music, there was no form, no rhythm, and the water vole squirmed as tritones – devil's intervals, – assailed his ears.

He got up, swaying wildly on his feet, the water beckoned. He watched it swirling in kaleidoscope eddies, the primary colours all around his boat took the form of flowers, vivid against the stark, black water.

With his arms outstretched, he placed a foot on the gunwale, and the boat tipped to the side. He raised himself on one foot and somehow, quite miraculously, placed the other beside it. He was doing the impossible, standing and balancing on the gunwale of the boat.

Three metres down Esox rose just clear of the tangled roots, the eyes at the top of his head were cold and implacable. He waited.

This effort of balance, of maintaining balance, became a joy. It became everything, it was simplicity itself, so when the music began, he barely noticed. It came upon him as might dawn's light and grew slowly in intensity. The vole began to walk about the gunwales as would a tight-rope walker, he did not look down. Around and around, he circled the little craft never once faltering as pipe music filtered through the mist and rippled mellifluously, as might a stream. He was dimly aware of a silvery sheen as the primary colours began to fade away, yet now, the pipe music held him entranced.

He stepped from the boat. He stepped onto the island and before him stood, shimmering in fragmented, scintillating, silvery light, his lost friend. To stand within his body and remain, for how long he would never know, unified him, completed him. Together, if now, as one, they were enveloped in a glistening, diaphanous haze. Then did the mist and the music fade away as softly as it had come. A tremor then ran through him, his senses returned and with all the courage he could muster, he raised his head. Did he capture anything in fading mist, some form, some ethereal presence? He had sensed an other presence, not of this world, he had heard the pan pipes...hadn't he...hadn't he?

The water vole sat and watched the sunrise. The wind had shifted about to the south. He knew this island of course. It was Esox's island and yet, it had once been, if legend had it correctly, a holy isle. He gazed upon the river and a huge, dull silver flank broke the surface and disappeared leaving a swirl of water in its wake. Esox had found breakfast. The water vole shivered and with the utmost care, climbed aboard his craft. He looked for the other oar, there was only one, whatever became of it? He had no memory.

'Just have to scull back upstream,' he muttered aloud. Strangely, this did not put him in a bad mood. He stood in the back of the boat, shoulders set square, and began to work the one oar and scull his way home. A near-empty bag of weed and mushroom he cast over the side. Never again? He was not so sure of that, but today. No.

Quite what had happened to him, he was at a loss to fathom. Evidently, he must have been away with the fairies given that his bag was all but empty. So why, he wondered, did he feel so serene? Why did he feel bolder, stronger? Try as he might, he could not recapture what must have been a dream and with each passing willow, the memory receded back into the mists from whence it had sprung.

Halfway home a small dog-like head popped above the surface followed by another. The water vole knew them both, Nipper and Clamp, and a greater pair of tykes he had never encountered.

'Ere Trev, you all right mush?' shouted Clamp.

'Old man's been worrying 'bout yer,' said Nipper.

'Old girl too 'un all,' added Clamp.

The water vole, who was slowly getting used to Trevor, replied light-heartedly.

'Oh, yes, I'm fine and please tell your mum and dad they have no need to worry on my account. Oh, and thank them for their concern…err mush.'

'Ain't you s'posed to have two of them?' asked Clamp, nodding toward the oar.

'Ideally,' replied Trevor.

'Reckon you was as wasted as a coot and lost it,' said Nipper laughing.

With that, the pair of brawny young scamps plunged and were gone.

Waiting on the riverbank when he finally reached home were two old friends, Brian and surprisingly, the badger. The vole sculled them over to his abode.

Chapter Five

What Sauce

'For Pan's sake, what does it matter? Names are not the issue here Rat,' the badger asserted, hotly. The vole and mole begged to differ. 'If I may, Quincy...' the water-vole ventured tentatively, keeping a weather-eye on his large, volatile acquaintance, '...I consider names to be of the utmost importance.'

Brian, who had been in a frivolous mood all morning, now suppressed a snigger. The discovery that the badger, that redoubtable bulwark of propriety, was named Quincy, tickled him.

'Oh, yes, I quite agree with Trevor-Stan, where would we be without them?' Brian concurred, airily.

The water vole, Trevor, had introduced the vexed question of names. He now felt himself to be an amalgamation of his former self and, his lost friend, Stan. Although he couldn't offer a concrete reason why this should be, he was nevertheless determined to be addressed as Trevor-Stan.

This type of amorphous conversation was not what the practical-minded Badger had come for and it was testing his patience to the limit.

'Now look here Rat, and you too Mole...'

The two animals in question crossed their arms in defiance and turned their heads away; baiting the badger was good sport. Badger stamped his heavy foot crossly.

'What in the name of blazes has got into everyone? Right, right, have it your way. Just what, Brian and Trevor-Stan,' issued the badger sneeringly, 'are we going to do about it?'

Since the water vole's return, the badger had been pacing about the small riverside cabin like a bull in a china shop, inadvertently upsetting the vole's dainty furniture.

'Do sit down Quincy and we'll run through it all again, from the beginning,' Trevor-Stan implored.

'Brian, you start please,' Trevor-Stan requested.

Brian told of his sighting of a *Montgolfiere* and his narrow squeak with an outsized hawk. 'I thought I'd eaten my last worm.' He shuddered at the memory. Then he told of his surprise at meeting with, what was apparently called an otter. Next, he glossed over his encounters with Taupe as his companions had already heard all about her virtues- *ad nauseum*.

The badger, having identified Taupe from the description, had made disparaging remarks. Luckily, Brian was in good humour that morning otherwise he might have taken umbrage. The badger's account of their testy exchange had only endeared Taupe further to Brian and nothing could dissuade him of her charms. The badger had been so disagreeable all morning that he had probably got his just desserts, he concluded.

'Your turn Quincy old chap,' the water vole encouraged, ignoring the scowl that the use of his name provoked.

'I will not, I repeat, will not be evicted from my own wood by a bunch of foreigners!'

The badger reinforced his point by banging his paw down heavily on the arm of the vole's favourite chair.

'My family has owned those truffle grounds since time immemorial, and they will not be plundered on my watch!'

With the badger so hot under the collar, the vole thought better of contesting his claims to the ownership of food resources. Animal etiquette had it that each according to his need was the ethical code to live by. If these newcomers were demonstrating greed, then of course that was wrong. However, the badger's present corpulent state was indicative of hypocrisy.

'Might I ask again Quincy, how you know these animals to be foreigners...as you put it,' Trevor-Stan asked.

'Well of course they are. Not English, are they?' Quincy barked, with a censorial glance directed at Brian.

The water vole was beginning to find the badger's presence irksome, he had yet to mention his own problems with the mink. It was all self, self, self with the badger.

'I mean to say, they've no right to be here, have they? We don't go over there, wherever there is, and steal their food do we? No, no, no, something must be done about this,' the badger stated categorically, adding 'I mean to say, first it's a couple and then they'll breed of course.' He shot another accusatory glance at Brian. 'Then there will be more, you mark my words, and we'll end up being pushed out. No, no, we can't allow that. We'll have to push them out first.'

Brian raised a paw. 'Umm, exactly how would we go about *pushing them* out? I mean, you said they were large animals, oh, and would that go for the otter too? He seems like a decent sort to me.'

The badger sniffed audibly and thought for a moment-

'Where's he from?'

'I'm not sure,' Brian replied, adding 'from a clean river, he said.'

'Does he speak English?' the badger pressed.

'Yes, perfectly...well, after a fashion.'

'Makes no difference,' the badger asserted after a brief pause, adding 'two of them arrived, now there are four of them, next year it'll be eight and on an on. The river hasn't got enough fish. Rat, you know that,' concluded the badger looking expectantly toward the water vole for affirmation, but the stony-faced vole made no reply.

'Blast it all! Trevor-Ann, or whatever you call yourself,' roared the badger; he left his seat and stormed out onto the landing. Brian shrank back into his chair as the large animal brushed past. The water vole said nothing, but walked into his kitchen, took down a box from his shelf and began to roll a joint. Brian joined him in the kitchen.

'I thought you were giving that up.'

'Just the mushrooms old chap, I think we all need to calm down, this is the only way I know how, these days.'

'Perhaps you should make him one too,' Brian suggested, nodding toward the landing.

'He'll calm down in his own good time, he's best left to stew in his own juices.' The vole lit his joint, toked deeply, and offered it to Brian, who took the most tentative of puffs.

'You see,' began the vole, 'old badger never wants anything to change and if there is one certainty in this life, it is change. Animals come and go and I am not saying that I like it because I might be one of those on the way out.' The vole looked down at the smouldering joint and concluded dolefully 'That's just the way of things.'

'If you don't mind me saying, I think you're being a little defeatist,' Brian began. 'You told me that in your ancestors' time, otters lived on this river. Well, now they're back. Who's to say water voles won't return?'

'Mink,' replied the vole forlornly, quickly adding 'not that Stan and I did much to help our cause.' He then wandered out to the landing to placate Quincy, the badger.

So much for spring, Brian thought. Still, he reasoned, his old friend was trying to keep off the mushrooms at least, that was a start. Perhaps there is something I could do to help, perhaps Taupe might have an idea- With this thought in mind, Brian made his excuses and started for home.

**

Ideas rarely troubled Brian and seldom did they coalesce into a plan but when they did, he tended to act impulsively. Quite what possessed him to make such a rash promise he would never know; he fixed the blame firmly on his friend's weed. He'd had no more than a half-hearted puff and yet he was not quite himself and not quite, someone else. If this is what a vegan diet does for you, he thought, then it might be best to steer clear.

He now found himself seated on the riverbank organising a romantic dinner for two, on the water vole's terrace, for an otter couple-

'Trout you say Brian? We're not talking rainbow, are we? Not a patch on the wild brown, different kettle of fish all together.'

'Oh, brown every time I can assure you Reg,' replied Brian, categorically, attempting to conceal his bafflement; he had never heard of such a fish.

'And the crayfish, ain't gonna be the ones in 'ere are they? Me and the missus is sick to the back teeth of 'em. Kids don't know no better 'course. Cor blimey I'd kill for the old white claws, take me and the missus right back that would.'

'Only the very best,' assured Brian with as much certainty as he could muster.

'Then, it's a deal mate! Next sunset you say?' Webbed paw joined clawed, and all was sealed.

Walking homeward, the effects of the weed were beginning to wear off and a worried expression now replaced a gormless grin. Where, in his locale, was he going to find brown trout and white-clawed crayfish and more importantly, what did they even look like?

**

Meanwhile, the badger and water vole had not parted on the best of terms. The vole's assertion that it would be better to attempt to befriend the newcomers rather than evict them, had led to an outburst.

'Where's your fighting spirit man? You're a pale imitation of the rat that took up arms with my forebear. If we don't make a stand here, we shall be swamped!'

'That is an exaggeration, Quincy. Don't you think your concern is more for your stomach than it is for others?'

'Confound it all man, they're my truffles!' The badger stamped his heavy foot so hard that he holed one of the floorboards. 'You'd better row me back over before I lose my temper.'

The water vole did as bid, although he was sorely tempted to refuse. A refusal would have meant a ten mile walk to cross at the nearest bridge for the badger and he was a terrifying prospect when riled. Besides, the badger had a nasty cough, a hangover from winter, he claimed.

'Aren't you supposed to have two of those?' the badger asked, attempting a conciliatory tone.

'I need the other one to mend my floorboard.' The vole replied, acerbically.

'Humphh!' was the response and the crossing was made in silence.

'I intend to hold a meeting,' declared the badger, coming close to capsizing the boat as he got out. 'I'll send a message.'

The vole rested chin in paw as he watched the badger stomp away. He still hadn't mentioned the mink. Perhaps there was something in what the old curmudgeon said, perhaps the cudgel was mightier than the word. He shook his head, he would not betray his principles, not for badger's bloated stomach at least. He yawned, he'd barely slept a wink and needed his bed. All was peaceful as he reclined and drifted into a deep sleep to the accompaniment of a reed warbler, warbling nearby.

**

'What are you doing Brian?' Taupe asked coldly.

Brian, surprised both by Taupe's return and the chill of her delivery, almost jumped out of his pelt. He straightened and felt immediate guilt at having been caught red-pawed rummaging through her belongings, of which, there were many.

'Oh, I err…was just err. Hello,' blabbered Brian. He moved to embrace her, but crossed arms and a tapping foot arrested him.

'You were looking for somesing perhaps?' Taupe asked, inquisitorially.

'No, no just trying to, you know…How do you cook fish?'

'*Quoi?* What you talking of now…Fish? I'm bloody-fucking mole, how I supposed to know? I never eat a fish!' she replied belligerently.

'Of course not, no, I don't think I have either.' The mole stated uncertainly.

'Brian, eezer you know, or you do not know. *Tu dis n'importe quoi* – talking crap – Taupe brushed past toward the kitchen. 'You do know I try to gestate here, I do not have the time for you and your…' forgetting the word, she used the French, *conneries* – bullshit.

Rooting about in a cupboard, Taupe produced a thick tome entitled *Je sais Cuisiner – I know how to Cook*. This she promptly lanced at Brian who caught it with difficulty.

'Every French girl 'as it.' Taupe fixed him sharply. 'You can read *n'est pas?* – feigning casual interest, Brian began to flick through the pages, although he felt his cheeks redden.

'Yes, yes, I'm a bit slow but I can read all right...pretty well actually,' he replied, attempting nonchalance.

'Hmmn...me too, I slow when I 'ave book upside down.' Taupe said facetiously. Brian's face was burning now.

'Just looking at a picture,' he spurted.

Shaking her head, Taupe disappeared into her bed chamber to begin unpacking and carried on the conversation from there.

'Why you cooking fish anyway?'

'We're having a dinner party and I've promised trout,' adding importantly, 'that's a type of fish by the way, only I don't know where to get one.'

'I know what is trout Brian, *merci*,' Taupe replied wearily, then in a raised, censorial voice cried ''Ave you been looking in my knicker box Brian?'

Taupe reappeared to confront the guilty mole who had not been able to help himself.

'I was looking...' he began, searching for a valid excuse, then promptly gave up.

'*Bon, formidable*, first I 'ave idiot, now I 'ave pervert.'

Brian was sent packing with a flea in his ear. However, all was not lost. First, a todger inspection, at Taupe's insistence, gave him cause for hope. He had been scratching it absent-mindedly since his arrival. More garlic leaves required.

Secondly, she had reminded him to scan the sky and thirdly, she advocated a white sauce to disguise the flavour of the fish. 'The trout do not live in zis river,' she assured him.

That she had delivered all the above in a terse voice and that she had yelled 'now bloody fuck-off and leave me gestate!', Brian, being an optimistic soul, took for positives.

After all, romance for a mole did not consist of staring at one another doe-eyed, rather it required an inordinate amount of tunnelling, it was combative and all in the thrill of the chase.

Making his way back downhill toward the river, Brian felt a familiar stirring down below. That's odd, he thought, it's not February. Perhaps all the scratching had induced this tumescence, or was it the thought of Taupe in the skimpy green panties? The swelling soon abated however as another thought followed hard upon.

'Why does she have all those pelts?' he muttered aloud. He had counted seven at least, all differing colours and there were hats to match. More perplexing still were the array of little triangular-shaped flags of varying patterns and colours. He shrugged his shoulders, hugged the hedgerow and the cookery book, which he sincerely hoped the water vole could read, and marched onward.

Smitten though he be, there came upon him a nagging sense of injustice. Hadn't he just been shown the door to his own home? – 'The sauce of it all!' he said aloud and broke into a laugh at his own joke.

Further on, the mole encountered a hedgehog with whom he was on nodding terms.

'Afternoon,' said Brian cheerily, expecting nothing more than a nod in return.

'Aren't you coming then?' the hedgehog quizzed.

'Coming? Coming where?' asked Brian, blankly.

'The meeting, everyone's going, well all wild-wooders anyway'.

The hedgehog described how one of his kinsmen had been obliged to remain in a curl all morning. 'Bruised but unharmed,' the hog looked gravely at Brian, adding 'this time at least. He was pawed all over the lea like a puffball.'

The mole posited that an Upright's cat had most likely gone feral, but this was met with a scoff from the hog. 'It was twice the size of an Upright's cat,' he said soberly.

The mole bid the hog adieu, checked the skies, and hugged the hedgerow, here he was safe – or used to be. It was therefore with some relief that he stood opposite the water-vole's abode and hailed the ferryman.

Chapter Six

A Table for Two

It was late afternoon when a bleary-eyed water vole, somewhat reluctantly, sculled the mole over to his abode. Brian's insistent cries had broken into his boating dream in which, he and Stan were sailing gull-winged – that is to say, boom and mainsail set at right-angle on the starboard side and forward gib billowing out on the port side – with a following wind of course. But this was the stuff of romantic fantasy for a river-vole, a sailing boat was next to useless in the narrow confines of a river. So the vole's fancy soon ebbed away to be replaced by irritating petitions from a mole, named Brian.

'Apologies once again old friend it's just that I did promise…remiss of me not to have asked you first,' Brian said, sheepishly, as he appraised Trevor-Stan of his dinner plan.

Trevor-Stan sighed.

'Better get the rods into the boat, never thought I'd be using one again. Perch might just swing it, as for the white-claw crayfish, we're scuppered there I'm afraid.'

The mole had quickly amassed a small tub of worms and the vole, standing at the back of the boat sculling with his solitary oar, was keeping a beady eye on his companion.

'May I remind you this was your idea and if you eat any more bait, we'll have nothing left to catch a perch with!'

Suitably chastised, the mole put down the tub of worms and did his level best to think of something else.

Casting their swan-quill floats into a likely-looking pool, beneath an overarching alder, the pair settled down to wait.

Brian found angling to be a veritable pleasure, other than when his reputation of being a mole of his word hinged upon a result. They had been at it for more than an hour without as much as a nibble.

Despite angling not being a vegan pursuit, the vole was nevertheless, enjoying himself. He had taken the precaution of not attaching any bait to his hook.

'For some reason I can never fathom Brian, the Upright anglers desert the river at this time of year, so this is the best time to go fishing. They'll be back in mid-summer of course, disrupting everyone...BITE!'

Brian, who had surreptitiously sneaked another worm from the tub as his friend waxed lyrical, grabbed the butt of his disappearing rod just in time. This was not a small fish; this was a mighty fish. The cat-gut line sang and whined under the strain, the old split-cane rod creaked and groaned as the fish, whatever it was, dived and tugged manically in all directions.

'Don't let him get into the roots Brian!' hurled the vole. 'Side-strain mole!' he lanced critically, temporarily forgetting the niceties. 'Now pump and wind….no, no, no let him run, he'll snap the line. Don't wind mole! For Pan's sake! You've let him get under the boat now, get aft – quickly!'

All this conflicting advice had Brian flustered, and, on several occasions, it looked like the fish would get the better of him. His right arm ached, oh, how it ached, he now felt as if he were in mortal combat with a fish likely to weigh as much as he did. But Brian had powerful arms, a season's tunnelling had honed his muscles and finally, the fish broke surface.

'It's a perch, an enormous perch,' cried the water vole excitedly as he slipped the landing net into the water. Sure enough, there it was; this mighty green fish with banded black, vertical stripes, blood-red pectoral fins, and fearsome spikes on its dorsal. With a huge forbidding mouth gaping and gills flaring, it took one look at the landing net and anglers then dived for freedom once more, almost wrenching the rod from Brian's grip. And so began the tussle again, yet the fish was marginally more tired than Brian and resurfaced a spent force.

'Well done old chap, well done!' commended the water vole. 'I couldn't have handled it better myself. Now, you hold him, and I'll get the hook out.'

The perch had one last, parting shot however, as Brian clasped him with his paws, the perch shook violently and impaled his palm with his spiky dorsal fin, and with the razor-sharp point of his gill, he managed to spike his other paw too. Brian yelped in pain.

With the hook removed, the water vole fished in his kit bag for the priest, a short, dense rod. Now was the noble predator to meet his maker.

'You'll have to administer the last rites old chap; this is not a job for a vegan.'

Sculling homeward (this one fish was considered ample for two diners) Brian felt a pang of remorse as he marvelled at the beauty of this once fearsome predator now expired in the bottom of the boat. He wondered at the purest white of its belly and the flame red of the underside fins. The spikes of his great dorsal sail now lay limp, he had hunted his last. Brian examined the puncture marks in his palms and considered them well-merited.

**

'We ain't going empty-handed Reg, don't you know nuffing?' berated Trace Otter.

'Wot we 'sposed to take then, flowers? There's some primroses up on the bank, reckon old Trev will go for them,' replied Reg, placing his paw on his hip camply. This had his two boisterous boys in stitches but earned Reg a whack about the ear from Trace.

'I ain't standin' for none of that tonight, and don't you go givin' the boys ideas like that, you're 'sposed to set an example for fuck's sake. And we are walking, and that's final.'

Trace had spent over an hour preening her dense fur and 'doing' her whiskers. About her neck, she wore a daisy-chain and intended to wear violets behind her ears.

'If you fink I'm swimming after all this, and arriving all wet, then you've got anuvver fink comin', Reginald Otter.'

The boys, Clamp and Nipper, saved the day concerning a present to take; they had spotted the water vole's oar a mile or two downstream and now went to fetch it. With the boys out of sight and his partner looking so glamorous, Reg's thoughts bent on romance.

'Get awf will ya?' Trace warned, adding 'and get yerself ready, we gotta be there soon.' She threw Reg the fish-bone comb. 'When did you last use that eh? Scruffy bleeder!'

Diamonds didn't come much rougher than Reginald Otter, but that is not to suggest that Reg did not have a softer side. He couldn't remember when he had seen his mate looking so lovely. 'You look beautiful Trace,' he said tenderly, taking her paw. The paw was however quickly pulled away. 'Fuck-awf, you ain't getting around me like that,' chided Trace, as she turned away and tried to conceal a little smile.

Back at restaurant *'Vole-au-Vent'* – the name having been hastily inscribed on the wood panels of the shack by the vole in red paint – the two chefs were hard at it, all too aware of the dipping of the sun and the imminent arrival of their guests.

On the landing stage, a table for two resplendent with green cloth and tallow candles was awaiting. On a board, propped against the doorway, a menu was written:

> *Aperitif – Eau de Navet a la Maison*
> (House Turnip Hooch)
> *Truite – Brune avec Ecrevisse dans sa sauce Velouté.*
> (Brown Trout with Crayfish in a rich fish sauce)
> *Rayon de Miel.* (Honeycomb)
> *Digestif – VieuxWobbler*
> (Oldwobbler Hooch)

The water vole was exceedingly happy with his *Velouté* sauce, he had seasoned it heavily and was confident that it would disguise the flavour of the perch. The perch was a fine-tasting white meat as opposed to the pinkish hue of trout, but in the dim candlelight and coated with his sauce, to which he added hawthorn berries to provide colour, he was hopeful he would get away with it.

Brian was dispatched to forage for crayfish. There was no hope of his finding the white-clawed, native crayfish, the water vole had disabused him of that idea. The vole knew this because he used to eat them and the invader, the American signal crayfish, was a poor substitute in his opinion. Digging in the banks of a small side-stream, Brian came upon his prey and his prey came upon him.

With paws full of the, not-so-tiny, lobster-like creatures, he chanced his luck for one more. With his head deep in the hole he had dug, an irate crayfish attached himself to his snout and refused to let go. With his paws full, nose smarting with a crayfish attached, and eyes watering profusely, Brian made a dash for the kitchen.

'In there, smart as you like!' cried the vole who indicated a pan of boiling water and then promptly creased himself up in laughter. The mole threw his pawful of unfortunates into the rolling boil and then lowered his snout into the pan…too far.

With the water vole rolling on the floor in laughter, it took a while for Brian to see the funny side. Being then dispatched to a known source of honey, did nothing to improve Brian's humour. With him, he took a smouldering stick designed to placate the bees and the advice was to make a rapid grab. The smouldering stick worked a treat, and the bees became drowsy. Brian got his honeycomb and then forgot the water vole's advice – 'should you get stung, ignore it and back off slowly.' Turning tail and running was not considered best practice. Quite how many times the mole was stung on any available non-clothed area, he couldn't say, and he returned to the kitchen in a sorry state.

'Bravo, well done that mole!', enthused the vole to his moping companion.

For some time, Brian sat not knowing which area of his body to nurse first; his painful paws where the perch had exacted his revenge, his smarting and scolded snout, his arms, neck and back where angry bees had taken issue with him, or his niggling todger, which was still playing up.

'No, no no, this isn't right,' declared the water vole as he lowered his head to sniff the pot. 'This will never pass muster.' The vole peered down at his moody friend slumped on the floor, who was scratching his back against the rough wall planking.

'Come on old fellow, chop, chop, they'll be here any minute,' the vole insisted. Gingerly, the mole lowered his smarting snout to the pot. He didn't care much for the aroma, but then, he didn't know what it was supposed to smell like.

The vole insisted that the perfume coming off was unmistakable, the now oh-so-common, American crayfish.

'One sniff and they'll know it. They can probably smell it already, good snouts I shouldn't wonder,' the water vole concluded, anxiously.

Rooting and rummaging about inside his trousers, Brian produced a handful of wild garlic leaves with a flourish.

'That ought to disguise it,' he declared, and without waiting on the head chef's approval, he slung them in the pot. A potent odour assailed the water vole's finer senses.

'Cheese, I'm getting blue-cheese and…' – the vole screwed up his eyes and turned his head away – '…a hint of fungus I think…yes.'

'Job done,' declared Brian, having now lost all enthusiasm for the project.

At the water vole's insistence, Brian was to discard his ancestral pelt coat and don a smart white shirt and black trousers. The vole did likewise and looked every inch the *maître d'*.

Brian, on the other hand, had difficulty in doing up the buttons over his bulging stomach. The water vole was built on a slender basis and his portlier friend struggled to get the trousers on. The fly had to be secured with a knot of rough twine.

Compliments on Trace's beauty abounded, flushing her face to red. Proud as punch, Reg, who had scrubbed up well himself, took his seat opposite his mate and beamed at her. A sharp kick to his shins reminded him.

'Oh, yes Trevor, I quite forgot. The boys have a present for you.'

It did not go unnoticed that Reginald, under strict instruction, had modulated his language for the occasion. He slapped his paws together and looked expectantly toward the river. Nothing doing, he repeated the exercise, again without result. Temporarily forgetting himself, he got up from his seat and walked to the edge of the landing, muttering as he went.

'Where are yer, yer little fuckers? Two heads popped up from the water and between them, they held aloft the missing oar.

'There you go Mr. Trevor,' announced Clamp cheerfully, whilst his brother followed up with 'yeah, safer to sit down Mr. Trevor when you're pissed as a fa...' but Nipper's contribution was cut short by a withering look from his mother.

Following three glasses of *Eau de Navet,* tongues loosened. Try as he might, Reg had difficulty in remembering his elocution lessons and his frequent slips resulted in badly bruised shins.

The fish course was adjudged a towering success. Neither otter had eaten a cooked fillet before and certainly not accompanied with a sauce.

'You must let me have the recipe Trevor, and where, oh where, did you get the trout?', Trace enthused and then touching on the crayfish, she looked directly at her partner, adding somewhat dubiously 'The sauce tasted familiar.'

Reg was unusually taciturn concerning the meal and shot a few quizzical glances toward Brian, yet as his partner Trace was having such a wonderful time, and indeed holding his paw on occasions, he joined in the praise.

'Done us proud both of yer,' he beamed. 'You, not yer,' corrected Trace when the vole and mole were out of earshot.

Honeycomb, although not an otter staple, was devoured greedily and particularly by Reg who wondered why he had never tried it before.

'You see my darling, we can try new things. We just need to get out more,' Trace said encouragingly. The mystified expression on her partner's face did nothing to curb her enthusiasm.

'May I try a puff on one of your cigarettes Trevor?', she asked, baffling Reg further.

'How do we smoke with these?', Reg said, holding up his two webbed paws. 'Can't hold a fag with these can yer?'

The ever-attentive vole and mole duly obliged by offering thin, rolled tobacco with only the slightest pinch of grass, to their lips. Both otters coughed and spluttered so much that the experiment was abandoned.

'Fuck-me, me 'eads spinnin'', declared Reg who escaped sanction due to Trace being affected similarly.

A pause ensued and the vole and mole retreated to the kitchen leaving the two lovebirds some privacy. It was then that Brian noticed his friend was a little subdued-

'Anything the matter old chum?', he asked, gently.

Trevor-Stan shook his head sadly- 'Nothing that can be rectified I'm afraid.'

The sound of giggling and laughter floated in on the night air and the two friends looked out upon the candlelit scene. The night was still and unseasonably warm for April.

'You know Brian, I have always lived my life alone and until now, have never been lonely. Since Stan...well, you know, I find myself looking at couples and feel a terrible envy of them.'

Brian touched his paw tenderly, he couldn't think of anything to soothe, so he said nothing.

The vole sighed, then straightened and said smartly- 'This will never do, we are forgetting our guests. Fetch the *digestif* old chap.'

With that, the vole picked up a battered old Spanish guitar left to the family following the fabled visit of a sea-faring rat and strode out onto the landing. To the astonishment of all, he began to play an old Spanish air.

Quite how the otter couple made it home, topped-up with Old Wobbler and on foot, was subject to much debate and hilarity for weeks. That they had to hold each other up, was evident. That it took them all night, they arrived at dawn, was puzzling. The distance was no more than half a mile.

The planned boat trip, which had been chalked in for the morning after the dinner, did not occur.

'Mate, I'm still wankered,' Reg groaned, dipping his head in the river to try and clear his senses. "Ave to be tomorrow Brian…sorry.'

Chapter Seven

A Voice in the Wilderness

'Paltry turnout,' commented one of four weasels present. 'Look out,' said another. 'Here come the Fenians.'

The foxes, Fergal, and Molly Fenian, were ambling toward the mounds that generations of badgers had created about their setts.

'Haven't I better things to do with my time Molly than listen to that great windbag giving out the pay?', complained Fergal.

'Such as what?', Molly enquired sharply, knowing full well that her apathetic mate would only spend the morning dozing on his favoured grassy knoll.

Fergal rolled his eyes, five seasons with Molly had taught him not to argue, he hadn't the stamina for it.

'Well, even I expected a few more,' Fergal said.

In dribs and drabs the numbers swelled; Rabbits, stoats, hedgehogs, weasels, grey squirrels, roe deer, tawny owl, and a solitary dormouse on the periphery. Even before the arrival of the speaker, tension within the assembly was evident. A group of grey squirrels were passing on nudges and nods in the direction of two red squirrels. Roe deer were deliberately obstructing the view of a few muntjac deer and each time the smaller deer moved, the larger moved to block their view again-

'Did you see that, Jack?', questioned Jill Stoat of her mate. 'Not one of us is above the other here. What are things coming to? I've got a good mind to go and have a word with madam over there,' said Jill, indignantly.

'It'll settle down when the big-I-am turns up…eventually,' replied Jack, hoping upon hope that Jill would not be making one of her scenes that morning.

It was a rarity for the woodland animals to gather. The old custom of assembling on the mounds on the evening of the shortest day of the year was now only observed by the older animals. With the dipping sun, it had always been the last social meet before the onset of true winter following which, many would go beneath ground or hunker down. It was however accepted by all, even by the younger generations, that the mounds were a place of sanctuary. All in this place, were welcome, equal, and safe.

Badger, who was practicing his speech before the mirror, went to his window to check on numbers. This was disappointing, he had expected more. What was the matter with these animals? He noticed a few drifting off and decided to make an appearance before it was too late. His speech was incomplete; too bad.

'What is it, this place we call home? What does home mean to you?' The badger stood foursquare, feet parted, shoulders back, chin up, and with his mighty paws turned outward to emphasise his power. His voice boomed out.

'And ask yourself this – to whom does my home belong? Generations of you have lived in these woods, on this land, it belonged to your fathers and their fathers before that. Does it still belong to you today?'

A murmur sifted through the crowd, they were listening, and emboldened; the badger went on, importantly.

'I'll tell you what my home means to me; my space, my fireside, my warm bed, my kitchen, my little piece of England…'

'My truffles and my fat belly more like!', cried a weasel. Not renowned for their ability to concentrate, weasels are disruptive and make for habitual hecklers.

The badger scowled as a ripple of laughter passed through the assembly and Fergal the fox cried out. 'You're on the money there weasel, sure enough!'

But there were those who tutted and shushed, allowing the badger to resume.

'We have in our midst, newcomers – foreigners; you know who they are. Who asked them to come? You? Let me assure you of this, it certainly wasn't me! Oh yes, today you mention my truffles…'

'Who mentioned truffles? He's obsessed!', cried another weasel and a wave of laughter circulated.

'No, No, let me speak,' shouted the badger raising his great paws. 'Today my truffles, and tomorrow your berries, your…' The badger faltered, he hadn't thought to make a list of other animals' sustenance.

'My what?', shouted a ferret. 'My acorns!'

This intervention caused hilarity among the other strict carnivores and the badger decided he'd better change tack.

'Who here feels uncomfortable to hear strange accents and foreign languages, here in this wood, in their own home? I know I do. Then what happens? Those very same foreigners try to push us out, they take our food, take our homes…'

'Does that include us?' Molly Fenian-Fox intervened sharply. A brief silence fell and the badger, no friend to Molly, was temporarily lost for a reply. 'I mean to say,' Molly continued, 'himself and I never had any choice in the matter, some eejit of an Upright brought us over as cubs and we escaped.'

'That's the way of it,' Fergal added. 'Now the same feckers chase us with dogs.' A great murmur of sympathy circulated for the couple. You killed to eat, not for the fun of it. Those animals who persecute, and there were a few, were generally shunned.

'You're both welcome here as far as I'm concerned,' reassured a stoat who reddened at the focus of attention upon him. A warm wave of approval swept through the gathering at his remark.

'That's lovely my friend, that's all grand,' persisted Molly. 'It's just that I don't understand what the big fella is trying to say. If we are welcome, and I'm tankful for it, and we had no choice in the matter but to be here, then how do we know these others had any choice? I mean, has anyone taken the time to speak with them?'

Comments, such as 'She's got a point', and 'Have you spoken to them?' were then drowned out by a straggle of animals, chiefly stoats with the odd ferret, newly arrived from a neighbouring wood. The most vociferous among them, a ferret who was evidently their mouthpiece, began by shouting.

'You can't talk to them because they don't speak our language!' She went on in a similar vein, railing against the newcomers and as to how they made no effort to integrate and how their numbers will only swell.

A much-reinvigorated badger puffed out his chest and declared pompously:

'It is the inalienable right of every English animal...' – but once more, he was interrupted.

'What does that mean?' came the raucous cry of a pheasant. The badger struggled to define the word succinctly and when the pheasant cried out again 'I still don't get it' the badger lost support from those nearby who heard him muttering crossly 'Shut-up birdbrain!'

Here had the badger transgressed. Cries of 'shame' went up from those at the front. However, the straggle of incomers now seemed to be gaining the upper hand. The meeting was becoming unruly which was grist to the badger's mill. He raised himself to his full hauteur and boomed.

'I say our friends here are right. If we don't make a stand, then we'll all lose our homes, our food, our way of life.' Above the ever-increasing din he hollered 'Foreigners out!' A roar went up by those who would roar at anything, followed by the refrain 'Foreigners out.'

'Will you come along now Molly,' Fergal cajoled, but his partner was reluctant to move. 'Did you ever hear such a bunch of feckin' numbskulls?', Molly seethed. Fergal tried again. 'Come along now, I don't like the look of that lot at all, there's more of them every minute.'

Certainly, the number of incomers was increasing, some of whom were patting the badger on the back and all of whom wore angry faces.

Quite how such a diminutive animal as Taupe could then make herself heard and silence an unruly crowd was remarkable. Dressed in a pelt coat of the brightest orange and with the mole's spectacles perched on her snout, Taupe had the bearing of a schoolmarm. Nevertheless, at the outset, she had to contend with jibes and barbs from the rabble.

'Letting them all in!' 'We're flooded.' 'Only here to take our food.'

Taupe was assisted by Molly Fenian who cried out 'Let her speak.'

'Merci madame, like you and your mate, I 'ave no choice, I come in the root ball of a tree, I wake up and I find myself here.'

'Hid in it to get here more like!', shouted an incomer. 'Go back home to where you come from', hurled the ring-leading ferret, adding 'Can't understand a word she's saying! Can you?' A clamour went up for Taupe's removal and Molly Fenian had had enough. Dragging Fergal by the paw, she made her way up the mound.

'Are you forgetting where we are?' Molly shouted. 'We all have the right to be heard in this place.' Turning to the badger, she added:

'And you should be ashamed of yourself, great lump that you are.'

Taupe stood her ground and let the commotion die down. She began quietly, necessitating a hush to catch her words.

'Badger, you speak of the old times, you speak of the traditions, but the big pigs, the *sanglier*, were here in the time of your ancestors. *Et alors*, you are here today. What that mean eh? If they eat all your food and push badgers out, then how you are here today, huh? *Non*, who push out the big pigs? Uprights. They hunt them, they cut down forest, so they have no home.'

Whispers in agreement spread through the assembly with one plucky hedgehog yelling out:

'Always was a greedy beggar old badger, got it from his father they reckon.'

Fergal Fenian noticed the ring-leader ferret in conference with his comrades and he was pointing toward the hedgehog, he gave the ferret his hardest stare and received one in return.

'You little gobshite, you wouldn't be so brave without your mates,' muttered Fergal.

'Who is it who take our land, take our food and cut down trees?' – Taupe persisted, scanning all the upturned faces. 'Who is it who shit in our river killing fish?'

A hush descended, largely because the woodlanders had scant knowledge of the river. Taupe went on. 'Who spray poison on our fields killing our herbs, our insects, our bees?'

Muted murmurs grew. 'Uprights,' voiced a hare timidly from the back of the gathering and soon 'Uprights' resounded about.

'*Voila*! It is not fault of animals, it is fault of Uprights. And what we do here eh? We make the division between ourselves. You think we are stronger like that? I say we are weaker.'

'Don't listen to her!', shouted the ferret. 'They're only trying to take over, we make the rules here.' He cried defiantly. 'Everything was all right before they came!', he added fiercely pointing toward Taupe. A sizeable portion cheered his outburst; however, they were fewer in number.

'A small body does not mean a small mind, only a closed mind is small,' continued Taupe deliberately avoiding eye contact with the ferret.

'If we imagine a world where Uprights are pushed back, where the forests grow, where meadows return, then we must start somewhere. This mean animals come back that we are not used to. We must learn how…'

'I say no, never, never, never!' bellowed the badger, losing all restraint, and leaving those who were prepared to listen drowned out by a cacophony sent up by the incomers.

'Bloody-fucking wonker!' hurled Taupe as she tried to shake off Fergal who, sensing danger, was trying to pull her away. The meeting had descended into chaos and a few of the incomers seemed to be spoiling for a fight.

The Fenians led Taupe down the back of the mound and then, somehow, she disappeared. One minute they had her and the next she was gone; they had only taken their eyes off her for a few seconds. Utterly perplexed they craned their heads this way and that but there was no sign of her.

'How in the name of all that's holy?' Molly exclaimed.

The din coming from the other side of the mound didn't help Fergal who had pricked his sensitive ears to listen. Both foxes then used their noses and followed a trace for some fifty metres.

'Now, would you look at that?' said Fergal, smiling in wonderment. 'Just look at that.'

'What? What am I looking at exactly?' Molly demanded.

'Ah, you're too late now.'

'Too late for what?' cried the vexed vixen, irritably.

Fergal caught but glimpses of a disappearing mole, one moment green, the next brown and, then violet. His last sighting came as a retreating Taupe merged into a bed of newly flowering bluebells.

Chapter Eight

Mink Ahoy!

Brian had put together a hamper consisting of reeds, grasses, berries, and freshly sprouted leaves. He looked at, what for him, was an unappetising selection of vegetable matter and turned up his nose in disdain. How long can he keep it up, he wondered. To augment his friend's lunch, he decided upon duckweed. He had no idea whether the water vole ate it or not, yet it was green so why not?

As he was making the perilous descent of the riverbank to harvest the weed, his attention was caught by flying objects. 'Montgolfieres!' he cried. 'Some of them!' That is to say, there was more than one – the mole had never learned how to count. As he gazed skyward, he slipped and plunged feet first, through the duckweed and into the river. He surfaced and splashed about frenetically; he could swim as most animals can, yet he had never adopted it as a pastime. Luckily it wasn't deep. As mischance would have it, Rear-Admiral Canard and his flotilla of mallards then hove into view.

'So here we have it ladies, our burrowing lothario is cooling his ardour,' quacked the Rear-Admiral.

'Maybe she pushed him in,' replied the head of the harem, jokingly.

'Small wonder he only mates once a year, he's not going to impress her with swimming like that,' added the Rear-Admiral, derisorily, and his remark was greeted by a raucous racket of quacks and general hilarity.

Scrambling back up the bank, his pelt coat sodden, and sporting a crown of dripping duckweed, Brian turned and saluted the ensemble with his middle digit. 'Fuck off!', he hurled. Much affronted, the Rear-Admiral ordered the flotilla to about turn and once more, issued the order, 'present arse!' Brian scrabbled in the earth for projectiles.

'Why can you never find a stone when you need one?', he grumbled, but it was too late, the Rear-Admiral had led his troop away, joking at the mole's expense.

Back in the water vole's abode, Brian was attempting to rouse his still-sleeping companion. This was to be the day of their boat trip upstream and yet, the vole snored soundly. He tried a number of techniques to wake him, he sang, he whistled, he clattered pots and pans, all to no avail. Quite what made him do it, and he wished later that he hadn't, he couldn't say. All he did know was that he had fixed a time with Reg the otter and that was when the sun topped the far field oak.

'Mink!', hollered the mole and the effect upon the somnambulant water vole was electrifying. He shot bolt upright and cast about wildly, in his confusion he leaped from his bed, fell to his knees, and scrambled beneath the bed panting heavily. The poor animal then began to hyperventilate leaving the mole both at a loss and wretched.

Thinking on his feet, no small feat for Brian, he picked up a cudgel, stormed outside and whacked the weapon upon any solid structure that came to hand. 'Take that' – BANG – 'Want some do you?' – WHACK – 'Come back when you're man enough' – CRACK – culminating in- 'You need to grow a pair mate, yeah, go on, that's it, run away!'

The mole went back in to be met with a still tremoring vole peeping out from beneath his bed. His expression was a mixture of incredulity and fear.

'Are...th...th...they gone B-b-b-b-b Brian?'

'Who?', Brian began, casually brushing himself down. 'Oh yes, the min...you mean the pests' – he continued breezily – 'Oh, they won't be back. I made mincemeat out of them actually,' he concluded, unconcerned.

'I was just looking for my cricket bat,' the water vole said unconvincingly. 'I could have sworn it was under here.'

With the utmost caution and a wary eye on the door, the water vole edged out from under the bed. 'Gone you say?', He tremored.

'Who?', replied Brian, over-egging the pudding.

'The blasted mink!', screamed the vole.

'Oh, like I say, quite gone old friend,' he soothed, taking his companion by the paw.

'Listen, I've made us up a glorious hamper of all your favourite nibbles. It's a beautiful morning, fresh breeze and barely a cloud in sight, how about taking a row on the river?'

'With mink about? You must be joking,' retorted the vole, as he attended to his toilette.

The vole noted the look of disappointment on his friend's face, and he now took a good look at his own in the mirror. What was it the badger had said of him? Not half the animal his illustrious ancestor was, or something like that. Hadn't the mole, whose own ancestor was reputed to have been a timid creature, beaten off a band of mink single-handedly?

Still, he considered a boat trip foolhardy. He frowned as he preened his whiskers, sighed as he brushed his fur, and his shoulders slumped when his reflection returned a frightened, spineless animal. He continued with his ablutions nonetheless until the swan mussel shell he used for shaving, cracked in his paw.

Then, did he sense the presence of an old familiar, a shadowy character who occasionally got the better of him. He crushed the swan shell into a hundred pieces and welcomed the character in. Now, in his mirror-glass, did he see a different vole, a vole with lips drawn back to display teeth. Gone was the wet, doleful eye to be replaced by a fierce glint. Trevor-Stan Vole had got back in touch with his anger.

'Brian, prepare the boat, we are heading upstream,' he commanded, adding determinedly 'and find my cricket bat if you would.'

With the boat loaded with hamper, cricket bat and an array of cudgels, the vole pulled on the oars. Brian was admirative of his dapper friend; dressed as he was in cricket whites, a polka-dot cravat about his neck and all topped off with a straw boater. The mole's subterranean world did not lend itself to such elegance. His ancestral pelt-coat had a touch of mange here and there and he now felt conspicuous in his shabbiness. It really didn't help when the mismatched, nautical couple chanced upon Sir Edwin Preece-Moog, his wife Constance and their five cygnets. Sir Edwin, a swan of the purest white wore a double-breasted jacket with gold buttons and sported a monocle-

'Immaculately turned out as always Mr. Rat, allow me to congratulate you on maintaining river standards,' he proclaimed haughtily. His monocle fell from his eye when he turned his attention on Brian.

'Gillies were once suitably clad,' he intoned, now fixing the vole in the eye. 'My sympathies my dear fellow, so difficult to find staff these days.'

'Two things,' began the vole. 'No, make that three; first, Mr. Brian Mole is a direct descendant of the illustrious mole of yore, secondly, dress doth not make the animal and thirdly, I am a water-vole and not a rat!'

Sir Edwin's wife assisted in the replacement of the monocle allowing her husband time to formulate a response.

'Do accept my apologies, Mr. Mole, I am aware of the constraints living below ground must place upon one's attire. But, as to this modern fad of playing with nomenclature, I really can't say I approve.' He tilted his head such that sunlight glinted in his monocle forcing the vole to avert his eyes.

'Oh, like the adoption of *Sir* I suppose,' retorted the vole, acidly.

'Good day to you,' Sir Edwin replied. 'Come Constance, we have appearances to maintain,' he said, haughtily, as he led his family away.

They sculled onward in silence with the vole seething, and the mole scratching periodically. It was only a small boat and Brian's itching had begun to grate.

'Brian old chap, have you a problem in the nethers?'- The vole demanded, tetchily.

Brian sighed, buried his head inside his pelt-coat to investigate, then resurfaced.

'Yes,' came the matter-of-fact response. 'Still.'

'I see.'

Once more they carried on in silence which became burdensome to Brian.

'That swan get your goat old friend?'

'Somewhat,' replied the vole tersely. 'Thinks he's royalty. He believes he can trace his lineage right back to King Upright Henry's table.'

'I should have thought it ended there,' replied a puzzled, Brian.

'Pity it didn't,' the vole added dryly.

As the boat rounded a bend in the river, the water vole's attitude stiffened, his sculling became metronomic and his eyes flitted left and right. Brian picked up on it realising that they must be entering territory held by the mink. He inadvertently emitted a pungent, musky smell. This odour, unpleasant as it is, serves to protect moles from predators who can't abide the stink. The water vole, polite creature that he was, could not but help ask-

'I say Brian, have you let-off?'

'No, but I've got one brewing,' Brian replied candidly, pursing his lips.

On they went and then Brian, without thinking asked:

'These mink, are they big chaps?'

Trevor-Stan stopped rowing instantly. 'Repeat that would you?'

Immediately recognising his gaffe, Brian tried to back-track.

'I mean...I mean, the chaps, the ones at this end of the river,' he quavered.

The vole, a very smart and intuitive creature, stared at his companion intently.

'There were no mink this morning, Brian, were there?' He interrogated, coldly.

At a loss, Brian shrugged his shoulders.

'Not many,' he lied, unconvincingly.

The boat, midstream, began to drift back slowly. Suddenly, a sharp voice piped up from the bank.

'Hey, limey, you got some *cojones* to come up here again.'

The water vole froze in terror. Brian let one go but had the presence of mind to pick up a cudgel. The vole and mole made no reply but stared wide-eyed at each other.

'Hey, yous guys, come and looksy what we got ourselves here!', shouted a mink in an appalling American drawl.

Soon the bank was crowded with mink, all laughing and hurling abuse.

'Geez, smell that? I reckon those limeys are crappin' themselves.'

Shrill laughter filled the air as the vole picked up the oars, turned the boat about in panic and began to row.

'It's no use,' cried Brian. 'Look behind you!'

The water vole looked over his shoulder, on the bend of the river, where they would have to pass, were more mink. A few were on a tree bough that overhung the river. The mole and vole were trapped. Some had taken to the water and were heading directly for the boat.

'I'm gonna chew me some ass!', screamed one, and many on the bank began to make whooping cries. 'Go get 'em Jack!' 'Bust his ass!' 'Haul his ass outta dere.'

Brian, cudgel in hand, got to his feet wobbling unsteadily and quavered.

'I may have the feeble body of a mole…' Forgetting the rest in his terrified state.

The water vole took his cue. 'But we have the hearts of lions!', he screamed, brandishing his cricket bat.

Turmoil then ensued, the water began to swirl in huge eddies, mink, one by one disappeared from the surface. Many began swimming for all they were worth for the banks. All around the boat the water boiled in bubbles. The boat rocked alarmingly as thud upon thud resounded upon the hull. The water-vole and mole had to cling to the gunwales.

The sudden flash of a huge, silver flank rolled on the surface as another mink disappeared.

'Esox!', mouthed the water-vole in disbelief.

'Wotcha cock,' had the beleaguered nautical pair turn in unison to be greeted by a friendly, familiar head.

'Fuckin' lovin' this Trev. Ain't 'ad such a good ruck in years.' Reg grinned, then promptly dived back under.

Brian, whose plan this had been from the outset, took on a confident air as with cudgel in one paw, he beckoned the mink with the other. 'Come on then, just one, just one!'

Some of the mink were scrambling, hobbling up the bank only to be pulled back in the water by Clamp and Nipper.

'Now that will do boys, they've had enough,' shouted their mother Trace, sternly.

'Oh dad, come on please, tell mum,' whined Clamp. 'Let me at the cunts!'

'Right!', screamed Trace, making a bee-line for her wayward son and clipping him fiercely about the ear.

'You'll come and apologise to Mr. Trevor. I ain't standin' fer language like that!'

A struggling Clamp was tugged toward the boat with the nape of his neck held firmly by his mother's teeth. His younger sibling Nipper, now floating on his back, found the spectacle hilarious and he slapped his stomach in glee with his paws.

'Honestly Mr. Trevor, I don't know where they get it from,' a flushed Trace bemoaned. She cuffed Clamp about the head saying 'now what do you say?'

The exuberant, young otter muttered something along the lines of 'sorry Mr Trevor,' and when his mother released him, he dived immediately and came up beneath his younger brother and a tussle ensued. 'Who'd 'ave 'em Mr Trev?', an exasperated mother otter wailed.

**

With the mink routed and solemn promises extracted from their chief by Reg, that those remaining would take up home at a day's swim upstream, the water vole and Brian sculled onward. The mole settled himself back in the stern wearing a self-satisfied look upon his face. The water vole watched him intently as he trailed his paw in the water.

'That was all planned, wasn't it?', the vole said.

Brian grinned and hunched his shoulders. 'I hadn't counted on the pike, that must have been Reg's idea.'

'Good to see them getting along, they don't make ideal bedfellows,' the vole said, adding abstractedly 'that poor devil Esox must be hungry.'

Brian had hoped for something in the way of thanks from his friend, and for some minutes he felt ignored. One does not do a good deed in the expectation of gratitude, he reminded himself. Perhaps Trevor-Stan feels humiliated, he further thought, a chap might feel belittled, might want to fight his own battles…

The water vole stopped rowing and shipped the oars. He was gazing at a derelict home in the riverbank. Brian noted him swallowing hard and rubbing a tear from his eye with his upper arm.

'I'm so sorry Trevor-Stan,' Brian said, tenderly, but no reply came. At a loss, he added 'well, at the least, we have some retribution.'

The water vole sighed heavily and fixed the eye of his friend. 'Retribution? That is not the way of we animals. Retribution is the cursed domain of the Upright.'

Lunch on the bank passed largely in silence and Brian took solace in five particularly juicy lobworms. He stared at his sombre friend and wondered where the old water-rat had gone. He now longed for old ratty, the *bon-viveur* always full of vigour and enthusiasm. This, he told himself, is what love and a diet of greenery does for you, it only makes you sick and listless. His thoughts then bent on Taupe, and he frowned, hadn't she brought him to the same pass? But he brightened when he recalled the conversation he had had with Reg the otter.

'Mate, don't go getting me wrong, I love Trace to bits, muvver of me kids and all that, but there's a difference between love and being in your condition innit?'

Brian had spent some time extolling Taupe's attributes, but these he had confined to her physical charms. So, when he pressed Reg on what condition he considered him to be in, the answer was typically forthright.

'Cunt-struck,' Reg affirmed. 'That's wot you are mate.'

A smile played at the corners of Brian's mouth, and he wondered if Reg's designation was accurate. He had thought himself to be in love, but then he also felt put out, literally put out of his abode.

By nature, Brian was a solitary creature. The season came and the chase was on, he had chased tail with varying degrees of success, he had been bitten more times than he cared to remember, and then, quite abruptly, the season ended. Love had never had anything to do with it. If he was in love with Taupe, and he couldn't decide one way or the other, then it was an unsatisfactory arrangement if she didn't love him back.

Brian had packed a bottle of Old-Wobbler into which the water vole had made great inroads; he was now unsteady on his feet as the two friends clambered back into the boat. It was decided that Brian should take the oars as they continued upstream. Brian's beefy forearms were well suited to the task, although his lack of coordination meant for constant course changes.

The water vole settled himself back in the stern and gazed upward at the passing clouds, there he sat contentedly, until, rubbing his eyes in disbelief, he shot bolt-Upright.

'What in the name of Pan is that?', he exclaimed, breaking into Brian's daydream of next season. Brian followed his pointing paw and glanced upward.

'Oh, that's a Montgolfier.' He looked more closely and concluded offhandedly, 'some of of them, actually.'

'I know what they are Brian, and by the way, there are only two, but what is that hanging beneath?' The vole picked up the bottle of Old-Wobbler and sniffed the contents-

'Did you put anything in this Brian?', he quizzed.

Attempting to act casually Brian replied, 'Oh just a few leaves you know, give it a nose.'

But all of the water vole's attention was upon the balloons.

'Curses!', exclaimed the vole. 'I've forgotten the field-glasses.'

It appeared to the vole that the large baskets suspended beneath the balloons were carrying animals and that atop the baskets and in a cradle of their own, were Uprights. Brian, certain that his companion was once again rat-arsed, replied simply 'Oh, quite likely.'

The balloons drifted into the distance leaving an inebriated water vole wondering if he had not been imagining things.

Chapter Nine

Damned Odd

'You know Brian, I haven't been up here for a very long time. The old place is still standing at least,' said the vole, wistfully.

The pair were gazing upon unkempt lawns, now all but ceded to briar and shrub, and set far back, the faded grandeur of Toad Hall, once home to generations of the Toad family.

'How are the mighty fallen,' declared the water-vole, adding 'now home to a legion of house rats below and squirrels and bats above I'm told.'

'Dear me, whatever would our illustrious ancestors have made of that?', posed Brian.

'That's odd, the boathouse is flooded, unusual for this time of the year,' observed the vole, adding 'and the steps, there used to be a flight of steps down to the river's bank, they must be submerged.'

'Everything changes,' said Brian, dismissively.

Why, what, and how, did not figure largely in the mole's thought processes. Causality, why one event impacts another, was more the preserve of the water-vole.

'Something's out of joint here Brian,' ruminated the vole.

Yet, the sun shone brightly, damsel flies flitted back and forth, Rudd and Dace rose to errant hawthorn-flies and the air was fresh with the promise of spring, so the pair rowed on leaving the crumbling, red-brick, seventeenth-century pile behind them.

Draining the last dregs of Old-Wobbler, the water-vole declared himself to be agreeably pissed. He began to mutter and hold a conversation with himself leaving the mole side-lined. That his friend sought solace in the weed, mushroom and bottle, Brian found disappointing. He hoped this was only a temporary situation because, at times, he felt excluded, even bored, and wished he were somewhere else.

He was about to turn the boat about and head for home when his inebriate friend sat Upright once more and peered over his shoulder.

'Obstrussion ahead mole,' he slurred.

No sooner had he garbled these words than did a tree creak and fall with a huge splash, adding to the obstruction. They rowed onward at a cautious pace, the current had slackened, and the going was easy.

'Those reeedsh Brian, look,' the vole slurred, indicating a bank of reeds practically submerged with only their green tips visible. 'Wotsch you make of jat?'

True to form, Brian simply shrugged and cautiously edged nearer the obstruction.

It was Brian who saw the animal first as the water vole still had his glassy eyes on the reeds. Brian started, was startled, and stared in disbelief. He took off his spectacles to clean them. One of the lenses wasn't ideal as it tended to magnify everything five-fold while the other diminished an object by half. Still, somehow, or other, the mole's brain managed to compensate, if not altogether reliably.

'Oh, my giddy aunt!', declared Brian, tremulously.

'Washt is jit mole?', asked the vole. 'Not Uprightshhh is jit?'

No reply came from the speechless animal at the sculls, just an inclination of the head in the direction he had been looking.

'AGHHHHHH!' cried the water vole and all hell broke loose in the boat. The vole knocked Brian backwards, down onto his back and into the prow, he wrested the oars from the stricken animal's grip leaving the portly mole, beetle-like, with limbs flailing in the air.

During this un-seamanlike manoeuvre, an oar was lost over the side. 'GET IT BRIAN!', hurled the captain. Brian did his utmost, however, his utmost consisted in struggling to his feet by which time the oar had drifted off. One further look convinced the vole that speed was of the essence and with his one oar, he stood in the stern of the boat and began to scull frenetically away from the obstruction. He had sobered up in an instant, yet still his litany of utterances was indecipherable to Brian.

Exhausted, and with some distance between them and the obstruction, the water vole slumped to the stern seat to regain his breath. In between heaving pants, he managed-

'What in the name of blazes?' – 'How is it possible?'– and uncharacteristically – 'What the fuck was that?'

Brian was at a loss and only managed 'Well, my mother always said, it's the little ones you have to be wary of.'

The water-vole looked up in incredulity. 'Brian, that animal...that beast, pushed down a tree! Is that all you have to say?'

Brian cogitated on this for some time as his friend, head bowed, regained his puff. Contemplation carried with it several physical ticks that aided the strain of thinking; he would pick his nose, examine the fruits of excavation, and stick it beneath the bench seat; he would shift his weight on to one buttock and scratch his anus – pick inside his ears for wax, sniff the result, and marvel at the resemblance in perfume to the rear-ends he chased in season and now, as it was uppermost in mind, he made a cursory examination of his todger's bell-end to check on recovery.

It was in this attitude, head buried deep in coat, that inspiration struck.

'It's normally Uprights who bring down trees,' came his muffled voice.

'Is that it?', enquired the vole, incredulously.

Brian reappeared from the fetid depths of his pelt-coat.

'Could do with finding some garlic,' he stated, absently.

In the realisation that meaningful conversation would have to be sought elsewhere, the water vole pulled the boat into an inlet in the reeds. The pair had been hailed by a moorhen and a coot, who asked for any upstream news. Brian was first out onto the bank asking the two birds where he might find garlic.

'Knob-rot?', enquired the coot casually, taking a cursory sniff at the air.

An embarrassed Brian scuttled off as directed considering, as he went, the snags of the solitary subterranean life and as to how, one became used to one's own, particular, aromatic fragrance...

'Twice this month already,' bemoaned the moorhen.

'Rising damp? I've been flooded out three times,' added the coot scornfully.

'Doesn't make any sense,' continued a moorhen, looking up from her knitting as she shifted position on her eggs. 'Been no rain to speak of.'

The water vole, himself a solitary type, would not usually socialise with common fowl, however the news that the birds had to continually build their nests higher and higher up the bank due to rising water levels, intrigued him. After all, although a few miles downstream, his own abode had to be at risk. He began tentatively.

'My friend and I chanced upon...some creatures. Creatures who were felling trees, believe it or not, into the river.'

'Uprights,' came in unison the chirped reply. All birds cocked their heads when the vole failed to confirm their supposition. 'What creatures then?' quizzed the birds.

The water vole sighed as he had begun to doubt the evidence of his own eyes.

'Imagine me, if you can, only twenty-times bigger,' he said hesitantly.

He did not notice the knitting hen look toward her mate, nor did he notice an exchange of glances all around. He did not observe them roll their eyes in concert. One neighbouring coot feigned the lifting of a glass to lips and nodded in the direction of the vole. If there was one thing a coot was famed for, it was for going on the piss and recognising fellow pissheads. To be 'cooted' was animalese for pissed.

The birds made their excuses, leaving the water vole to lay back on the high bank and stare at the sky. A lark was singing high, high above and for a moment, the vole forgot the turmoil of the day. He dozed and drifted in and out. Presently he heard Brian return.

'Peregrinations at an end old chap?', the vole murmured lazily. A sudden yelp was unexpected as indeed was Brian's headlong dive into the thick of a gorse.

'What on earth?', exclaimed the vole, as he sat bolt Upright and searched for his friend. Presently a familiar snout appeared from the thicket, eyes darting in all directions, his spectacles on the skew.

'Where, where...has he gone?', he demanded anxiously.

'Who?'

'The bird, the peregrine of course!', Mole replied, irascibly.

That his current social possibilities consisted of moorhens, coot, otters and a mole, the water-vole lamented. How has it come to this? he asked himself. Was he a snob? He hoped not, but sometimes, oh, sometimes he yearned for more. How fondly he remembered his fireside conversations with the erudite Stan, how stimulating had been their talk and yet, Stan would have been the first to upbraid him now. In this bedraggled, smelly, myopic mole, did he not have the stoutest of companions?

'I promise I shall never use the word again in your company old chap,' the vole pledged sincerely. For the vole's laughter, at Brian's expense, had been taken, as was just, badly.

Back on the water, the pair headed homeward. Slack for a time, the current had picked up a little making the sculling downstream less onerous. It was dusk and bats flitted just above the river, darting this way and that as they dined on the bounty of spring. As they passed by, again, the decrepitude that was the former residence of toads, Brian remarked-

'Look, there are lights in the windows.'

'By Pan you're right!', exclaimed the vole in a mixture of excitement and intrigue. He then screwed up his eyes. 'And what is that thing on the roof? It wasn't there this morning, was it?'

Squint as he might, and when he did Brian's front teeth projected keenly, the mole couldn't make the thing out.

'Some sort of…I don't know, tower, is that the right word old chum?', asked the vole.

Not being able to see it, let alone know what a tower was, Brian gave his habitual shrug to the chagrin of his companion, but this time the water vole made no adverse comment.

'Let's investigate tomorrow. What say you old chap?', the vole enthused.

Pleased that a note of optimism had returned, Brian readily agreed.

**

Seated back in the vole's abode, the pair were puffing and exchanging a joint. Brian was becoming accustomed, perhaps too much so as he now looked forward to the water vole's ritual rolling. It was a slow process and he tried not to seem too eager to engage. He feigned a nonchalance when he saw the vole take down the small, wooden box from the shelf. This insouciance he found hard to maintain when, habitually, the vole would hog the joint for what, to Brian, seemed an inordinate length of time. Is he doing this on purpose? he asked himself, is he tormenting me?

'Brian,' the vole would say offhandedly as he proffered the 'doobry', as he termed it.

Then would Brian affect mild surprise, lean forward and accept the prize. For a moment or two, he would engage the vole in meaningless chat ignoring his strong desire to puff the hell out of the remainder.

Eyes glazed and pleasantly stoned, the two animals would watch the river flow and listen in contentment to the chirruping of grasshoppers and the lonely calls of coot.

Attuned as he was to all matters concerning the river and its inhabitants, it came upon the vole of a sudden, he sat forward and rested his chin upon the back of his paw.

'Oh. Oh, I see,' he said softly.

He had no need to go outside and look downstream, no need to see Sir Edwin-Preece-Moog and his family glide past, nor Rear-Admiral Canard and his retinue, nor a host of others heading for the spot. It was the appointed hour for the coronach – or requiem.

'I should go,' the water vole said gently, and he took to his boat and let it drift slowly, silently downstream.

No explanation was required, Brian, although not a river-banker, understood immediately.

On a grassy bank, by the side of an inlet, were assembled all of the creatures to whom the river was home. The grasshoppers fell silent as a cloud passed over the moon, it was a fleeting silence, then, and only if you were a river-banker, would you hear rise a chorus, a melody sweet to the ears in which each animal sang his part. This was the coronach. This was the dirge for the departed. There was no remorse, for how could there be? Predation was as natural as breathing itself. Neither did the predator, who was most obviously and dutifully in attendance, feel any remorse. This was the natural order of things and the ceremony lasted but moments.

As Brian sat and awaited the return of his friend, he too knew, even in his befuddled condition, that the old rabbit had bought it. He felt himself present in spirit, he could see it in his mind's eye, hear the coronach rise and sense the lonely march home. A time of safety, a time when no animal need look over his shoulder, the march to and from the gathering was peaceful, was sacrosanct.

Gaffes, faux pas, indiscretions, call them what you will, of course occur. In the Upright world, this may be akin to a noisome fart in church and Brian now dwelt on a coronach he had attended recently: the culprit was a falcon who had provided his ravenous offspring with a kit rabbit. There did he perch in all due solemnity; all was hush until he inadvertently emitted a sonorous belch. Decorum at these gatherings is everything.

But what was this unease Brian sensed? So finely attuned was he to those who share his neighbourhood that he could not but help pick up on it. When all should be at peace, there were those who were decidedly not. He took a deep drag on the joint in the hope, more than the expectation, that these troublesome thoughts might dissipate.

Chapter Ten

Makes no Seance

The water vole did not take kindly to being awoken from his slumber, and Brian through bitter experience, knew not to. So, when a badger hammers on your door with his gnarled walking stick, as the dawn mists still swirl on the river, there is little more guaranteed to put the vole in foul humour.

'What did you let him in for Brian?', demanded the vole, in vexation, as he buried his head beneath his reed-woven blanket.

'Come on Rat, rouse yourself animal, half the day's gone already,' boomed the badger.

'Fuck off Quincy,' the vole muttered into his pillow.

'Heard that!' thundered the badger. 'Come on, up and about, we've got problems.'

'Is it your truffles again?', asked Brian, sympathetically, hoping to pacify the overbearing animal.

'No, it's not my bloody truffles!', blared the badger as he began to pace about with a scowl. 'No, no, well not completely, but that's part of it,' he conceded.

Bleary-eyed, the vole presented himself, resting his shoulder on the door jamb and yawning – 'must be exhausting'– he yawned again – 'to be so angry all the time.'

The badger, untypically, ignored the remark and took a chair by the window. 'Do sit down,' said the vole, sarcastically. The badger turned his gaze to the window and was evidently trying to compose himself. The vole was testing the badger's patience to the limit and Brian shot him a worried look.

'Toad Hall,' announced the badger grimly with his gaze averted. 'Toad Hall is crawling with Uprights.'

'We know,' came the unified response.

Turning his head about sharply, the badger demanded- 'What do you know?'

An explanation was provided, albeit scant as far as the badger was concerned.

'That hall, that monstrous testament to riverbank wealth' – and here the badger eyed the vole (he viewed him as an entitled idler) accusingly before continuing – 'belongs nonetheless to animals, even if it pains me to say it, to toads,' he concluded resignedly.

'Toads haven't lived there in generations,' the vole said, wearily, mid-yawn.

'Statement of the ruddy obvious!', roared the badger making the vole's Limoges China teacups rattle on the dresser. 'Hardly the point, is it?

A dismissive shrug of vole shoulders only incensed the badger more.

'Damn it all!', he slammed his clenched paw down on an occasional table making it leap from the floor. 'Doesn't anyone care about anything around here?'

The vole did care about his slender-legged table, an heirloom, and he eyed it with concern.

It was Brian who answered.

'There has to be change, it is the only inevitable thing...actually,' he concluded timidly, then edged behind his friend as the badger's countenance darkened.

'Why?', trumpeted the badger rising to his feet. 'Why must everything change?' He fixed the mole intently who was unable to provide a reason – he'd never examined the assertion further.

'I don't want change and as sure as acorns; I don't want it foisted upon me! I don't want to hear foreigners in my neck of the woods.' Again he fixed and unnerved Brian.

'They can go back to where they've come from. I won't have it. We wild wooders will send them packing, make no mistake about that!'

The badger had worked himself up into a lather and began to wheeze; for a moment or two he had difficulty in getting his breath. He then began a coughing fit, his face turned puce, resulting in the mole and vole exchanging anxious glances.

'Quincy old chap, take a seat,' said the vole and, assisted by the mole, they took an arm each and helped lower him onto a chair.

Once the fit subsided with large globules of mucus deposited in the badger's capacious handkerchief, it was a more measured, thoughtful animal that resumed-

'Sorry about that. Not been quite right of late.' He coughed again.

'Damp old winter. I'll be right as rain when the warmth arrives.'

He looked up to see concern writ large on the faces of the mole and vole.

'We badgers are prone to chesty coughs.' With that he arose. 'Need a spot of air, that's all.' He went out onto the landing where the damp chill of the morning air, rather than help him, caused more wheezing and coughing.

'Oh dear. Oh my, that's not good,' Brian began as he tugged the vole's sleeve, drawing his attention to the floorboards. 'I've seen that before I'm afraid.'

There were small spots of blood on the boards. 'What is it, Brian?'

'Cow disease,' replied the mole authoritatively. 'Cows give it to badgers and badgers give it back to cows. My mother told me never to eat brandlings beneath a cow pat, tempting though they be.' He looked vacantly out of the window. 'Those little rosy-red wigglers make a lovely snack,' he concluded wistfully.

Further discussion on the badger's health was curtailed when he summoned them to the landing. Pointing upward, he demanded brusquely 'what is that?'

'That, that is a Montgolfier,' declared Brian proudly.

'Thought as much,' replied badger, unconvincingly, before turning to Brian and adding 'those Upright symbols, what do they mean?' The blank expression returned met with a pat on the back. 'Quite right Mole, just so. No right-thinking animal reads Upright. Rat, what does it say?', he commanded.

The vole, in less than charitable mood given the damage to one leg of his heirloom, accompanied by the slur of evidently not being a right-thinking animal, only complied as a concession to the badger's health.

'First, we have a large letter 'M' which I surmise to be an initial of the vessel's captain, secondly, the words "Wild World, A Better Life for All." This I deem to be a slogan to promulgate some notion or other dear to the skipper or owner,' delivered the vole in an air of superior and exaggerated boredom.

'Hot air!', contributed Brian emphatically, not noticing the vole shoot him a withering look.

'What?', demanded an exasperated badger.

'It's kept up there with hot air,' replied the mole, importantly.

'How?', quizzed the badger, fixing the mole's bespectacled eyes.

'Just is,' replied Brian, evasively, shifting from foot to foot.

'Thermo-dynamics,' began the vole. 'All to do with the differing density of hot and cold air,' he continued airily, until being pulled up abruptly.

'And there we have it!', roared Badger. 'There we have it. I might have known it. Why didn't I think of it before? Damn your thermowotsits Rat, there is your answer,' he declared pointing upward with his cane. 'There's your ruddy answer!'

Brian's front teeth were at their broadest reach yet as spellbound, he gaped upward through his bottle-bottomed glasses. The badger, whose eyesight was keen, clamped the vole's head between his heavy paws and tilted his head upward to the balloon.

'One word Rat, one word explains everything.' But words deserted the loquacious water-vole as he too now gawped.

'Toad!', bellowed the badger, jettisoning the vole's head- 'Toad is behind all of this, I'll be bound,' he ranted as he commenced to pace back and forth the length of the landing.

'Well, I'll be...' began the vole.

'No doubt you will be Rat if a gentleman toad has anything to do with it,' declared Badger.

Drifting serenely above the river, the balloon's volte-face had revealed another face, a countenance from another age. Humbly emblazoned to encompass no more than half of the globe's surface, beaming down from on high, were the unmistakable features of a gentleman toad.

**

The gentleman toad, although the breed had been missing for generations, still cast a long shadow over river, field and wood. Legion were those who recounted the old fables with nostalgia; the one animal who was the equal to the Uprights, the breed who got the better of them. Legend even had it that one had escaped an Upright's cage dressed as an Upright female. Then there were those who saw nothing of merit in a breed who lorded it over other animals and never wanted to see their like again.

The badger's gut instinct told him that toads spelt trouble. He had learnt the fables of the ancestors at his mother's knee in the same way had the water vole and the mole. However, their learned accounts of the merits and deficiencies of the gentleman toad differed widely. The badger had the breed down as being duplicitous and villainous, the water vole as vainglorious and impulsive and the mole, as being charismatic and amusing.

It was then to the book of ancestors that they turned. Together they would undertake an odyssey and assume the minds of the illustrious forebears to learn more of gentlemen toads.

This voyage of discovery had been instigated by the water vole and it required a minimum of three participants. He could count upon Brian's participation, of that he was sure, however, he was utterly amazed at the badger's acquiescence-

'Know your enemy mole.'-The badger advised sternly tapping the side of his snout. This was not at all in keeping with the vole's spirit and loftier ideals, yet a participant nonetheless, the badger would be.

That the odyssey had always resulted in abject failure in the past, the vole kept to himself. Now, in the dimmest corner of the vole's abode, candles, arranged in a circle upon the round, heirloom table, were lit. This occasional table had had its surface polished to a sheen. For, it would be in this sheen that the memories of ancestors would play out. Furtively, the vole added seed heads from his grass crop to the herbs burning as incense, in the hope that its influence might mollify the badger's propensity to anger.

'Come along Quincy, it won't work unless you join in,' chided the vole.

A lengthy sigh had the badger reluctantly join hands with the mole and vole. They were all detailed to concentrate on nothing but toads. They then all stared intently into the warm patina of the table.

It all happened so quickly, and they all felt it, an electric spasm running down their spines. Co-joined it grew in intensity as nebulous imagery, multi-coloured, swirled and eddied upon the table. Forms, indistinct, hove into and faded from view.

And then they had it, distinct and clear, they were aloft in an Upright's old flying machine as it descended rapidly toward the ground, they could sense the terror, feel the panic, see the mottled-green hands pulling furiously, desperately on a stick, hear the cries of anguish as the lofty top of an oak tree loomed, larger and larger, until-the image cut out.

Next were they at the handlebars of an Upright's motorcycle hurtling along narrow roads, cheering crowds flashed past. All three animals tensed hands as the machine sped to the summit of a hill and the stomachs of all three were in their mouths as it leaped into the air and came down on the other side. Through lanes and streets, houses flashed past- 'Left here – now right – right, left, right, sharp left coming up.' All of this could they hear until 'Left. No right! Aghh!' The image vanished.

Then followed a myriad of short-lived images: two mottled-green hands were holding a bar, two flat sticks below skated over blue water. Now were they flying down a mountainside, snow beneath with green pines ticking past. Then were the same green hands at the wheel of a tall sailing ship; they saw a vast, white sail bulging, the starboard gunwale awash and heard the toad's voice exhorting 'More sail, hoist more sail!

Next were they suspended high above ground holding bed-sheets knotted precariously together. They could feel their hearts pumping, see the ground far below and could hear a toad's voice incanting 'Hold out, hold out knots and I'll be a changed toad.' Now could they see the incandescent face of a burly Upright female, see her great arms reach out, feel their heads spin into dizziness as about and about her head they span only to take to the air and come to earth with a bump that they all felt, only too keenly. Then was there darkness, dankness and despair. They all felt it. Now came the inflamed face of an Upright with white hair and finger pointing accusingly. 'Prison, theft, scoundrel, reprobate, down, down, down.' These and many other words muddled into one until the spell was broken, shattered abruptly and irretrievably.

'Stuff me, what a pen'n'ink! Nah, its alright Trace,' shouted Reg back out through the door. 'Just old Trev and his hippy-dippy mates, it ain't on fire or nuffink.'

Three startled faces turned in unison and flushed quickly to crimson. A baffled Reg stood for a moment not knowing quite what to do. But when a surly badger got to his feet, he decided to beat a retreat.

'Sorry bout that Trev,' said Reg as he turned sharply about. 'Mind you, if that's all the thanks I get...' he muttered looking back over his shoulder at an approaching badger.

'Shows you what I know about hippies,' he said as he slipped into the river. 'Thought you lot was 'sposed to be peace lovin'.'

Hopping mad on the landing, the badger bellowed something along the lines of 'bloody foreigners,' to which a retreating Reg, floating on his back, replied 'up yours 'un all mate!', which was accompanied by a crude salute.

All seated back at the table, the trio, try as they might, could not reconnect with the ancestors. As a collective, they had witnessed the mad exploits of Toads stretching back into antiquity, but each of them had also seen his own, unique, vision. Piecing together a mosaic of abstract imagery, they conjured up the lives of their own, illustrious, forebears.

There were no recollections of cosy evenings in company by the fireside. On the contrary, the vole's imagery was of rearing horses and rage, the badger's of cudgelling the heads of weasels and stoats, whilst those of the mole focused on being lost, cold and frightened.

A fatigue set in, the experience had been emotionally draining and they slumped into chairs, lost in their own thoughts. The vole skinned-up, lit up and exhaled.

'What, if anything, have we learnt?', he asked, taking another deep pull on his joint. 'I mean of toads.'

'That they are all reckless, thoroughly disreputable scoundrels,' declared badger severely.

'Hedonists certainly,' allowed the vole. 'And yet one must admire a certain spirit, a *joie de vivre*'. He tilted his head back and blew smoke toward the wood-boarded ceiling. 'A sense of adventure,' he concluded, wistfully.

'I'd say they are jolly good fun,' spouted Brian, earning him a disapproving scowl from the badger. 'I mean they dare. I wish I was daring like that; I just live in a hole.'

Brian's comment, on his uneventful life, resonated with the vole particularly, and with the badger somewhat. A melancholic mood then pervaded, broken moments later by Brian himself.

'Anyone else see the tunnel?'

'What tunnel?', asked the badger and vole in unison.

'You know, the one we all…I mean the ancestors – the one that leads up into the Toad Hall,' he replied, matter-of-factly, adding:

'Comes up inside a food-store…didn't see any worms though…lots of jars, pickles and hanging meats…all dead though, nothing wiggling,' he concluded disdainfully.

The badger and vole exchanged a glance and within that glance, the seed of an idea germinated.

'Reckon you could find that tunnel Brian?', asked the vole.

'Could you, old chap?' asked the badger, already beginning to salivate.

With a growing sense of confidence in his own worth and importance, Brian replied casually

'Oh, no doubt at all, probably find it in my sleep, pretty good at tunnelling actually.'

Chapter Eleven

Toad Aloft

Taupe scanned the skies above Brian's abode before venturing out to hoist another coloured pendant. Fluttering in the stiff spring breeze, on a tripod two metres high, were pendants of many colours, orange on top through all the colours of the rainbow below. Falcons, buzzards, harriers, and kites had all circled this curious addition to the landscape and departed, baffled. Rabbits, hares, foxes, stoats, and weasels had all taken a peek, shrugged their shoulders, and moved on. Opinion was unanimous, Brian's new mate was decidedly odd. The less charitable considered her barking mad.

Back down below, Taupe busied herself connecting a myriad of *mycelia*, tiny white fungal roots, inside a wooden box. In a small, earthen cup she had mixed a saline solution into which, two thin strips of metal scavenged from the earth, stood. Next, she connected two thin, fibrous roots, one to each metal strip, and sat back to wait. Within seconds, the meadows, fields, and woods came alive. Pleased with her handiwork, she put her head inside the soundbox to listen. Such a cacophony of sound, she was accustomed to. It was music to her ears.

Taupe was not pregnant. Indeed, Taupe was chaste – 'Chased for bloody-fucking kilometres' – you might hear her complain each passing season. Of a scientific bent, she was ambitious and had no time to waste on childrearing. To that end, she did one hundred pull-ups a day to keep her strong arms at the ready. She could tunnel faster than any mole who had chased her to date. And yet, this season, Brian had come close to catching her. At one point she thought all was lost, but happily the chimes of the earth (which moles alone can hear) sounded to declare time at the rump, and the end of the mating season.

Of a caustic disposition, she had scant regard for males who were driven by their genitals alone. And yet, this Brian, this dim-witted little fellow had all but caught her, might he not prove to be a suitable mate? The idea flashed across her mind. She would like to have at least one litter before her time was out. She began to evaluate his credentials: good strong arms, plenty of stamina…and then she struggled, what else? That he had had the wherewithal to fashion a pair of spectacles was in his favour, then again, the design had been passed down to him by his predecessors, so it didn't count. With a sigh, she shelved the notion.

With her head back inside the soundbox, she began to tune in to a conversation. The *mycelia* web, feeding back electrical pulses stretched for miles around, but the wood was her focus.

'Fergal, I'm warning you now, get off me you big eejit or I'll…' Molly Fenian's laughing voice brought a broad grin to Taupe's face. 'I mean it now…will you get off, right, I warned you!' Taupe threw back her head and laughed as a howl of pain, almost wolf-like, resonated within the soundbox. 'That's the way girl!' Taupe said aloud, clapping her paws together.

Now that her wood-wide-web had been established, Taupe's great challenge was to discover how to transmit. This one had hitherto defeated her. Yes, she could eavesdrop, and this alone was a triumph, but she had been engaged on the understanding that she could send as well as receive. She had lied of course. What use a spy, if not of a duplicitous nature? The summer lay ahead and in Brian's conveniently situated abode, she determined to crack it. And if she failed, well then, she would simply lie.

The Upright was, all things considered, an inferior class of animal in her opinion, an animal divorced from nature. For all their technical abilities, they were too dependent on ravaging resources when it was abundantly clear that nature provided all they required. She, Taupe, would make such discoveries that would earn her international accolades. Why could not a mole, she reasoned, be the first animal to win acclaim in an Upright dominated world?

Reversing the polarity on her battery was bound to fail, as it had before, and it did again. Taupe sighed, there had to be a way of connecting into the loop, back to the drawing board. One thing she could do was to broadcast a symphony and this she now did for the devilment of it. Deftly, she turned back the two fibrous roots upon themselves and connected her battery to slender *mycelia*. The resulting symphony would now spread far and wide. This had been an accidental discovery and initially, she had thought it to be her Eureka moment. However, with no means of controlling it, or adding her own input, it had proven a false dawn.

She leaned back in her chair as the symphony swept over her, a fungal consonance that only those below ground could detect, she cast her eyes about the abode. What was that? Taupe moved over to Brian's bed. She had not slept in his bed as it smelt fetid, and she was minded to haul it above ground and set fire to it. The spine of a book perhaps? From beneath the mattress of woven reed, she pulled out a book, the pages of which were made of large, pressed leaves. Charcoal drawings charmed her initially, that is until she got to a section where the artist, evidently Brian, had sketched numerous rear-ends of what she took to be his conquests.

There were a great many explicit drawings and the unimaginative title to the page was Molasses. Taupe sighed profoundly at the oldest and most juvenile of all mole jokes. She shook her head. '*Quel branleur!*'– What a wanker! – she murmured.

Every twist and turn of Brian's abode, each and every possession he owned, aggravated her. What antagonised her more was that he kept entering her thoughts. There had been a pleasure in bandaging his little todger for him, his boyish look of expectancy charmed her. Taupe was confused; did she desire him sexually? If so, how? His personal hygiene left a lot to be desired. Or was it a mothering instinct?

She replaced his seedy rag beneath his mattress, picked up two coloured pendants and went aloft to hoist them.

**

He cuts a strange figure, thought Horatio, as he puffed on a Cuban cigar and observed the figure holding the binoculars at the window. That suit for starters, he considered, is woefully tailored. What did he say again? It was made from hemp and dyed green with broccoli juice; Horatio shook his head in disbelief. And then the shoes, canvas? They belong on deck. Oxford, wing-tip brogues, that's the footwear for a gentleman, Horatio had always maintained. But he made no comment, not to this all-important new business partner.

Standing at the window on the third floor of Toad Hall, Georges Montgolfiere was scanning the horizon. He noted with satisfaction that workmen were unloading glamping-pods. Another delivery had arrived, huge coils of fencing wire which were being rolled off the back of a wagon. 'Good, good, not before time,' he mouthed. His scrutiny then turned through one hundred and eighty degrees to a distant hilltop, he smiled and consulted a pocketbook briefly before declaring:

'Excellent work Agent Orange, excellent!', he enthused, turning to Horatio, and adding 'Ingenious types, moles.'

Scepticism spread over the broad face of Horatio Toad and his prominent, copper-coloured eyes, narrowed.

'Moles? Utter dimwits in my opinion. Servile though… make for a half-decent valet I suppose,' he concluded disparagingly.

Quickly noting Montgolfiere's disapprobation, Horatio added conciliatorily 'not to say there aren't exceptions… I suppose.'

With a stout pull on his cigar, Horatio Toad tilted his head far back to exhale, thereby reducing his surplus of chins to a double.

'What exactly is ingenious about this fellow, if I may ask George?'

'She,' corrected Montgolfiere emphatically. 'She, our Agent Orange, if not our eyes, is most certainly our ears. She is using a network of *mycelia*, fungal roots, to listen in and communicate with every living animal and plant on our great estate…'

'Err, my estate old boy, we haven't signed the lease yet on your bit,' interrupted Horatio sitting forward quickly in an old captain's chair and thereby multiplying his stomach folds, four-fold.

'Yes, yes, yes,' Montgolfiere resumed, with a dismissive wave of his hand. 'We will know the thoughts of all living creatures on this estate. We will be able to plan for their wellbeing.'

'Thoughts of that lot?', Horatio stated arrogantly with a cursory wave toward the windows. 'Shouldn't have thought you need a genius to find that out – still live in mud holes.'

As a legal beagle prepared documents on a large mahogany desk in the library, Horatio Toad, bored with proceedings, took time to study the portraits of his ancestors. No fewer than fifteen oils clad the oak-panelled walls. He had made a cursory study of the family journals, passed down through the generations, and although the exploits of most of his forebears were remarkable, it was one in particular that grabbed his attention.

He stopped before the largest painting and smiled in appreciation at the most feted of all, his Great-three to the power of three-Grandfather. So great a figure in family lore was he, that he was known only as Toad. He had seen copies of this original in the journals and indeed, had emulated his apparel, and he hoped, his style.

But now, before this illustrious ancestor, Horatio felt humbled. Yes, he came from a long line of derring-doers, but to date, Horatio had done precious little in comparison, he had dared little. Oh, he'd got into plenty of scrapes back in Bermuda where the remainder of portraits hung, however, an ample supply of the old necessary, as he termed his bankbook, had always got him out of a pickle.

Of his Eton education, Horatio was thankful, for within it he had forged many a useful contact. 'Many a toad has passed through Eton,' you might hear him say. England was not as alien a landscape as it might otherwise have been to an animal who had spent the bulk of his life in sunny climes. The clearing of a throat broke him from his reverie.

'All in order?', Horatio enquired lazily of the officiating solicitor, a thin, pallid, sharp-nosed fellow smelling of mothballs, named Snipe. 'Perfectly Mr. Toad'.

Horatio Toad made a cursory scan of the document, pretending to understand the legalese, and hovered with the nib of his fountain pen above his full name.

Horatio Calidus, Superbus, Dimidium-Nelson Toad.

With a flourish, Horatio applied his signature and was immediately followed by Georges, Sauvage-Montgolfiere, who did the same.

A broad grin on Montgolfiere's face had Horatio wondering if he hadn't leased out for too low a price. Whatever the fellow found of value in two hundred hectares of scrubby heath, woodland, and second-grade farmland, he had no idea. Montgolfiere's undiminished grin had Horatio beg the question:

'Pleased with yourself Georges?', he asked in curiosity to a man transfixed upon the document.

'Oh, very much so,' spurted Montgolfiere, as if taken by surprise. 'Indeed yes, a very fair deal for us both.'

A short, awkward silence ensued during which Horatio Toad wondered if he had not been a chump in getting into bed with Montgolfiere. Horatio had been a chump before and would doubtless be a chump again for attention to detail was not his forte, he simply could not be bothered with it. The detail was what fusty, little types such as Snipe were for.

Montgolfiere, sensing some unease, broke the silence.

'I was just thinking of how unimaginative my parents were in naming me…no middle name you see.'

'Does seem a bit rum,' Horatio replied abruptly suspecting that his bright-eyed, indeed one might say, wild-eyed, business partner was deflecting attention.

'I note,' continued Montgolfiere, playfully, 'that one of your middle names is hyphenated.'

'And so, what of it?', Horatio replied, defensively. He had never been entirely happy with his full moniker.

'Idle curiosity, nothing more, none of my business of course,' placated Montgolfiere quickly as he turned to a member of his staff and asked him to bring two large glasses of what he assured, was a very fine nettle-wine.

Gentlemanly manners, although pressed upon Horatio from a young age, had never found fertile ground in which to flourish, indeed they had withered on the vine. More used was he to *grand cru* clarets, and what he now had a mouthful of, he wished to dispose of by a speedier route than nature had designed.

By contrast, Montgolfiere's aquiline nose was interred deep within his glass, eyes closed in ecstasy as he savoured perfumes. These same aromas reminded Horatio of latrines and so he took the opportunity of tipping his glass on the bare floorboards and emptying his mouth in the guise of a sneeze.

'My hyphenated middle-name,' he piped up to deflect attention. 'All to do with an uncle, you see. Famous wrestler back in Bermuda don't you know?', he spouted, noting Montgolfiere's attention drifting toward a wet puddle on the floor. 'Oh, yes, renowned throughout the Caribbean. Mother was very fond of him, but father insisted that half-nelson wouldn't be fitting so the Latin-Dimidium-Nelson- was used instead.'

Montgolfiere proffered the bottle toward Horatio's empty glass.

'Oh, dear me no, I never drink before the sun is over the yardarm,' he lied. 'In any case, I prefer red.'

'I have a truly excellent elderberry,' replied Montgolfiere, brightening and, without noting a look of pure disdain on his partner's face, scurried off to get it.

Horatio decided to make himself scarce, leaving a message with Mr Snipe that he had to go and check on progress with the zip wires. In fact, he had decided that he, Horatio Toad, the brain behind the idea, would be the first to give the apparatus a go.

Towering ten metres high on top of the roof of the three story, Elizabethan Toad Hall with its red-bricked, spiralled chimneys, was a structure not dissimilar to a mini-Eiffel tower. A steel rung ladder within it led up to the pinnacle from which steel hawsers splayed out at all points of the compass. These cables stretched far into the distance only coming to earth at a distance of some six-hundred metres. The westerly route criss-crossed the upstream, meandering river. It was this route that Horatio elected to try for the inaugural flight.

'No, no, no sir, I can't allow that today. There's a storm brewing, look,' declared the chief engineer.

Since a toadlet, Horatio had struggled with the word *No*. To hear it in repetition, was insupportable.

'Who, may I ask, is paying your wages sir?', Horatio asked, imperiously, adding quickly 'and who, if I may be so bold, has paid for this contraption?'

'Why, you sir and you did, but it's too dangerous to be connected when there is a risk of lightning.' The engineer indicated an ominous, lowering sky away to the west, adding for good measure. 'Besides, not one of these trolleys has been tested yet.'

Horatio fixed the engineer with a steely eye. He then clambered up to verify that the pulley trolley was free running.

'It is perfectly obvious to me my good man that this trolley, brand new as it is, is in fine fettle.'

'I mean, tested under load,' the engineer qualified hesitantly, trying not to cast aspersions on the weight of the corpulent Horatio. He failed.

'My good man,' Horatio retorted haughtily, peering down with an accusatory glare. 'Uprights of considerable bulk must use this equipment, are you telling me that you have failed to make adequate provision?'

'No, no, not at all Mr Toad, it's just that we always send down a heavy weight to make sure a bearing doesn't malfunction under duress,' the engineer explained courteously. 'We'll attach the cradles tomorrow. Best to come back then,' he concluded. However, Horatio had taken nothing on board, save for the repeated negative- 'No.'

A howling NO! This was all Horatio heard behind him as he expertly flicked off the safety catch, for he had used one before, and took flight holding on to nothing more than a strap attached to the trolley. 'Yippee!' he screamed as the trolley picked up speed in seconds. Down he hurtled following the river below which took on the appearance of a live, silver, sinewy snake as he progressed along it at breakneck speed.

So exhilarated was Horatio, so pleased with his act of defiance, so self-congratulatory, that a couple of points escaped his attention. Had he but looked up, he might have noted a trail of smoke emanating from the trolley. He might have spotted dark clouds approaching at the same speed that he was approaching them. But on he went, proclaiming the family motto joyously.

'Not for us the well-trodden road, the life mundane, the humble abode, the only animals who truly live are the well-travelled, death-defying toads!'

A sudden piercing screech brought his knees above his head and his head below his knees as he came to the most abrupt of halts. So sudden a shock was it that he came close to losing his grip. Looking up he now saw the trolley's bearing block glowing a faint red as it issued clouds of smoke. The sky had turned beetle black. He looked down at the river, ten metres below, and averted his eyes as it reflected a blinding lightning flash. Horatio's heart began to pound as he counted the seconds, pound, pound, pound. On the count of three, an ear-cracking peal of thunder rent the air.

'Oh, lumme,' he muttered, as a familiar sensation took hold, a *melange* of injured pride, regret, and cowardice. Once more, he had fallen foul of chumpism, his life-long foe and nemesis. With another flash, another peel, the storm was ever closer. Now panic took hold and his arms began to ache.

Aware that he was now in peril, his bulging eyes grew to twice their normal size, if he had teeth, then they would have chattered. The river below was nothing more than a thread of grey as the wind began to gust, and he began to sway. At one moment he was above the river, the next, above the land. Chilly rain, goblet-sized, began to fall chilling his hands and weakening his grip.

What could he do? He racked his brains, help was required, but from what quarter? Another flash of lightning had him extract, with his mouth, a large handkerchief from his top, jacket pocket, and this he waved with vigorous shakes of his head.

Sheltering from the ravages of the storm, a group of swans had found refuge in a small, reeded bay.

'Edwin dear, whatever is that?', Mrs Preece-Moog exclaimed, indicating upward with a sweep of her long, elegant neck. Sir Edwin squinted upward for a second or two before his monocle fell out. Dutifully, his wife fished the glass from the water and replaced it. Peer as he might, Sir Edwin could not make head nor tail of the strange apparition.

'It's a toad,' stated Mrs Preece-Moog, categorically. 'A flying toad,' she added less assuredly. Sir Edwin, ruler of the roost, chuckled at the prospect and in habitual, condescending manner 'Cobsplained' – 'The toad, my beloved, is an amphibian and whilst there have been reported cases of amphibians raining down to earth, indeed in such storms as we have today, I am unaware of any report of a hovering toad.'

'It is a toad,' maintained his long-suffering wife, 'and it appears to be in some distress,' she emphasised, raising herself in the water with two, hefty beats of her wings- 'Someone ought to go up there and take a look.'

Sir Edwin knew that the someone in question was him. Another flash of lightning and an ear-splitting crack of thunder, exacerbated by now torrential rain, had him delay.

'I'll go,' Mrs Preece-Moog stated, curtly, as she glided out in readiness for take-off. She had no intention of doing so but knew this ploy to be effective. Dignity for the Cob of the household was everything and as a self-appointed knight of the realm, Sir Edwin knew he would never live it down if he didn't comply.

It always takes the line of least resistance, Sir Edwin told himself as he prepared his run-up. The teachings of his ancestors flooded back; the likelihood of a bird being struck is negligible. Nevertheless, Sir Edwin, monocle fixed firmly, did not relish this flight one little bit. Fortune favours the brave; he panted as he skated along the river's length beating his powerful wings. Undercarriage up, he reminded himself, as he took to the air.

Clearing the treeline, he circled widely and then made a broad sweep past the hovering object. It was of no use however as his monocle was all but opaque, steamed up, and spattered with raindrops. He elected to make another pass in the opposing direction so he could get a look with his good eye. 'Undercarriage up' saved the day as he had to undergo an emergency procedure to avoid an obstacle, some form of aerial wire he had never seen before.

On his second pass, he was convinced that his good eye was deceiving him, on his third, and this, of course, was fleeting, that the suspended object did indeed resemble the form of a toad. On his fourth, his monocle dropped out as he swooped close past the face of a terror-stricken, gentleman toad. Sir Edwin then made a wide circle as he considered a course of action.

Meanwhile, Horatio was at the end of his tether. The lightning now sent bolts to earth all about, his hands were numb, and he was convinced that any second now he was going to die. 'I'm done for – I'm fried – I've had my chips!'

'Let go!', came the first of Sir Edwin's exhortations as he swept past.

'Jump!', came the second, loud and insistent.

'Let go you damned fool!', was the last.

Horatio's grip gave out and down, he plummeted. A toad who'd had his chips was about to take a battering and be united with the fish.

Chapter Twelve

Jigs and Reels

It had been a day of mixed fortune whether on river, in field, or wood.

Off to a promising start, Trace had agreed to send the boys, Clamp, and Nipper chubbing; a filling, if fatty fish for growing lads and one that Reg could barely stomach. Reg, being on a promise, was doing all he could to keep his partner sweet, and to that end, he had cleared out the boys' section of the couch.

'Filthy little bleeders, I'll be glad when they're gone,' he grumbled in a low voice; he didn't want Trace to hear. 'Any uvver jobs love? he asked helpfully, too helpfully perhaps.

'Nah', Trace replied, adding teasingly 'thought we might take a swim upstream together. I mean, when was the last time we did that?' Reg's face fell. Trace was adept at playing a hopeful Reg along, he was putty in her paws.

'Oh, um yeah, you've got a point love,' Reg spluttered, failing miserably to keep the disappointment from his voice. Trace threw back her head and laughed.

'Come 'ere, you horny git!'

Now, all of this would have been, to use one of Reg's colloquialisms, 'randy and dandy', had it not been for a pair of Uprights in a canoe who just would not leave them be. The one in the front was pointing some apparatus or other at them and asking the one at the rear, to paddle and move in closer.

At the rear himself, and in a transport of passion, Reg was all for ignoring them, but Trace wasn't having any of it. 'Get orf fer fuck's sake.' She whined, pulling away.

Crestfallen and angry as he was, Reg gave the otter's version of the middle finger to no avail, understanding, or impact. The female Upright simply tipped her head to one side and smiled.

'Oh, Simon, aren't they cute?'

Reg was beside himself and let loose a tirade of insults, mined from the deepest pits of his rich vocabulary. But the female Upright simply made little kissing sounds and kept smiling at him as if he were an idiotic pup.

It was Reg's fervent hope that he might resume where he left off, but Trace had lost the impetus. Besides, she could see the bow waves of the boys returning and the chance had gone.

**

'It's still sounding Fergal,' said Molly Fenian to her husband as she got from her bed to answer a call of nature. 'My legs are like jelly,' she laughed as she kicked Fergal playfully in the butt. 'Come on, up you come.' Fergal rolled onto his back, paws in the air, and then back onto his other side. 'I'm not able for it Molly, I'm fair knackered,' he complained good-humouredly.

The previous evening, the Fenians had discovered music, more precisely jigs, and reels. It had been an accidental discovery and had occurred when Molly decided to chew through an unsightly root protruding from the roof of their den. Standing on her hind legs she had just begun when her ears were assailed by first, a discordant din and then something altogether more rhythmic. To the utter bemusement of her husband, she began to dance about the room with her front legs clamped to her sides and her hind legs skipping about the floor.

'What, in the name of the green man, are you up to Molly?', demanded a perplexed Fergal. And that was that. Molly pulled him up, tuned him in, turned him on, and away he went. 'Will it ever stop?', Fergal had cried, three hours in.

'I never want it to stop. I love the diddly-dee, I want it to go on forever!', Molly cried in ecstasy.

**

Molly and Fergal were not alone, for down in Jack and Jill Stoats' place a party had been in full swing and only now, as daylight filtered through the canopy above, did weary and intoxicated stoats make their unsteady way homeward. But this had been sound of a different order, thrash-metal. A mosh-pit had been raging all night leaving many bruised and utterly bemused.

'What got into us Jill?', Jack asked, pleased to have their cramped abode back to themselves.

'Drink I think,' came the less than fulsome answer from a still-dazed Jill.

'That's not how it started; it was more than that. The noises, where did they come from? I mean, I went up to get some fresh air and they stopped,' explained a mystified Jack.

'Was it the green man then?', asked Jill, searchingly.

'How would I know?', replied Jack. 'Never seen him. Anyway, they say he sticks his finger in his ear and makes a horrible racket through his nose. No use for a party.'

Quincy Badger, although deaf in one ear following a dust-up with a neighbouring badger who tried to commandeer his nut store, was not immune to the classical strains filtering through his roof. In between bouts of coughing, it always did affect him badly at night disturbing his sleep, he listened in wonderment to the sound. It got to him. Initially, he had turned his head gruffly to one side, deaf ear uppermost believing it to be a storm outside, but, bit by bit, he tuned in. Eventually, he drifted into the most contented sleep he'd enjoyed in years.

Taupe's attempts at transmission had taken a great leap forward. Yes, it was only music, and no, it would not suffice, but it constituted progress, nonetheless.

She had spent the whole night connecting *mycelia* in random patterns, thousand upon thousand, and had then scurried off to the end of a burrow, twenty metres away, that she had dug herself, to listen to the results. The results were confusing. No matter what connections she made, she heard the same genre of music – reggae. It was the only type of music she was familiar with and so, she wondered if that was why she picked up on it. Could it be that she was transmitting thousands of notes, but only selecting and piecing together those that made sense to her? Rather like listening to a foreign language, she asked herself, am I not appropriating a strange word to fit my lexicon, just to make sense of it?

Deciding that she needed rest, she slumped onto Brian's bed and despite some olfactory objections, she sensed a proximity to him which was not entirely repugnant.

Chapter Thirteen

All the Young Shrews

All the young shrews carry the news, and today was no exception.

'You've got a shrew, Trevor-Stan,' called Brian through to the water vole who was preening his whiskers and attending to his toilette. For the life of him, Brian couldn't fathom such fastidiousness toward personal hygiene, particularly as that night they were to use the secret tunnel. White trousers, it seemed to Brian, were inappropriate attire.

'Send him through,' replied the vole, abstractedly, as he noted with relief the regrowth of fur on some of the bald patches on his back. He quickly donned a sky-blue shirt before the shrew arrived.

Being of diminutive stature, it was necessary to get down on one's hands and knees for the plug-in. Young shrews had always plied their trade as messengers, and they were ideally suited to the task. Fleet of foot and small enough to avoid notice, they had a reputation for discretion. The accepted payment was wasp grub, and the vole always kept a jar of these ready on his mantlepiece.

The vole presented his ear, and the little fellow poked his pointed snout in to impart the news.

Meanwhile, out on the edge of the landing, Brian was in a quandary. 'Once you've eaten one, you just can't stop,' he muttered to himself as he frantically excavated the bank for wasp grub to replenish the jar. 'Sodding typical,' he cursed. 'When you want to find one, you can't.' In exasperation, he stopped for a moment to scratch at his nether regions. The healing process was taking an eternity this year and he had resorted to maggots inside the bandage on his todger. They usually did the trick, and the tickling sensation was not unpleasurable.

'Really?', came the sound of the vole's voice from within. 'And he was quite, ok?', questioned the vole. 'Well it seems as if I may have misjudged them...' he continued. 'Do send my regards to Sir Edwin.'

'I say Brian old chap,' called out the vole. 'Do give the little fellow a couple of grubs, would you? No, make that three – He's brought heartening news. You'll find them in the jar.'

Without wishing to incur the wrath of his friend who was liable to anger when his stocks were plundered, Brian had to think on his feet. He fished inside his bandage and brought out a small paw full of wriggling maggots. At first, the young shrew turned up his snout as the pungent ammonia hit him square in the face. Nevertheless, he had a nibble then made a small squeak of surprised satisfaction, then quickly devoured the lot.

Brian sauntered into the vole's abode, hands inside his pelt pockets and declared casually:

'I know you said 'some' old friend and I did tell the little chap 'just some'. I only turned my back for a moment and the little beggar had devoured the lot!'

'But the jar was already empty Brian,' replied the vole searchingly, as he stood with paws on hips.

'Was it? Was it indeed?', a reddening Brian spluttered. 'I hadn't noticed...I mean, I did give him some titbits...as a tip from me.'

The vole simply sighed, turned his back, and continued with his ablutions leaving Brian to shift from foot to foot.

'Err…good news, was it?', he asked awkwardly.

'Interesting, I'd say,' came the teasing reply.

'Oh.'

A booming voice then heralded the arrival of the badger.

'Why must he always shout? Uncouth animal. Scull him over, would you Brian?'

Keen to get back into his friend's good books, Brian obliged.

It had been decided that they would wait until dusk to make their foray into Toad Hall. The badger had come equipped for a fight. He wore a wide leather belt into which every manner of offensive weapon had been tucked.

'We have no way of knowing what we are up against in there,' he declared gruffly, a comment which occasioned a surreptitious roll of the eyes between vole and mole.

'I've got the whole wild wood behind me,' the badger continued, menacingly. 'One word from me and we'll rid this place of foreigners for good.' Emotion then caught in his throat instigating a bout of wheezing and coughing.

'Really Quincy, I'm sure there'll be no cause for that,' replied the vole soothingly, but his reply had the opposite effect. Between fits of coughing, the badger made it abundantly clear, baring his teeth frighteningly at times, that the wood belonged to English animals. Whenever the vole tried to remonstrate (Brian didn't dare to), he was shouted down.

'No, no, let me speak…' would he shout, holding up his great paw to stay the vole before lancing more vitriol.

The shrew's news went unsaid. The vole was still processing it and given that the badger's views on gentlemen toads were well known, he thought it best not to inflame him further.

**

The exact account of what happened to the hapless Horatio Toad differed somewhat from the account provided by the shrew. Reliable animals though they be, a relay system operated by young shrews can result in a Chinese whisper, exaggeratory effect.

Sir Edwin Preece-Moog's account to fellow river- dwellers was this: -

'At great risk to my own personal safety, I took flight in response to a distress signal, namely the waving of a handkerchief. As a knight of the river, I insisted that my wife and family remain grounded'. Murmurs of approval greeted this. Constance Preece-Moog turned her head away in disbelief.

'As misfortune would have it, a storm was raging at the time and as I gained altitude, lightning passed over my wings. But, a fellow animal, a gentleman toad no less, was in peril, clinging to an Upright's aerial wire, so I did not heed the consequences.' Gasps of admiration.

'Having attained a high altitude, I made several passes to reconnoitre the situation. In a petrified condition, the poor animal was clinging on for dear life and in no condition, indeed in no position, to make an informed choice. Clearly, it was my sole responsibility to save him.' Sir Edwin paused for dramatic effect and to take in the plaudits, of which there were many.

'I gave express instruction for the animal to jump upon my back as I passed.' Cries of wonderment from wide- eyed, transfixed animals.

'Now, I knew this manoeuvre constituted a grave risk to both parties, yet with the storm worsening and lightning bolts shooting all about us, I had no choice. On my fifth pass, or was it my seventh? You will forgive the inexactitude here given the pressure I was under, not to mention the danger of collision with the wire, I managed to dislodge the animal's tenacious grip. I did this by flying on one engine – on one wing so to speak.'

Huge intakes of breath resounded all about. A glance expressing incredulity from Constance went unheeded.

'With one wing beating at a pace to rival a lark, I managed to flip the animal onto my back. "Hang on" I cried, and immediately felt the weight. He was heavy, very heavy, and it took all I had, with the lightning flashing all around and the rain torrential, to bring him down to a safe height. Because, and only because I was spent, did I then ease him into the safety of the river for splashdown.'

At the end of Sir Edwin's epic account, a huge roar of approval went up, obsequiously led by Rear-Admiral Canard. Canard was a naval man, knew his station in the river's hierarchy, and deferred to Sir Edwin as Admiral of the Fleet.

**

Horatio Calidus Superbus Dimidium-Nelson Toad's version of events differed in key aspects.

'Due to the infernal contraption seizing, something to do with the engineer having fitted the wrong type of ball bearing, I was left, suspended a good fifty metres above the river in a bit of a quandary. I always carry with me a multi-tooled army knife and having hooked my feet about the wire, I began to disassemble the faulty mechanism. By necessity, I had to hold component parts in my mouth…'

Horatio failed to notice quizzical looks being exchanged between staff of his forthcoming business venture. Some of his six wives, the later recruits, were nevertheless enthralled and he was now in vainglorious flight.

'Having located the faulty bearing, it became evident that there wasn't a jot I could do about it. Then the idea hit me in a flash – and by the by, there was a lot of flashing going on what with the lightning, thunder, and rain, but I didn't pay it any mind.

'*Carpe Diem* Horatio, I told myself! Why not saw through the blessed cable and swing down to earth like that Tarzan chappie? Well, there I was sawing away quite merrily when some infernal bird started strafing me. Big old swan type.'

Gasps of 'Oh no!' and 'You poor dear' emanated from wives four, five and six. Horatio took a puff on his cigar, a swig of his wine and continued.

'Well, I was pretty miffed I can tell you, *Acta, non verba*, I told myself, action this day! So, on his umpteenth strafe, I fetched the fellow a sharp one on the beak. Only snag was, I over-reached, lost my grip, and down I went.' Sharp intakes of breath as palms shot to mouths. Horatio then held up his own palms, expelled a long puff and continued.

'I'll confess, I'll confess that for a moment or two, I thought I was in dire straits. But then, the old dive training kicked in. I used to be a champion cliff-diver back in the day in Bermuda...did I ever mention it?' Younger wives cooed whilst pay-roll staff, wishing they were somewhere else, snorted quietly.

'Oh, yes dire straits indeed, what with being sixty metres up, but a*udentes fortuna iuvat* and all that. I adopted the old semi-pike, then the full-pike and down I went like an arrow, hit the water with barely a ripple. "Still got it old boy", I congratulated myself as I struck out for the bank. I say, do forgive the false modesty here, won't you? Bit of an ordeal, don't you know?'

A faint ripple of applause grew to a clamour as Upright staff members dug each other in the ribs in a reminder to laugh when the king laughs.

Mrs Tabatha Toad, wife number six, unable to contain her emotion, was the first of the six wives to embrace the hero of zip-wire one.

'Yes, yes,' Horatio spouted, keen to free himself as she showered praise and wet kisses. 'It was nothing really Martha,' he said, pushing her away. 'Tabatha!', she countered crossly and fixed him in the eye.

'What? Oh, yes, quite so my dear, Tabatha, quite right-emotion and all that.'

The account of the incident on zip-wire one, as witnessed by a pair of beavers from their lodge, was this:

'Moira, Moira!', called Jock. 'Drop what you're doing and come and take a look at this.' Moira shouted back 'I'm busy.' Jock persisted. 'Ach, you'll no' want to miss this one hen.' Moira, dressed in her housecoat, made her way up grumbling as she went. 'This had better be good Jock McTavish.'

Moira was not disappointed. Flashes of lightning illuminated the great wings of a white bird that appeared to be dive-bombing some poor, hovering, unfortunate.

'That's no' the great stuck-up ponce, is it?', Moira asked, squinting upward.

'Aye, that's him all right, Sir Edgar Stooge, or whatever he calls himself.', replied Jock, derisively.

'But what's he doing? Whatever is that thing up there?', pressed Moira, and just as she did so, down plummeted the thing, the object of the swan's attentions.

Far from the heroic Olympian dive as recounted by Horatio, the transit to water was more akin to a tumble and flop, accompanied by a scream that could be heard above the rages of the storm. Entrance to the river was by way of the back, flat on the back.

It was a few moments later, as it became apparent that the object couldn't swim (it surfaced, arms stretched, gulping for air, then promptly sank again) that Jock McTavish took to the water in rescue.

Bedraggled and covered in weed and slime from the riverbed – for Horatio had plumbed the deep – Moira was, at first, unwilling to permit access to a filthy, gibbering wreck of an animal.

'Plunge him and wash him off first Jock,' she commanded.

Although Jock considered this harsh, Moira could be harsher still when roused, so he did as bid. Holding him by the scruff of the neck, for Jock was a powerful animal, he plunged a discombobulated Horatio time and time again in the central pool of their lodge. Then they plunged together, coming up inside a surprisingly spacious, well-appointed apartment.

The translocated Scottish couple sat and surveyed the dripping object fished from the river. First impressions were not favourable.

'You know what that is Jock,' said Moira curtly. 'Aye, that I do pet,' replied Jock, stuffing his pipe.

'A landowner, a landowning amphibian no less.'

Horatio, aware that certain social niceties ought to be extended to a couple who may have saved his life, could not, however, tolerate the term *amphibian*. On the verge of making a polite correction to the effect that he was, first and foremost, a gentleman toad, he was beaten to it by Moira.

'An amphibian who can't swim, I've no' seen the like of it!', she declared joyously clapping her paws.

Horatio sat simmering as the pair of beavers had their fun until he could bear it no longer. He then launched a withering verbal attack and consequently, the second impression of the day, and one that left an indent, was of Jock's heel upon Horatio's backside. Once again, Horatio took to the air, landing in an undignified heap on the bankside.

'And dinnae darken my dam again, ye great, fat sassenach amphibian!'

Chapter Fourteen

Eden Awaits

It was dusk on the riverbank, most birds had gone to roost, bats took flies in flittering dives and the only calls were those of the raucous coots. Somewhere off, a tawny owl hooted.

All was still as the water vole beached his boat between some reeds at the edge of the lawn of Toad Hall.

'This, Pan damn it, is a covert operation Rat. White trousers, whatever are you thinking of?' hissed the badger for the umpteenth time. He himself wore improvised military fatigues and had gone to the extent of blackening the white stripes of his muzzle with mud.

The badger became very anxious in the proximity of Uprights, Brian nervous, while the water vole, wearily accustomed to their presence on the river, was cautious, but calm.

Lights were now on throughout the building and even in the attic rooms, the former servants' quarters. Knowledge of what went on inside was scant. Some of the squirrels, who had long taken up residence in the lofts had left, complaining of the noise. Bats, with an established colony, were loath to leave and so they put up with it. House rats, now obliged to go beneath boards, found easy pickings and enhanced variety in their meals. But that was about it. There were no great insights into the purposes of Uprights or indeed of a new, gentleman toad.

The intrepid trio remained in the boat until night fell and then, upon badger's command, they followed their stealthy leader over to the spot where the entrance to the tunnel ought to be. Except it wasn't of course – nothing but lawn. The water vole wagered on a count to ten, but it was only seven before the badger lost his temper.

'If you've got me out here on some damn fool's errand Mole, I'll wring your neck!'

'No need for that Quincy old chap,' chastised the vole.

'Shut up Rat! Get behind that bush before you're spotted,' barked the badger who began to cough.

'We'll be heard,' retorted the vole quickly, unable to help himself. A glare and show of teeth had him edge behind the bush.

'Has to be here,' began Brian uncertainly. 'Has to be'. He paced about leaving neither of his comrades confident that he had the faintest clue of where to locate the tunnel.

'Find it with my eyes closed,' spat the badger sarcastically. The overbearing animal was making Brian nervous, and in such moments, his mental faculties deserted him.

Eventually, he had a flash-back. 'There was a tree!', he declared triumphantly. Fortunately, Brian didn't notice the badger's paws curling into fists, the vole, however, did.

'What type of tree old chap? asked the vole, encouragingly.

'A big one,' declared Brian.

A low grumbling sound began somewhere in the pit of the badger's stomach and slowly grew in intensity, the vole knew they only had moments before he would blow his top.

'Like that big oak over there?', the vole posited, rapidly.

Now, 'over there' to a myopic mole is tantamount to indicating an ant in the uppermost branches of a tree. Squint as well he might through his spectacles and with his front teeth protruding alarmingly, Brian was looking in the wrong direction.

'Probably,' was all he could muster. The vole took him by the shoulders and pointed him in the right direction.

'Could it be that one Brian?', he asked, forcefully.

'Oh yes...most probably,' came the response, lacking in all certitude.

The disgruntled badger led the way, he had adopted a crouching position with his head turning from side to side to check that the coast was clear. Brian followed in his footsteps mimicking his actions, whilst the water vole sauntered at the rear, hands in pockets.

As soon as they reached the giant oak, Brian began to sniff the air. He then got down on all fours and sniffed the earth.

'Truffles,' he exclaimed. Only for the briefest of moments did the badger forget about tunnels.

'We're here to find a tunnel Mole!', he bellowed.

'Shush!', from the vole, didn't help matters.

'There's a tunnel too,' stated Brian brightly, adding 'right below our feet'.

He slipped off his pelt, and took off his spectacles. 'Here, hold those,' he commanded, as he stuffed his belongings into the arms of the badger whose nose reacted violently to the cargo. He hurled them as far as he could.

With a speed the badger had to admire, albeit reluctantly, Brian, digging like a mole possessed, disappeared below ground leaving only some garlic leaves and what looked suspiciously like maggots crawling on the grass.

Molehills then sprouted left, right and centre.

'Canst move in the earth so fast old mole?', murmured the water vole.

'What's that?', barked the badger.

'Oh, just a line,' replied the vole, dreamily.

'Well, shut up!', commanded the commander.

'Yes Sir!' replied the vole sarcastically, earning him a cautionary stare.

Perhaps it was minutes or even an hour before the mole resurfaced, animals don't count time as Uprights do, but pop up he did, and speedily did he impart good news.

This rapidity in reporting saved him from the cudgel because the badger had long since tired of watching molehills sprout, he was determined to clobber the little blighter the next time he popped up.

Brian had found it, with one caveat, he had found the tunnel's curved, red-bricked roof.

'Right under here you say?', demanded the badger sternly, divesting himself of his arsenal and great coat. 'Leave it to me.' And so did the badger begin his own excavation, hurling up earth behind him.

Seated with his back to the giant oak, the vole produced a joint and lit up. As ever, Brian cast furtive glances from the corner of an eye. Eventually, a nudge to his shoulder bade him partake.

'You know Brian, I can't help but think it would have been easier to have knocked on the door.'

The two animals fell into fits of giggles as brick after brick shot into the air from below. However, a sonorous bout of coughing dampened the mirth, amplified as it was in the deep hole, the dread thought of their witnessing a comrade digging his own grave, cast a pall.

'Come on and bring my weaponry,' issued a hoarse and panting badger.

With tallow candles in hand, the vole and badger followed Brian who assured them he had no need of light. Dank and pitch black save for the eerie candlelight, the tunnel's floor was uneven causing the followers to stumble and stub their toes. Brian, on the other hand, was in his element, the badger also to an extent, but the water vole felt claustrophobic, and the tunnel seemed to go on forever. At last, they began to ascend until they came to a boarded, wooden ceiling, akin to a hatch or trapdoor.

'Now what?', growled the badger.

'We could always knock,' the vole replied, facetiously.

Barging his way past the water vole and Brian, the badger pressed his muzzle to the boards and sniffed loudly.

'Food in here,' he remarked, attempting complacency. Bracing himself, he placed his great paws on the boards and pushed upward. With a creak and groan the hatch lifted enough for the badger to poke his head cautiously through.

'Hey, like, what's de notion bro?', piped up a house rat, busy hauling a cob of corn.

The badger ignored him telling the others that they had come up in an Upright's food store.

'Told you so,' replied Brian, casually if, greatly relieved.

'Don't go casting no shade on me bro, this is our store,' claimed the house rat.

'Fuck off!', barked the badger, who was scowling at the rat.

'Easy, easy boomer, like I need beef on my strip right now,' said the house rat, backing up.

Brian poked his head up beside the badger wearing a look of confusion. 'What's he talking about?'

'Haven't a clue,' replied badger. He then fixed the house rat.

'Where are the Uprights?', he demanded, tersely.

The house rat, seated on his hind legs, made simmer-down motions with his front paws, and then indicated the shelves above.

'Simmer bro, you sure is one hangry dude, avail yourself, ain't no need to be so salty.'

A perplexed badger called down to the water vole.

'Rat, get up here, see if you can understand this twerp.'

The water vole poked his head up through the hole and spoke.

'Yo bro don't go botherin' 'bout the tool, I ain't hangin in that squad, spill the tea, where they at?', he then lit his joint and proffered it to the house rat.

'Dem's havin' a rager up high dude,' replied the house rat with a laugh as he approached cautiously to high-five the vole and take the joint. He took a long toke, then spoke.

'So, you the plug bro?', he asked, in curiosity. 'Just I heard a simper you voleos was the main man,' he said, searchingly.

'Nah, ain't no plug dude, just bum a zoot now and den. Slow me down. You catch?', replied the water vole, amicably.

Without the slightest inkling of what the house rat and water vole were talking about, the badger and Brian were left to exchange puzzled glances. So, when the vole said 'come on, we're off, ' both were taken by surprise.

'Where?' they cried in unison.

Now they had a guide, and a more adept guide they couldn't have wished for. The whole of Toad Hall was lit by candlelight, casting shadows in which to conceal at every turn. The house rat moved stealthily, quickly, and held up a paw when a halt proved necessary.

They all concealed themselves behind a large tapestry. On the other side, a large dinner party was in full flight. Periodically, the house rat would scurry out and return with a paw full of food scavenged, or taxed as he termed it, from beneath the table, which he offered up to all. Brian accepted this gleefully and the water vole, breaking his vegan regime, enjoyed with a guilty pleasure, fragments of pate on toast. The badger thought it beneath his dignity.

At length, the chiming of spoon on glass brought silence to the room and the trio pricked up their ears to listen.

'Ladies and gentlemen, thank you for coming,' began a toastmaster reading from a card handed to him by a relay of Horatio's wives.

'We shall hear two speeches tonight: the first from the esteemed naturalist and architect of Project Sauvage, Mr Georges Sauvage-Montgolfiere.'

A ripple of applause arose from the long dining table at which thirty guests were seated.

'And the second from Mr. Horatio Toad, much-esteemed owner of this estate, brain and inspiration behind, Toadland, Nature & Adventure Parks Incorporated...' The speaker stayed the applause as he squinted at the remainder of the verbose inscription on the card, adding

'...and so very much more.' Polite applause was accompanied by a quiet ripple of laughter.

Horatio, seated in between his six wives, raised his goblet to the ensemble, puffed out his fat cheeks and slowly expelled the air, nodding at faces about the table as he did so. He then pushed back his chair and settled back to listen.

'Mr Georges Sauvage-Montgolfiere,' announced the toastmaster. In his late fifties, dressed in his trademark green hemp suit, the tall slender figure of Montgolfiere stood and surveyed the table with his wide, wild black eyes set deep in a narrow, pallid face. His grey, shoulder-length, hair was swept back behind his ears.

He took in each face, in turn, breathed in audibly through his aquiline nose, and began-

'Listen.' He paused as he cast his gaze over the ensemble. 'Just listen.' A dead hush fell. 'You are listening to a silent spring,' he said quietly and then raised his voice.

'Is this the sound you remember from your youth?' A murmur went about the table. 'Probably! Oh, yes probably unless you had the good fortune to be raised in, let's say Romania or Bulgaria.

'Now look out over the vast estate of our dear friend Horatio Toad. What do you see? I'll tell you what I see, I see shadows, I watch them move. And who are they, these shadows? Why, they are the shadows of animals long since gone. Ghosts of the noble beasts that once ranged here when there were forests, wetlands, and meadows.

Did you know that if we were to take our spades and dig down, we would unearth bones of bears, bison, lynx, beavers, wolves, and even lions? Oh, yes, they all roamed free here…once. Lions? I hear you say, here in England, really? You might then respond "oh well then, that was because it was hot here at the time". But you would be wrong. In fact, the temperature then was not so very different than it is today. No, no, these noble animals are no longer here due to human agency – because of us.'

Mongolfiere then placed his hands on the table, leaned forward, and bowed his head. In a low voice that necessitated his audience to lean in and listen, he went on.

'We cut down the forests, we drained the marsh, we enclosed the fields, and we grew our crops. Yes, we grew our crops. Time and time over we grew the same crops until we needed fertilisers because the soil was so poor that they wouldn't grow without it. Then in our hunger for more, we sprayed them with herbicides and pesticides killing off the insects – the very base of the food chain. Where go now the bees for nectar in this sterile desert?'

He took up a glass of water and examined it at length. 'Our lifeblood, looks pure, doesn't it? But the nitrates and pesticides that wash off our farmlands and into the rivers, lakes, and reservoirs, where do they go?' He picked up a spoon and tapped the glass.

'In here, they're all in here. Oh, but in vanishingly small amounts, I hear you cry. Who tells you this? The governments, the same governments who presided over the rape of the land, the same people who polluted the rivers, the same people who pay sheep farmers subsidies for their animals to denude the hills until they are nothing more than barren wastelands.'

Montgolfiere lifted his head and cried aloud. 'Sheep shagged! Where once there was verdant flora, now virtually nothing grows and the tragedy of it all is that people find beauty in this barren, hostile landscape, they think it normal, they think it natural.' He thumped his bony fist on the table and cried:

'It is anything but natural!

A murmur of agreement, nodding heads and 'he's got a point' circulated the table. Montgolfiere tipped his glass of water theatrically on the floor and continued.

'Land ownership', he declared loudly. 'Did you know that of all the countries in the world, only Brazil has more land under private ownership than Britain?'

'Nothing wrong with that!', piped up Horatio Toad importantly, temporarily throwing Montgolfiere off his stride. Horatio puffed out a few chins and added:

'Leave it to oiks and see what a mess they'll make of it.' The two wives sitting on either side of Horatio patted him on the arms and the remainder murmured dutiful if bored assent. Montgolfiere smiled and only the keenest of observers would have detected a hint of disingenuity in it.

'Horatio is a landowner with courage and vision, I wish that they were all the same.' Horatio accepted a ripple of applause with false modesty and a dismissive wave of the hand.

'Yes, would that they were all the same. So much land is given over to grouse shooting and deer stalking for the pleasure of the idle rich,' Montgolfiere continued in derision, quickly qualifying his remark by adding:

'And Horatio is far from idle, witness the transformation that is about to occur on these lands, of which he will expand upon shortly no doubt. No, I'm talking about an unbalanced landscape where animals are allowed to multiply unchecked. But what harm a surfeit of deer? Aren't they the most charming of creatures? I say no, no they are not!

Once more, the raised voice and the fist upon the table captivated the assembly as Montgolfiere, in passionate flight, continued:

'Just consider for a moment the damage deer do when their numbers go unchecked; they strip the leaves, the bark, and the shoots of trees, they forage in the undergrowth and deny the regeneration of trees and the result is, a stifled biodiversity, choked off at birth. They are second only to the dratted sheep in the damage they do.'

Montgolfiere paused, looked about the table and in a low voice, went on.

'Now, some would advocate culling them…and I agree.' He then raised himself up and declared in sonorous voice: 'But not with men and guns, I intend to do it with that most glorious, most effective predator, nature's own intended, absent from these shores these past three hundred years, the wolf!'

Behind the tapestry, Brian and the badger were looking to the polyglot water vole, that most erudite of animals, to translate. 'Upright' was little more than a caterwauling of discordant, jarring sound to most animals. Rodents, however, including house rats, had their own unique take on the language and were competent in the subject.

'Like, I was with the dude,' said the house rat, spitting crumbs as he leaned into the water-vole's ear. 'But, that wolf thing? Dat's de big howlio innit? That's some heavy shit going down there bro.'

He turned a crust between his paws and examined it, then added before taking a nibble:

'Ain't never thought living below boards was all that, but you're sure gonna get beef on your strip, things is going to get butters dude!'

'What in the name of Pan is he going on about Rat?', the badger, red-faced, hissed, doing his utmost to suppress a cough.

'I'll tell you all later,' replied the vole, keen not to miss out on the speech.

'Oh, I see your alarm,' continued Montgolfiere. 'Wolves are dangerous, aren't they? Isn't that why we hunted them to extinction in the first place? Let me tell you that the wolf is dangerous yes, especially if you are a deer or a sheep! But to us? No.'

A clamour arose about the table, necessitating Montgolfiere to raise his voice. 'Provided they have enough on which to predate, they will leave us alone, they are shy animals, in fact, we will be very lucky to see them at all.'

'Don't tell my tourists that!', exclaimed Horatio, adding emphatically 'We'll damn well feed em if we have to!'

Horatio Toad's intervention sent a muddle of confusion about the room and Montgolfiere chimed his glass with his spoon, coming close to cracking it.

'Yes, yes, at first, this may be necessary, but as our territory grows in size, and we are already in negotiations...'

Horatio, puffing out his cheeks, affirmed this to be the case as Montgolfiere went on.

'We will have sufficient land...albeit fenced at perimeters,' Montgolfiere qualified, with a note of dismay, but he brightened hastily.

'Wherever wolves have kept deer numbers in check, there have we seen a resurgence of flora and with this growth in wildflower and herb, we have seen the return of butterflies and a rich panoply of insects. With the return of insects, we have the return of birds. All of this becomes possible when the apex predator resumes his natural place.'

Polite applause allowed Montgolfiere to sip at his acorn wine.

'But what if the wolf population increases too far, you might ask? Who is above the apex predator? Firstly, that most magnificent of animals, the wolf, controls its own population. Ladies and gentlemen, now that you have finished your meals, the alpha male, when he sees food resources to be scarce, will kill and eat the cubs.'

About the table some revulsion was voiced. Some – 'it's just nature's way' – and there were a few step-parents who dared not voice that they thought it an entirely desirable solution.

Montgolfiere raised his hands. 'Sentiment and remorse in the animal kingdom is always trumped by the need to survive. Secondly, we will reintroduce another predator, a big, beautiful cat, the Eurasian Lynx, to control rabbit, fox, and rodent numbers…'

'This dude got me all shook Voleo. Ain't gonna go down well my ends,' exclaimed the house rat with a shiver before adding:

'This geez gotta be havin' a giraffe innit? Me and my crew hate cats. Did the dude say big cats?' he asked, all of a quaver, only hoping that he'd misheard.

'Got me vexed too bro, ain't no jokes', replied the vole, his face now a study in consternation. 'My mandem ain't gonna like it neither.'

Brian and the badger were all at sea and the water vole's face, now pasty white, didn't help matters.

'Is it bad news Trevor-Stan?' whispered Brian, anxiously

'Later Brian', replied the vole.

The badger had had enough. 'I knew it, I knew it…come on we've heard all we need to hear', he declared in as quiet a voice as he was capable of. Yet, the others were not for moving as Montgolfiere brought his speech to a close with a flourish:

'Yes, you heard me correctly ladies and gentlemen, beavers are already at work creating new wetlands and soon will come the wading birds. A pair of lynx will hunt in these woods for the first time in a thousand years. These paltry woods will again become forests and within five years…'

Montgolfiere's voice rose to a crescendo of righteous excitement.

'For the first time since the days of the venerable Bede, brown bears will be seen on these shores! Yes, there may well be skirmishes between bears and wolves at first…'

A 'Hurrah!' went up from one Horatio Toad to the thinly concealed annoyance of Montgolfiere, who quickly picked up.

'But they will reach their natural accommodations, we shall have restored the equilibrium, the natural order to this barren land, a land fit for animals to roam. No more will our offspring visit the prisons of zoos, for we shall coexist in the new wilderness, we will recreate the wild world, a better life for all!'

Silence was then followed by hesitant applause, clearly many remained sceptical. Horatio Toad was not one of them and he stood and raised his glass, proffering a toast.

'I give you Georges Montgolfiere, visionary and…' Horatio was momentarily lost for words, and so added 'all round, top drawer, grade A, type of chappie.'

'Toad is speaking', the vole hissed at an increasingly belligerent badger. 'I know that! Why doesn't the blighter speak animal?', came the surly reply.

'Friends, if you are not excited by the prospect of gladiatorial combat between wolves and bears, then what are you excited by?', demanded Horatio casting his gaze about the ensemble.

Did Horatio note a slight shake of Montgolfiere's head as others did? Of course, not, and even if he had, he would have taken no notice. Puffed up with his own importance, he launched his money-making version of Wild World:

'I was sunning myself in my hammock, sipping my first pina colada of the morning, in the grounds of one of my villas above Horseshoe Bay – that's in Bermuda by the by- when my butler brought the letter…' Horatio sipped at his claret and went on.

'What's this?' I cried. 'Some mad fool wants to take on that crumbling old pile in England. Well, let him have it, I thought. Dreary, damp old country, dreary damp old house from all accounts. Only when I read through the memoirs of my ancestors, was my imagination sparked and I asked myself this question: what are you doing, Horatio, to rival their exploits? Oh yes, you are admired in Bermuda for your business acumen and generosity, but the island is a small place, and you are still young and virile Horatio.'

Some of the six wives, aware that they were under observation, smiled coyly, but a few exchanged looks from the corners of their eyes as if to say, 'really?' All went unnoticed by Horatio as he blustered on.

'So, I took the first boat for England. No sooner had I met Georges Montgolfiere and listened to his plans did I realise that the fellow was on to something. He won't mind me saying that whilst he's up on his animals, nature and all that caper, he's not so hot on the old pecunia. He didn't see the potential and he took a bit of persuading, but once confronted with a plan of genius, he had the wit to see the bigger picture, after all – *Pecunia non olet… et cetera.* –

Horatio paused and took a long swig of his claret, wiped his mouth with his sleeve, then spouted-

'Hands up who wants to visit Toads World of Adventure?'

Enthusiasm was muted, a few put their hands up, more in obeisance than enthusiasm.

'Come on, come on, let me tell you now, Toads World is going to be very much your sort of place. Bookings are pouring in. They'll be hot-air balloon rides for the old 'uns and zip-wire rides for the young 'uns, there'll be glamping for the vegetarians and boat trips for the bored, there'll be barbecues, there'll be candyfloss, there'll be jousting, there'll be pony treks, donkey rides and hot dogs, there'll be cocktail bars and restaurants and shops selling wolf costumes, bear costumes and all manner of tat. Now...'

Horatio stood foursquare eyeing the invitees and demanded: 'Who wouldn't want to invest in that?

Chapter Fifteen

Taupe's Tempest

Badger had worked himself up into such a state of apoplexy that his bed was called for. He could support himself, but only just, and it was all Brian and the vole could do to help him back through the wild wood and home. That the badger had shunned an offer of help from a wild boar named Gunter, had irritated the water vole.

'Rat, get that foreign brute – ' wheezed the badger, turning his back and leaning heavily on his friends' shoulders – 'away from me.'

'I'm afraid he's not quite himself this morning.' The vole's attempted apology was only met by a loud 'Humph!' from the badger, embarrassing his friend further.

'Herr vole, ' began the boar calmly. 'I think he is very much himself and that is his problem and not yours.' The boar, in parting, added 'I wonder if he merits your help.'

It was dark and dank in the badger's abode and so the vole lit the fire to bring some joy to the morning. He was desperately tired having been up all night and he settled back into an armchair in the hope of sleep. Hope was the operative word as the badger's coughing resounded horribly throughout the low-ceilinged sett. Brian was ministering to the stricken animal and rushed to and fro, washing out bloodied rags.

Discussions had carried on all night at the vole's abode. News of the plans, gleaned in Toads' Hall, had sped down the river like a winter current in spate. Shrews had been busy all night long carrying updates. Shock and initial disbelief gave way to cold, grim reality. What could animals do in the face of an army of determined Uprights? Fanciful schemes were hatched and summarily dismissed and as the night wore on, such plans became more outlandish. By daybreak, no conclusions had been reached save for a general resolution not to do nothing.

'I've seen this before,' stated Brian glumly, as he washed out an outsized handkerchief coated in blood. 'This doesn't end well,' he added, before turning back for the badger's chamber.

'You're a good fellow Brian, I'm not sure I'd have the same dedication. Quincy doesn't deserve you.'

Brian stopped to consider for a moment. 'We can't let him die alone.'

The possibility that old Quincy might be dying hit the vole of a sudden. Certainly, he was ill, but dying? You don't die from a cough, do you?

The vole had known the badger since he was a cub. indeed, as a pup, the water vole had bitten him on the nose when he came rooting about the undergrowth, for the vole was born away from the river in damp marsh. Seated by the fire, the vole now reminisced on that first encounter and allowed himself a smile. What had the badger's first utterance been, besides the yelp of pain? 'Why, you little fucker!' Something of that order, something oikish and wild-woodish.

This was how their relationship was born and how it had continued. Over the years there had been many such spiky moments, many shouting matches, many a storming out and yet, something akin to a friendship endured. Often, the vole wondered what such an unlikely relationship was founded upon, and his conclusion was mutual respect. For, in the final analysis, another badger might very well have polished off the vole and his siblings on that day long ago. As a tiny mite, the vole had stood up to the badger and the badger had been big enough not to retaliate and had walked away.

The vole helped himself to a measure of the badger's hooch. It tasted of armpit, yet it gave a kick to the throat. He swirled the muddied liquid about in the earthenware cup and tried not to listen to his friend's cough, which mercifully, was subsiding. On the verge of nodding off, Brian, as Brian invariably did, disturbed him.

'He's dropped off,' he announced, kicking the vole's foot. 'Thought you'd like to know.' The vole muttered 'Good…good.' But it was of no use.

'So, what have you got in there then?', he enquired chirpily, indicating the cup, and perching himself on the arm of the vole's chair.

'Brian?' asked the vole with as much patience as he could muster. 'Yes, Trevor-Stan?' he replied breezily. 'Don't you ever get tired? We've been up all night for Pan's sake.'

The mole tilted his head as if examining the question from all angles.

'Well, I'm used to that, I often move about at night, not that I'm nocturnal you understand, but I do wait for it to be quiet, and the night is usually quieter than the day. On the other paw, it is almost a quarter to May and springtime always gives me a second wind.' Brian then pursed his lips, lifted a buttock, and let go a freepy-fart. 'Bad worm,' he stated matter-of-factly.

**

Meanwhile, a heated debate was raging over in Toad Hall.

'Look, if you'll just let me get a word in edgeways…where are you now for mercy's sake?' hissed an increasingly exasperated Montgolfiere as he wheeled about.

'I told you to use the flags. You're not supposed to be here!'

'Ha! If I use the flags, it take you all day to decipher cretin! I waiting still for answer to message yesterday,' hurled Taupe as she made a sudden appearance, now wearing a green pelt before a brown curtain.

'At last, there you are! Now, as I was saying…stop doing that! Where are you now?', whined a pained Montgolfiere.

'I'm keeping low profile dumb skull. Why you didn't tell me about big, fat toad eh? Why you keeping all that secret? You think that I don't find out never?', lanced Taupe now stepping out from the cover of oak panelled walls in a brown pelt.

'How did you know about any of that?', came the cagey reply.

'You've got an informer, everyone know, whole bloody-fucking wood know now.'

Georges Montgolfiere slumped into a chair wearing a frown and began to drum his fingers on the table.

'Listen, Hor…the toad, is full of gas and wind, half of what you may have heard will never happen.'

'They think it will', stated Taupe, jerking a paw at the window. '*Mycelia* is smoking, you are in the *merde*, up to arse in crocodiles…you will have crocodiles as well?'

'Don't be absurd.'

'Toads have history here, none of it good. That's what they believe,' added Taupe.

Montgolfiere sighed, then sighed again as he lifted his eyes from the table to find that his interlocutor had vanished once more. 'We'll have to be more careful,' he concluded wearily.

'Ha! How? There is informer, I should know, I'm a spy, a mole, a taupe, clue is in bloody-fucking title! *Alors*, what all this shit about barricades, what you make here, zoo?', sneered Taupe, making another reappearance.

'Fences, the word is fences and I don't have any choice. When we get more land...' But Taupe was on the offensive.

'You know what you do? You make big zoo, but worse. You put in wolves and bears, and psycho cats and other animals can't escape.' Taupe gestured at the window. 'They know it. You told me just beavers, kites, and boars. I make speech in wood to tell them to make friends. What I tell them now eh? You make me look like big liar.'

'Look, none of that is going to happen tomorrow,' soothed Montgolfiere, adopting an emollient tone. 'I was just outlining my dream for the future.' He walked over to the window, stared out, and went on.

'Their future will not be in a scrubby patch of woodland hemmed in by arid farmland, their future will be a wilderness where a proper balance is restored.' He paused as he watched a red-kite wheeling above a distant field and his nostril flared in satisfaction.

'Not in a sheep-shagged, deer-denuded, rabbit-raided desert.'

'Tell that to deer and sheeps,' snapped Taupe. 'Who you think you are eh, Pan? You sit up here in tower of ivory to watch big cats hunt boar, *c'est ca*? It not just. Maybe you like to watch, eh?

Montgolfiere sighed audibly then opened his mouth to speak, but Taupe had the wind in her sails.

'*Et voila*, you like to watch the chase, you are the same as the big-fat toad, he should have shame, he is animal playing Upright's game. You told me just zip-wire and balloon, now it is boats and all other Upright shit. You make bloody-fucking cartoon park. Fat, idiot Uprights come to watch animal hunt, come to watch their intimacy like pervert. I hope big cats and wolves hunt them!'

'Have you quite finished?', asked Montgolfiere. 'I see little point in continuing this conversation until…' He hesitated. 'Not until…'

'*Allez, vas-y,* what you want to say eh? Until I calm down dear, *c'est ca*? Well, I not calm down *connard*, not until you stop plans for zoo', hurled Taupe in high dudgeon. 'Not until you stop arse-lardy toad!'

'Look, I told you', shouted Montgolfiere, losing his rag. 'None of this is happening straight away…there are things here you don't understand, things I can't tell you now!'

'*Et oui*, things I don't understand because I am just mole who live in hole, well I tell you something Georges Montgolfiere….'

**

Beneath boards, the house rat and his friends were being richly entertained.

'That sister givin' it straight bro, she stickin' it big to the Upright – respect girl!'

'Yeah, and he getting well salty with it, that bird is owning the booky Upright.'

As if watching a tennis match, heads were turning this way and that, all the young house rats had gathered to watch whilst the older ones, complaining of the noise, had shuffled off to the other end of the house.

'How she do that thing with the garms dude? I gotta know this shit.'

'Like she there one moment, gone the next. Well safe, innit?'

'Ain't no dench tho' bro.' This disparaging remark earned the brother a sharp dig in the ribs from the sister next to him.

'And like you are bro?', scoffed the sister. 'I could roll with that girl, she'd be in my mandem any day, she got class. She got that wasteman all vexed. Ain't all bout the looks, I like the way she par him off. Actually, I think she's a peng ting...for a moleo.'

**

With a host of fleas left in his ear, Montgolfiere was left to rue the day he had engaged Taupe and brought her over from France. He'd just wasted five minutes making what he thought was a rational case to a brick wall. Taupe had stormed out five minutes earlier.

Montgolfiere decided he had no great need of her. In any case, the fencing would take the best part of six months to complete and by that time he estimated that he would win Taupe around.

Nevertheless, he was troubled. His entire rewilding scheme was predicated upon procuring more land. His means were meagre and would soon be exhausted. Silas Snipe's legal firm – Filtch, Stripum & Tuckham – had all but used his cash reserves. What use a dream if he had not the liquidity to fund it?

That he had to rely on the largesse of one Horatio Toad, irritated him beyond measure. He had pinned his hopes on the fund-raising dinner, but thus far only one investor had expressed any interest and that was to create a chain of fast-food cabins with canoe hire along the riverbanks, anathema to Montgolfiere, but food and drink to Horatio.

Toad Hall made an ideal HQ for the rewilding project situated as it was in the centre of the estate. It was however far bigger than Montgolfiere needed. He now asked himself aloud 'could I sub-let it?' and 'might it possible to slip a caveat into the contract without Horatio's knowing it?' He laughed at his audacity. After all, the careless animal had signed an agreement on a one-hundred-year lease of house and land, in the belief that it only pertained to the land.

Georges sighed, it wouldn't be ethical, he thought. What he had already done was unethical, arguably dastardly. One day, people would understand, he then reasoned, history would not judge him too harshly and in any case, the ridiculous Horatio had more money than sense – what had he told him? That he owned five villas in the Caribbean, one in Florida and a mountaintop home in Switzerland. To be deprived of this dilapidated old country pile, that only now had he bothered to visit, wouldn't harm him.

Since a boy, gazing out from his bedroom window on a small, neatly manicured lawn with a nine-inch wide marigolded border, Georges had dreamed of adventure. With his shelves piled high with books depicting the wilderness of Africa and Asia, the constraints of a prim urban life in Hounslow just didn't cut it. Was it, he often wondered, his family name that inspired his lust for exploration and adventure? Perhaps. More likely it was his revulsion of all things man-made. Industrialisation – urban living, was anathema to him.

Forced through education by pushy parents (for which he was now thankful) and equipped with a degree in zoology, Georges, an only child, took off.

He remained 'only' and never married. He considered himself asexual and had no leanings in either direction. He despaired of a human race that denuded the forests and grabbed and polluted the land and oceans. Many a time had he wished he had been born another type of animal.

Reminiscences of his travels ran through his mind as he stared from the upper-story windows of Toad Hall. It's now or never, he told himself, *anno domini* would not provide another chance like this. Here would he create an Eden, his paradise would become a model to be replicated across a crowded Europe that had capitulated to industrial farming and sold its soul to consumption.

'Ah now, there she is,' Georges said aloud, reaching into the pocket of his hemp suit for his deciphering book. He fetched his binoculars to view the array of coloured pendants flying above *chez* Taupe and with his free hand, he began to note the order, size, and colour on a piece of paper.

Orange-large, blue-small, yellow-small, black-large.

Smiling, 'I knew she would come around,' he mouthed, he then sat at his desk and began to cross-reference his notes with the deciphering book, he wrote down the letters with a fading smile: '*basse-toi petit bon*!'

Although little tutored in French, even though his father had been French, he knew enough to translate. For some reason the b's should have been c's, the yellow pendant should have been green, but the meaning was all too clear:

'Fuck-off little twat!'

Montgolfiere snapped the book closed, took up his pen and began to draft a letter to Mr Silas Snipe, requesting an appointment at his London office.

**

Brian was starting to wonder if the object of his affections had a softer side. Whenever he surprised her with his presence, as he did now, he found her in a nonreceptive mood.

'What you want now Brian? I'm busy,' Taupe demanded brusquely, and returned to rummaging inside a large canvas sack.

A look of puzzlement made frequent appearances on Brian's face, and it settled in now. Where were the pups? Where was the fortress – the nest? He began to count his claws, a pointless exercise, as he always arrived at *some*. Mole infants never hang about for long, he knew that much, but surely, they don't scarper this quickly.

'Err, little ones up a tunnel…?', he asked hesitantly. No answer came from within the canvas sack save for a short-tempered, loud tut. 'Or, out playing perhaps…,' he added awkwardly, immediately wishing he hadn't.

'Oh yes, I send them out for kite's dinner,' came the sarcastic response. 'Where the bloody-fuck is it?', Taupe muttered. She straightened and turned to Brian.

'I wasn't pregnant Brian. False alarm,' Taupe stated, matter-of-factly.

Not overly concerned one way or the other, Brian thought it incumbent upon him to say 'sorry'.

'Well, I'm not,' she replied coldly, still preoccupied with her search.

'Can, I help?'

'No.'

Feeling something of a spare part, Brian, in curiosity, poked his head inside the wooden *mycelia* box and promptly got his spectacles entangled in the spaghetti of fungal roots. Hoping to deflect attention from his predicament, he said casually 'by the way, Quincy is ill.'

'Who is Quincy, your little *zizi*?', came the curt reply, as Taupe turned out a trunk.

The more Brian tried to disentangle, the more entangled his spectacles became. On the point of abandoning them, he heard voices, a myriad of voices. 'Badger is ill'. The voices echoed about the soundbox; he pulled away in alarm. Tentatively, he reached a paw in for his spectacles and received a shock, a mild shock, but it made him recoil with a little cry, his glasses had attacked him, had pricked him.

'What you doing now?', demanded a vexed Taupe, trying to fix Brian's eyes which he promptly averted.

'Oh, nothing,' he replied, attempting indifference as he shuffled his feet to conceal the soundbox behind him.

'As I was saying, the badger is ill.'

'Good,' she retorted sharply. 'Who care? Nasty animal!'

'No, I mean really ill…dying ill'. His voice trailed off. 'That sort of ill,' he finished weakly.

Taupe cocked her head quickly and then barged past Brian almost knocking him off his feet. She plunged her head into the soundbox and there she remained. Brian shifted nervously on his feet. 'Ah, yes, sorry about that, got myself a bit caught up.'

Taupe turned suddenly, her eyes were wild and wide.

'I have misjudged you Brian mole, you are not dimwit, you are bloody-fucking genius!', she cried, ecstatically.

Brian's muzzle was then showered with a hundred kisses, to his utter astonishment.

Taupe returned to the soundbox and became engrossed, she muttered a whole series of terms that meant nothing to Brian, touching on ohms, amperes, volts, resistance, impedance, and so on, alternating passing to direct, lunette wire acting as a coil…the list went on.

Once more feeling redundant, Brian asked 'Well, you see, I was just wondering if you had any ideas, you know, cures…that type of thing…'

But no answer was forthcoming from a preoccupied Taupe. So, Brian made his way to the door. Just as he was about to leave, Taupe cried out:

'Brian, are you wearing my green knickers?'

'I might be,' he replied, coyly.

Were he to have had his head in the soundbox, he would have heard guffaws of laughter from every corner of the wood.

'I'll come tomorrow,' Taupe said, casually, and carried on with her work.

Chapter Sixteen

A Boar for Badger

The vole sat beside the bed of the sleeping badger and, once more, reminisced upon their youth. Running a fever, the badger had thrown off his blankets to reveal a tattooed abdomen. The vole had almost forgotten that he had it. Now faded and distended the image was of a jug of beer. In his youth, the badger had been inordinately fond of ale and as a birthday present, his mother had tattooed it for him.

To witness this once, rumbustious youth, stricken with illness, saddened the water vole. If he was going to die, and the vole could not bring himself to believe it, then he would need a vestige of energy to make the trek. It came to all, as it inevitably must, and the final journey would be made in the dead of night. A quiet corner in some far-off field, quite alone, would he make his resting place. Most animals knew where they would go, well before that dread night arrived. The water vole knew his, and he would let the river take him there.

Alone with his thoughts, by the badger's fireside, the vole mused on what had brought on this illness. He had heard that it lived in all animals and that it only required a dip in morale to trigger it. That made sense thought the vole, the badger seemed more anxious than most by the new arrivals. In the hallway, next to a coat stand, was a full-length mirror.

The vole took every opportunity he could to examine his back. He undressed and turned to look and was shocked by the number of ovaloid, bald patches, the tell-tale marks of a stressed animal. He had seen them in foxes and pitied them their plight when the Uprights routinely chased them with dogs. Anger began to well within and a fierce cast took hold on his face, something had to be done, this was all the doing of Uprights, not to mention that idiot of a toad.

**

Walking back through the wild wood, Brian stopped to check the fly of his pelt trousers. Why were they laughing? He'd never cared much for the stoats, ferrets, and weasels, they were all piss-takers of the highest order, and your best bet was to ignore them. 'Challenge them at your peril.' That had always been the water vole's advice, and he tried to heed it now. Yet, his patience was wearing thin. Thus far, he had been subjected to jibes from every hole he had passed.

'Here comes Miss Mole' – 'Hide yer knickers girls'– 'It's pervy Brian!' – 'Oooh duckey!'– 'Leave her alone' – 'Get em orf!'

All this and a plethora of disparaging remarks questioning his masculinity, found Brian clenching his paws. This inadvertent, outward show of anger did not go unnoticed.

'She's getting riled lads, let's get the lady's knickers back!', shouted a boisterous stoat and before Brian knew it, he was surrounded.

Equipped with hefty forearms and strong shoulders, Brian reckoned he was a match for anyone, and he put up his paws now.

'Come on then, if you think your animal enough!', he lanced and began to prance about adopting a southpaw stance. That his tormentors were all laughing didn't deter him, for his dander was up. When a stoat made a sudden lunge for his trousers, Brian connected with a sweet uppercut knocking the fellow off his feet.

'Want some, do you, eh? Come on if you want some', hurled Brian as he wheeled about; but heavily outnumbered, he was brought down by a push in the chest, and he fell over a weasel who was kneeling behind him.

Then they were on top of him, pinning him down and he suffered the ignominy of having his trousers pulled down to reveal Taupe's green, lacy cami-knickers. Such was the hilarity that the womenfolk came out to stare and a face already red, turned crimson in embarrassment. Writhe as he might, he couldn't prevent two of the females from pulling them down-and immediately, the laughter stopped. It was replaced with howls of disgust.

'Oh, Pan, I'm going to be sick!', exclaimed one of the females holding her paw over her mouth. 'Urgh, the filthy little sod!', cried the other jumping up and backing away. 'That's, that's fucking revolting,' issued one of the lead tormentors wearing an expression of amazed revulsion. 'I ain't never seen nuffink like that,' said another disbelievingly, as he moved away in fear of contagion.

Freed from their grip, Brian took a cursory glimpse at his todger. Aside from a little puss and a polka dot of white spots on an inflamed helmet, the flies were to be expected, he reasoned. There were some chrysalises also matted in his pubic fur and several still writhing maggots. 'Have to give them time,' he mumbled. He pulled up the knickers smartly, followed by his trousers and stood to brush himself down with as much casual bravado as he could muster. The faces of the onlookers were a study of repugnance as they parted in silence to allow Brian on his way. With head held high, the knicker-wearing mole parted the fray with a vestige of dignity. This last vestige was then lost when he failed to notice a tree root which he tripped over, leaving guffaws of laughter and barbed comments on his personal hygiene behind him.

**

'I need a drink,' declared Brian. as he slumped into one of the badger's sumptuous armchairs, wearing a face like a slapped arse. The water vole studied his friend's countenance. 'Female trouble?' he posited. Brian responded with a roll of his eyes and a shake of the head.

'I don't want to talk about it,' he replied brusquely, adding testily 'where does Quincy keep his hooch?'

A fine spring this is turning out to be, thought the water vole, skinning up a joint, nothing but conflict, petulance, and anguish.

Brian had spat the badger's home-brew ale out, likening its taste to a hedgehog's latrine. For an animal that lives on worms and grubs, the vole considered, that comment takes the biscuit.

Several tokes in, Brian relayed his woodland experience to a vole who did his utmost to suppress a snigger. He failed.

'Glad you think it funny,' glowered Brian. 'They always had me down as dim, now they think I'm a perv too.'

But the water vole's laugh was infectious and coupled with the joint, both animals fell into a fit of giggles.

'Well, aren't you Brian? A bit of a pervert that is', advanced the vole jokingly.

'Might be…might be a bit,' came the candid reply.

A sharp rat-tat-tat on the door found neither Brian, nor vole, inclined to move. They were three joints in, Brian was stupefied, and the vole was drifting off. But the caller was persistent and so, with great reluctance, the vole heaved himself up and made unsteady progress for the door.

'Who in the name of Pan is calling now? It must be dusk,' he muttered, shielding a candle as he went. He opened the door to find no one there. He stepped outside and craned his head, shrugged his shoulders, and went back down the dark passageway to the fireside to find another mole slapping his friend Brian about the muzzle.

'Hey!', cried the water vole.

'Shut trap!' lanced Taupe, as she attempted to knock sense into Brian. 'What you do to him eh?', she asked accusingly of the vole. 'He was useless before, now he wankered. Total space waste.'

With one eye revolving and the other, like Venus, spinning in a contrary direction, Brian was indeed, spaced-out, and incapacitated. One might conclude fairly that he was indeed, wankered.

More used to the effects of his grass, which he maintained was due to his being a vegan, the drowsy water vole assisted Taupe in the kitchen. Spread out upon the table was a cornucopia of herbs and small earthenware pots containing powders. Upon badger's range, a large pot of what smelled suspiciously like urine simmered.

'Find me barberry stalk, barberry berries, golden rod and horsetail,' commanded Taupe bluntly as she added powder after powder to the liquid, muttering as she went. '*Pas de licorice...merde*! *N'oubliez-pas l'artemisinin…*' She turned to the vole, seemingly ready to scold him, and was pleasantly surprised. He had segregated the correct herbs from the remainder and was waiting on her command. '*Bon, tres bon*, now you chop them in little bits.' She turned back to her pot smiling.

'What is your name *Monsieur campagnol- d'eau*?'– Mr water-vole – she asked amicably, over her shoulder.

'Trevor, Trevor-Stan,' replied the vole.

Taupe continued adding pinches of powder. 'Bit of mouthful, TrevorTrevorStan. I call you Trev, *ca marche*? – Is that ok?'

The vole smiled as he chopped the herbs. '*Oui ca va*'– Yes, that's fine – he replied which had the effect of spinning Taupe about-

'You speak Pan's language, you speak the French?', she asked, intrigued.

'*Oh, quelques mots, c'est tout,*'– just a few words, that's all – responded the vole modestly. Taupe stared at him for a moment and then turned back to her pot.

'Big shame you are not a mole,' she said despondently, adding 'we could have mated next season. What choice I have?'

'I believe Brian is keen on you,' replied the vole, reasonably.

'Exactly, that what I mean, moorhen has more brains,' Taupe continued stirring, then asked '*et toi*, you mate this season?'

The water vole swallowed hard, unused to such direct and abrupt questioning.

'I don't,' he responded flatly. Taupe looked over her shoulder-

'You are sure you're not a mole? I wish you were.' She indicated the adjoining room with her ladle. 'Pants of passion over there, he think of nothing else...all brain is capable of, keep brain in *zizi*.'

It was not often that the water vole had the chance of enlightening conversation, and he made the most of it now. Water voles had a reputation for scholarship and Taupe, a direct descendant of the celebrated mole philosopher, Martin Idigger was his equal. Their conversation was wide-reaching and touched upon Oral Philosophy, that branch which passed down generations of animals; Animal Cave Art (which has been wrongly attributed to Uprights); and

Track-Literature – animal tracks that tell stories which too often, are effaced by the hiking Upright, and purported nature lover.

Brian was given short-shrift when he wandered in upon this heady conversation declaring an attack of the munchies.

'A little later perhaps old chap, we're in the middle of things,' coerced the vole politely to his still loitering friend, whereas Taupe's 'Bloody fuck-off Brian!' had more immediate effect.

'Well, if I'm not wanted…pardon me for existing,' he grumbled, as he slumped away with paws in pockets.

As Brian rooted about outside the badger's sett for grubs and worms, he felt a sharp pang of jealousy; was the water vole trying to pull his bird? In his stoned state, anything seemed plausible. He determined to have it out with him later.

Badger's coughing bout brought all paws to the pumps. There was more blood and here, Brian came into his own. He was called for by Taupe as the water vole proved hopelessly squeamish and inadequate to the task. The three animals managed to heave the badger into a sitting position and Brian dutifully mopped the ailing animal's muzzle.

Even in his stricken condition, the badger would not accept the medicament as proffered by Taupe. Between wheezes and bloodied coughs, he managed to speak. 'Don't let that oily foreigner poison me!', he pleaded, searching for the water vole's eyes as he clung to his arm. The vole couldn't bring himself to look due to the blood and mucus, but also because of his embarrassment. How could his friend sink so low?

By contrast, Taupe remained uncharacteristically calm, even soothing as she patiently waited for an opportunity to tip her preparation down the badger's gullet. At the last moment, anticipating resistance, she had added a quantity of honeycomb to the brew, and he had finally acquiesced.

Subdued after one jar-full, the patient was eager for more, he was allowed one jar extra, and no more.

Moments passed, animal moments (these cannot be equated to Upright moments) during which the badger's fever subsided. He was overcome with tiredness and fell into a deep, peaceful, sleep.

The three friends settled in by the fireside and made good use of the badger's logs and larder. It required dedication to drink the home-brew, but coupled with another few joints, it proved possible to imbibe without vomiting. With all three in a state of torpor, a loud knock on the door was a rude awakening. 'I'll go,' declared the vole sleepily, noting that moles seemed to have a low threshold when it came to narcotics.

Outside, night had fallen, and the wood took on a more sinister aspect. Gnarled trees that went unnoticed in daylight, transformed into demonic faces. One such face now presented itself at badger's door. The water vole stepped back in alarm at the towering figure before him replete with tusks and beady eyes. It was Gunter, the wild boar.

'*Guten Abend mein herr*, we understand the badger is ill.'

At his feet, he deposited a panier laden with truffles.

'Helga and I hope it is not too serious.'

'*Vielen Dank*, it is very kind of you both…probably more than he deserves,' replied the vole, sincerely. The boar threw back his head and laughed.

'You know Herr vole, badgers are the same wherever you travel, they have a conservative nature. They have, how do you say in English, a reaction in the gut. But we must all live together, even with badgers,' he concluded with another roar of laughter and turned away.

'*Gute Nacht* and if I may say, your German is excellent my friend.'

The vole watched a large mass disappear into the shadows.

'We shall be friends, if only we try,' it called back and was then gone.

Chapter Seventeen

Full of Hot Air

Horatio Toad opened his copper eyes on a bright, sunny morning, blinked, and promptly closed them again. He was not an early riser, but three of his six wives were. One, Tamara, the latest addition to the harem, was eager to start the day.

'Hory, oh Hory, time to get up,' she petitioned in a lilting voice as she caressed Horatio's knobbly head.

Not at all enthusiastic, Horatio humphed and turned onto his side.

'Oh, come on Hory, you said we would go up in the balloon this morning,' persisted Tamara. 'I've hardly slept a wink, I've been too excited. Come on Hory dear,' she implored.

Feigning sleep, Horatio played through the less-than-sober promises made the night before. Had he, he now questioned, bragged a little too much *vis a vis* his prowess with hot-air balloons? He'd been a passenger on a couple of occasions, watched the drill, and it all looked simple enough...but now, in the cold light of morning, his courage was failing him. Perhaps he shouldn't have told his wives that he was a qualified pilot, he now considered.

'Oh, don't be such an old grump,' whined Tamara, stamping a foot. She was the youngest of Horatio's wives and given to petulance. 'You promised!'

'What's that? Oh yes, soon my dear, soon,' he mumbled, sleepily.

The word *old* was not one that Horatio cared to hear. Each wife in succession was younger than the last. He was an uncommon, gentleman toad in having so many mates. Each new addition gave him a spurt of energy and renewed vigour, but it never lasted more than a season. Tamara was a striking, Caribbean, green climbing toad and initially, she had Horatio enraptured. And yet, as always, his enthusiasm was on the wane.

'Tamara is right Horatio, it's a beautiful morning and not a breath of wind,' chimed Melissa standing by the window (wife number four) with a conspiratorial wink to the other wives.

Horatio's harem, when working on him as a unit, had very much the better of him. Collectively, they had the guile to out manoeuvre him and the wisdom to make him believe that any decision was his own. Horatio did harbour suspicions that they hunted as a pack, yet so good was their play-acting, so realistic the inter-wife fights, that he was never sure and consequently, was putty in their paws.

Now in pretended slumber, Horatio began to wonder, not for the first time, whether that other chappie, Upright king whatnot, famed for the six wives, hadn't had the right idea; whittling them down a bit seemed the height of sagacity.

With his blankets stripped away, and the three latest editions to the squad jumping and bouncing on the bed about him in youthful glee, Horatio conceded defeat.

However, this left wives one to three to slumber on. Nothing would induce them to take to the skies with Horatio. Veterans of many a car and motorboat mishap, they now took with a very large pinch of salt any of their husband's boastful claims to competency.

A team of blinky, weary Uprights were summarily raised from their beds to assist in the launch. There was much grumbling from those put to work before breakfast. Many a hushed comment along the lines of 'does the idiot know what he is doing?'

'Didn't you ought to wait sir for Mr Montgolfiere's return?', questioned one of the older Uprights, whose primary concern was for the safety of the three wives.

Horatio brandished a small booklet. 'Qualified pilot my man.' A closer inspection would have revealed this to be his membership of the colonial club in Hamilton, Bermuda.

As the balloon inflated, so too did Horatio's ego. He stood back and watched proudly as his own image began to take form. Some ten metres high and five wide, his face began to lose its crags and wrinkles lending him a complimentary, youthful aspect. Tamara looked to the balloon and then at her husband's face, comparing the two, she wore a puzzled expression.

'Is it an old balloon darling?'

'You haven't sent up a pilot balloon sir,' shouted the older Upright. 'You ought to check the wind up there,' he cautioned.

One of the younger Uprights, who enjoyed sending little helium balloons skyward, had one already inflated.

'Go on, if you must,' shouted Horatio impatiently above the noise of the gas jets.

The little black balloon rose serenely. 'There, you see, not a breath. Don't go telling the captain what to do!', barked Horatio as he opened the gas lever to maximum and flared flame upward.

'Wait!', screamed the young Upright as he watched his pilot balloon gain height and then be whisked away by a strong southerly.

Horatio gulped as he saw the pilot balloon speed off, but it was too late, already the basket was clearing the roof of the ancestral hall.

'Yipee!', screamed Tamara, as she rushed to embrace her Hory. 'You clever, clever toad,' she enthused and she gave him a look, a look Horatio knew well: the promise of an early night.

Four were aboard *Toad One*, as he determined to name the airship – for he fully intended to have a fleet – *Horatio Toad, Tamara, Melissa*, and *Trudy* – wives six, five and four respectively.

That *Toad One* belonged to Montgolfiere was of no consequence to Horatio, it was only a matter of finance, and he would organise payment once the investment money poured in.

'No point in going up without a spot of wind,' shouted Horatio, optimistically. 'Just end up going up and down. Where's the fun in that?'

Along with the speed and direction of wind, there were a couple of other points Horatio had neglected: Firstly, crash helmets. Fearless Horatio had never sported one himself, hence the neglect. Secondly, he had not briefed his crew before lift-off – The Do's and Don'ts – concerning what to pull and not pull. Pilot Horatio couldn't see any purpose in any of that.

Suddenly caught by a strong gust, the balloon tilted and failed to gain altitude, it veered off course (if one had ever been plotted) at alarming speed. Horatio's bulbous eyes startled wide at the prospect of collision with a tall oak.

The snag was that the land rose steeply away from the river, and the balloon was not gaining height, rather, the land was coming up to the balloon. He flared the gas jets in panic, but such was the speed of approach that calamity seemed inevitable. In unison, screams went up, and Horatio blasting gas for all he was worth, found himself joining in the cries of 'Aghhh!'– which was the consensus.

As a noble, selfless captain, Horatio joined his wives in the bottom of the basket, for, they were his only concern. Never let it be said that he cowered. There was a jarring impact and the sound of cracking branches. The next sound was unanticipated and came from a large rook perching menacingly on the basket's rim.

'Sixteen sunsets,' rasped the rook. 'Sixteen sunsets me and the missus took to build that, you bloody hooligan!' And with that, the rook managed what doesn't come easily to a large bird in a confined space – he hovered like a hummingbird and delivered a series of painful pecks to Horatio's head.

But save for the pecking and the humiliation, all was well, the basket had cleared the tree. The bird left with a raucous cry of 'Vandal!'

Horatio got back to his feet quickly and again flared flame into the canopy above. Dabbing at his head, he noted that the bird had drawn blood. 'Cursed oik,' he muttered beneath his breath. 'Who does he think he is?'

The residue of faith in his proficiency as a pilot could be measured by the length of service of each wife. Tamara tended to her darling's injury, dabbing at it with her handkerchief. 'Nasty, spiteful bird, it's not as if it was our fault, was it Hory?'

Melissa and Trudy, veterans of near scrapes and not yet disasters (as had been wives one to three) exchanged anxious glances. The basket was swaying alarmingly, and the wind began gusting, seemingly from every quarter. Horatio elected to steady his ship. In his estimations, he needed to reposition the sandbags that hung on ropes to the outside of the basket. However, the bags were heavy, much heavier than he thought, and as he undid the clove-hitch knots, he lost two over the side. 'Blast it!', he muttered.

'Everything all right Hory?', Tamara cried, uncertainly.

'Perfectly my dear. What fun eh?', he replied, adding nonchalantly 'actually, I calculated that we would clear the tree, only a tad out, you know? *Fortes fortuna adiuvat* and all that.'

There was some relief in noticing that, although still at a low altitude, they would be making a wide berth of the wild wood which crowned the valley's ridge. There was, therefore, time to take in the view. Horatio crouched to light a cigar, then stood and indicated the wood with a dismissive wave of his paw.

'That wood is chop-full of oiks,' he declared derisorily. 'Usual suspects, weasels, stoats, foxes, badgers, and the ilk. Bad eggs the lot of them.'

The wives cast their gaze in the direction of the wood.

'They can't all be bad Horatio, oiks or not, they'll be some decent types,' remonstrated Trudy.

'Don't you believe it my dear, I've been reading up on them. Long history of nefarious deeds in this neck of the wood. Leopards don't change their spots. *Persona non grata* as far as I am concerned.'

All the wives, including Tamara, were tired of what they considered Horatio's gibberish. What did any of it mean for Pan's sake? Too often he would storm off having lost the argument spouting this non-animal nonsense. Only wife number one, Cordelia, versed in so-called Upright classics, would shout after him '*Ergo*, you lose again, doom brain!'

Short-lived was the respite aboard *Toad One*. Horatio's countenance clouded as he examined the gas bottle meter, he tapped it and tapped again. 'Damned rum, can't be out of gas so soon,' he mumbled, puzzled.

The wind shifted and so too did the mood onboard. Remarks questioning his competency to fly a balloon joined with the buffeting wind and came at Horatio from every quarter. Even Tamara wailed 'you might have checked Hory, really!'

Horatio's defence, that it was all Upright doing and that

they would be getting the chop when he returned, did nothing to relieve the anguish of his passengers.

Horatio's opprobrium was not limited to Uprights, Melissa, wife number four, had been clinging to anything that came to hand, and it happened to be the parachute valve cord.

'How long have you been clinging to that?', Horatio scolded.

'Since we took off,' replied Melissa. 'We've been swinging all over the place, I had to,' she protested.

A nervous tick, the twitching of his left eye, was a known precursor to a Horatio tantrum, so Melissa decided to get her retaliation in first.

'Well, you never told me that I couldn't. Some captain you are!'

The parachute flap, situated at the crown of the balloon, acts to release hot air, and now that it was closed, they maintained their altitude. Horatio blasted again on the gas jets, a fleeting flare of flame shot upward, then petered, then farted, then failed.

In as much as they were still flying, could be considered a success, yet the altitude they were flying at, could not. Pushed by a gusty south-westerly, the wild wood was in their flight path and it loomed large. Horatio more sandbags in desperation, but his canopy was beginning to sag along with his spirits.

**

One sunset before Montgolfiere's departure for London to keep an appointment with Filtch, Stripum & Tuckham, the house rats had convened a meeting.

While the bulk of the below boards' population had taken the news of increased predation with a resigned acceptance – 'Ain't no great jabs bro, like them Uprights been lacin' our bites with poison forever' – some didn't see it that way at all. A few key elders, and one in particular, was in a catatonic state. No one could calm her; she ran in circles parroting 'ain't no tin of Felix.'

An extraordinary meeting, known as a Rodeo, because it included all the households' rodents: squirrels, mice, and rats, was held in the lofts. The mice would never venture below boards as rats and mice do not make for good bedfellows.

The meeting had been rowdy at times, although valuable snippets of information had been gleaned and pieced together. The upshot was that one Georges Montgolfiere was up to no good. That he had been overheard to say that he intended to cheat the houseowner in some way had been key.

From a rodents' perspective, an empty house had been a joy, particularly for the squirrels. For the rats, yes, a newly stocked larder had been a boon, but they knew they were on borrowed time. Uprights had an aversion to them, which was misplaced.

It was well known in rat lore that the very fleas that caused the bubonic plague had first jumped on to them from Uprights. Said fleas then infected the rats with a host of horrid Upright diseases which duly mutated and then they jumped back onto Uprights making them a bit ill. –

'Ain't nobody talk 'bout how many brothers and sisters we lost back then, our ends,' stated an elder scholar, gravely.

When it came to toads: 'like I ain't got no beef. Not sayin' I gonna hang with 'em nor nothin', ain't never gonna be in my mandem, but theys don't go lacin' the bites like dem Uprights. Theys understand the tax-system.'

Espionage was called for, that was the conclusion – they needed to know more. A couple of the smarter young blades put themselves forward to make the trip to London with Montgolfiere, to eavesdrop. It would be a perilous mission no doubt. Neither had ever ventured more than a mile from Toad Hall. But that was the case for all but one of the rat squad, an ageing female, who'd been born and raised in a London sewer.

The old girl, now too old to make the trip, took the opportunity of regaling the youngsters with tales of the great city. She also laboured on about the hardships endured, and as to how youngsters today don't know they're born. 'Use the sewers to make your escape' was not advice that the youngsters wished to heed.

'Like dat's well gross ma, ain't soilin' me garms in no Uprights turdnuggets.'

Georges Montgolfiere was a man all too conscious of his personal carbon imprint. To that end, he would only ever travel by motorcar if someone else was driving. When travelling solo, he walked, cycled, or used a horse and cart. Given the distance, a good day's travel, he elected for the horse and cart. Unwittingly, he was not riding solo. Only the horse, a huge unflappable old Suffolk Punch, noticed the two house rats, Nibble and Gnaw, board. They found a snug just above the axle and settled in for the adventure.

**

Horatio's reputation as an aviator was in shreds, as was the prized balloon and quite possibly, three of his marriages. For what occasioned such a fall from grace, we must rely on the testimony of that most duplicitous of birds, the cuckoo. You may therefore decide to take what you read with a pinch of salt.

'I was perched in a copper-beech whiling away the time and having a laugh at the other twits who were knackering themselves out, feeding my baby. Blimey, I remember thinking, greedy little beggar, just like his father – although I only knew him for a few days.

'No, it gets me every year does this; how is it they can't make out that's my baby? I mean, he's only a few sunsets old and he's already bigger than they are – stupid or what? I mean, every year on the way over I think, same old scam ain't going to work this year – and then it does.

'Anyway, I lift me head and see this massive toad heading my way, put the fear of Pan into me at first, I can tell you. Then, I see it's not a toad at all, it's an Upright's picture of a toad – I mean, those toads are ugly buggers, all covered in warts and knobbles, nothing like this picture which made it look more like a frog. Anyway, where was I? Oh, yeah, so I take to the wing for a closer look.

'I'm circling away and having a chortle, because there's a proper domestic going on in this basket thing hanging underneath. Then I'm hearing shouting from the ground. There's a couple of Uprights bawling up "throw down the bags, throw out the bags!" Well excited they were, waving their arms about and all.

'My Upright is patchy, so I didn't understand what they meant. Anyway, the domestic is still raging – and if that don't prove our point, then I don't know what does – I mean, me and my mate meet up for a quick shag, I give him the run around for a couple of weeks to tire him out – I mean, one or two shags usually does the trick, I don't want him fluttering all over me for weeks do I? Besides, they only ever have one chat-up line: "cuckoo"– I mean come on, change it up a bit – same every bloody season!

'So why these idiots pair up for seasons is beyond me – Do the business and be on your own way, that's what I say. All this DIY and nest building – it's for the birds.

'Where was I? Oh yes – the basket and the domestic. Well, not that it would matter to me of course, but I suppose it's not the same if you can't fly…

'So, when the Upright is shouting up 'throw the bags out,' he kept shouting it over and over, so I got the gist, this toad, possibly a gentleman toad – worst type – starts to try and ditch a couple of his toads over the side. Naturally, they ain't none too keen and who can blame them?

'Now, this round thing, I think they call it a balloon, ain't got any wings so how in Pan's name are you going to get any height? Beats me. How is it going to weave in and out of the trees? Well, it doesn't, does it? It clears the copper beech, but it's heading straight for the tallest tree in the wood – I love that beech tree, see the whole wood from the top of that. I reckon it's twenty-four Uprights tall. Anyway, it crashes right into it, and that big balloon thing comes down like a cloud over the top of the beech.

'You should have heard the racket coming from that basket! The three toads, females they was, were beating the so-called gentleman on the head. I perched nearby and almost pissed myself. What's more, it wasn't just me, was it? Just about all the animals in the woods came out to have a laugh. This squirrel opposite was laying on his back and kicking his legs in the air, he was killing himself laughing so much that he fell out of his tree!'

**

'Now what Horatio Toad?', exclaimed an irate Trudy. 'You'd better get me down from here,' she warned as she wrestled with her wedding band which wouldn't budge and which only served to increase her ire.

'That's it!', she declared shrilly as she finally freed herself of the ring and threw it onto the basket floor. 'It's over, do you hear me? Over!'

'One down, five to go,' muttered Horatio. This was ill-advised.

Mellissa had less of a struggle in removing her ring and she spent the energy conserved in fetching Horatio a sharp slap to the kisser. She held the ring to his startled eyes and gave explicit instructions in which ring to insert it.

Tiffs will be spats and squalls will arise and pass, however when your husband tries to throw you out of a basket thirty metres up, it is just cause for rebuke. Such an action leaves little room for negotiation and apologies won't wash. Horatio's lame attempts, ended in abject failure.

Storming off is an instinctive manoeuvre, but of no use when there is nowhere to storm to. Horatio was stymied.

'Stuck in a nest of vipers', did he mutter all too audibly and once more, this was ill-advised. All it earned him was a clattering and a battering in the basket.

The cuckoo, rather expertly, relayed blow by blow commentary to the ever-growing assembly down below. 'Ooh, that one was below the belt'. 'Nice little uppercut, followed by a sharp left to the kisser'. 'Ooh no! That was a rabbit-punch, the referee should step in here…'

Tamara, being a green, tree climbing toad, had shinned down the tree in short order. She had been as angry as her co-wives when she left the basket, however on the descent it dawned on her that, six were now four, and that meant a greater share of the spoils. Although it was a shame that Mellissa had thrown in the towel, she thought, because she was the only other wife she liked. And yet, she didn't want to be the only young wife, for who would want an ageing Horatio spawning all over you every night? Perhaps she could get Mellissa to change her mind, she further thought, and then they could work together to get rid of the initial three.

Now on the deck, Tamara thought she'd better put up some defence of her husband.

'Do you mind?', she yelled. 'That's my husband you're talking about!'

'I'm sorry for your troubles', soothed Molly Fenian. 'But you're married to a grade-one eegit there. No offence mind…'

'He's not an idiot, he's…' began Tamara, defiantly, and many heads turned her way to hear her defence. 'He's, well he's…' she stumbled, causing ripples of laughter. It was not an easy task to defend a position you know to be untrue. Horatio was a fool, but a fool who kept on giving. A privileged lifestyle, the best of foods and adventure, all of this did the stricken numbskull provide.

'He's the kindest, most honourable toad I've ever met,' she managed, somehow.

'Honourable?' questioned a bemused Fergal Fenian. 'He's after trying to throw his wives out of the basket!'

Fergal's remark brought on a clamour of disapproval, all aimed at the hapless Horatio who was uncharacteristically subdued, and keeping a low profile above.

There was a consensus that something had to be done. The two poor wives, still aloft, could not be left alone with a dangerous idiot. And so, a party of squirrels volunteered to bring them down. Greys worked alongside the two red newcomers.

The wood was still divided between the badger's 'foreigners out' policy and those who considered the greater threat to be existential: Uprights were the problem, and so too, was a certain gentleman toad. But he was an animal and eventually a consensus was reached that he too should be brought down to terra-firma. Besides, he was under bombardment from a group of rooks who seemed to have taken umbrage against him.

Horatio's trek back through the wild wood toward Toad Hall was fraught with anxiety. He was goaded at every turn, followed, and menaced. Once more, he hadn't helped himself. When questioned by a grey squirrel, whose drey was situated in the beech and whose home was now occluded by an enormous cloud of material blocking out the sunlight, Horatio's flippant remark 'look on the bright side, it'll keep the rain out,' was met with scornful incredulity.

Yes, he was in an irascible mood, yes, he'd had a bad day, but to make such a remark and only extend a grudging, disingenuous thanks to his rescuers, was beyond the pale.

'Horatio!', chided Tamara. 'Apologise!'

'For what?' was, again, ill-advised.

So, Tamara and the two now confirmed, ex-wives Trudy, and Mellissa, left him to his own devices and they walked home, unmolested.

A toad's defence, when frightened, is to secrete an unctuous poison from glands on its back. Horatio felt it ooze and was happy for it because he was terrified. Stoats, weasels, and ferrets picked up on the scent and in the realisation that he was frightened, made sure his trip was as unnerving as it could be.

By some remarkable chance, his flight passed the badger's door. By the size of the door, he knew it to be a sett, a badger's abode. Although, chief-oik, in Horatio's estimations, a badger is regarded as one of the clever types, someone to reason with, and notoriously greedy. Bribery, Horatio thought in desperation, might just get him out of this, so he hammered on the door.

Chapter Eighteen

Rodent's Ride

'Like, everybody got their ends innit?' said Gnaw. 'Totes bro, but I ain't never thinking there be this many ends. Unreal,' replied Nibble.

The two house-rats were staring out on the wide world in wonderment from their niche below Montgolfiere's ambling cart. One was pretending to be a little more worldly, but in reality, they were both agape.

Montgolfiere had taken a circuitous route to avoid busy roads. The old Suffolk-Punch plodded along at a never varying pace and was imperturbable. Traffic, including screaming motorbikes, had not the least effect upon his serenity. As an ex-dray, he had seen it all before. Even the streets they would take in London, he had trudged before. The cart he now pulled was as nothing to those of his youth, laden with heavy barrels of beer. He did miss his beer though, often he would be given a gallon at the end of a day's labour. That it made him fart like a trooper the next day, his kindly driver never seemed to mind, he simply wore a scarf about his mouth and nose for the first hour or so.

Montgolfiere, dressed as always in his green hemp suit and today a wicker hat, as it was a hot day in early May, nibbled on a carrot as they progressed. It was too late now to turn back, he told himself, the deed had to be done. He needed money and the commandeering of Toad Hall and its sub-letting, would bring him in some of the funds he desperately required.

As the outer suburbs came upon them and the necessity to take busy, noisy, noxious main roads, Montgolfiere's face twisted into a leer. How he hated so-called civilisation and everything that went with it.

'Let the seas rise and engulf this place and everything and everyone in it,' he exhorted loudly in biblical fervour.

'Yo dude, like the Upright got a downer on these ends,' remarked Gnaw, digging his elbow into his companion's ribs, but his friend was craning his neck upward at the tall buildings, awestruck.

The cacophony of taxis, buses, lorries, and sirens had the two house rats cover their ears.

'Ain't no sense is this blood, like that old sewer-rat always givin' us beef when we rappin', like we ain't never blastin' like this!', complained Nibble.

The old Punch pulled up outside the offices of Filch, Stripum & Tuckham and Montgolfiere jumped down and hurried up the steps and through the door.

Beneath the cart, the two house rats, who had not formulated a plan, were in a quandary as to what to do. Had they thought to enter via the main door? Perhaps, but the speed of the wiry Montgolfiere had beaten them to it. To make matters worse, an Upright was loitering by the horse and writing something in a notebook.

In desperation they made a dash to the grill of a basement and were seen by a passing pedestrian who screamed, thereby alerting the loitering traffic warden. As they cowered just inside the grill, the warden attempted to kick them. 'Dirty, disgusting things,' he shouted as the points of his size twelves rained in. It was all they could do to avoid the blows and mercifully his feet were too wide to enter far.

There was no way into the building that they could find, not without a day's gnawing, and no safe way out.

'He heatin' me up bro,' said the rat to his comrade as he dodged the Upright's frenetic, crazed attack. 'Like, you gonna sink the gnashers, or me?'

'Psst,' came the sound. The house rats knew not from where, but they recognised it. In fact, it was more of an 'eek', someone was calling their attention. As they continued to dodge the incoming shoe, they spotted a tail waving in the corner – a rat's tail – and the 'psst' sounded again.

'I say, over here chaps, you might just squeeze through.'

'Wot's the dude verbin' bro?', said one rat to the other as they dodged this way and that. 'Catchin' empty bro but dis Upright ain't cedin' de bout.'

A fissure in the paving, more of an an ingress for mice, proved a challenge.

'Like my ass gonna be wearin' his shoe, maximise de speed dude!', Gnaw shouted to his comrade, who was almost through, as he weaved to avoid the incoming.

Miraculously, they both made it through unscathed. They found themselves on a brick ledge in a dank, dark cellar.

'Deese your ends dude?', asked the house rat to a particularly well-turned-out rat sporting a crimson jacket with tails.

'I'm sorry, I didn't quite comprehend old boy,' replied the smartly attired rat.

'Wot's he verbin?', asked a puzzled Nibble.

'Gleenin' empty bro, like he's verbin' some mashed up lingo dere.'

'My name is Jeremy', announced the rat proffering a paw. 'Positively awful scrape out there, you have my sympathies.'

Paws were shaken and names were exchanged, yet that was as far as they got. Communication proved impossible. The two parties simply smiled at each other in embarrassed, incomprehension.

Jeremy, a resourceful, clever, and well-read, city-rat, thought he recognised the incomers' language as being- 'Yokel.' And, to that end, he sent for an interpreter.

While they were waiting, Jeremy provided sustenance which endeared him greatly to Nibble and Gnaw. Broken biscuit, always a winner, and peanut butter scavenged from sprung traps was fell upon, hungrily.

The interpreter, Rita, an elderly city-rat, was an odd cove. She was dressed in a flamboyant, bohemian style with something of the aesthete about her. She brushed herself down, aided by Jeremy, and relayed some of the gossip from her neighbourhood, Bloomsbury. Having fixed her attire, which included a seagull's feather in her velvet floppy hat, she invited the house rats to speak. Yes, indeed, Jeremy was quite right, the incomers language proved to be 'Yokel.'

'Yo dudes,' Rita began, affecting an accent Gnaw and Nibble found too funny for words. 'Why you wearin' out de leather and truckin' on dis mile?'

Nibble and Gnaw looked at one another trying to keep a straight face.

'You empty or gleenin' bro?', Gnaw, baffled, asked of Nibble.

'Catchin,' replied Nibble. 'Catchin' bites.' He then passed comment on the near scrape with the Upright.

'You got real salt on dis strip sister, like dem Uprights got more beef dan Fray Bentos!'

Rita smiled and turned to Jeremy. 'Are you picking up on any of this darling?'

'I haven't the foggiest old girl,' owned her bemused friend.

Progress was slow and out of politesse, the house rats managed to maintain a straight face, even if Rita's grip on 'Yokel' was outlandishly overblown and outdated. The reason for the visit was, at last, understood. Jeremy and friends would escort the two-house rats to the office of one

Mr Snipe. However, they were under strict instructions not to be tempted by piles of cereal beneath boards, as Rita made clear (ish).

'Dudes, dem Uprights done gone lacin' de nourish. Man, ain't just no belly achin'. You digging de groove?'

Nibble translated for Gnaw, who was still having difficulty tuning in, and they set off with Jeremy.

Snipe's office was to be found on the third floor at the back of the building. Through an elaborate series of runs, they made stealthy progress upwards. They had to exit the building twice through gaps in the wall where soil pipes exited the brickwork, but the runs were well-trodden and the grips in the bricks proved easy enough.

**

Georges Montgolfiere had brought with him the contract as signed by Horatio Calidus, Superbus, Dimidium-Nelson Toad.

'You are placing me in an invidious position Mr. Montgolfiere,' declared Silas Snipe as he perused the document, looking for loopholes. 'Were my partners to catch wind of this...'

'Georges, do call me Georges, Mr Snipe,' Montgolfiere said, adding ingratiatingly 'I am aware that I am already in your debt for the inclusion of the Hall in the lease. However, as welcome as that is, the stipulation of not being able to sub-let presents me with certain difficulties...' Montgolfiere adopted a tone pregnant with connotation and continued, 'of a pecuniary nature.'

'I see,' replied Snipe, not oblivious to a simultaneous stroking of an attaché-case at the utterance of the word pecuniary. Silas Snipe sat back in his seat and stared through his half-moon glasses at the case which appeared to be fabricated from some reed or other. He then shifted his gaze to the oddball seated before him.

'Let us hypothesise Mr Montgolfiere…' began Silas Snipe.

**

Behind a dusty old wooden filing cabinet, an age-old hole had been made in the skirting and here, the two-house rats Nibble and Gnaw plus Jeremy and Rita, were listening in. Hushed tones were employed to share the discourse. Although both Nibble and Gnaw were reasonably proficient in Upright, certain words eluded them.

'Petuniary?' like why the dude verbing on 'bout gardening bro?' asked one perplexed brother of the other. 'Hype…hypoth…can't eeven verb it bro.'

Fortunately, help was at hand, Jeremy assured them, using Rita to translate, that minutes of the meeting were being taken.

'Like dis is wearin-on dulltown bro,' whispered Gnaw.

'Dem Upright minutes, drag time blood. Like dey is rat sunsets dude,' replied an equally frustrated Nibble.

**

'If', continued Silas Snipe, 'we were to insert a caveat as you propose, and I stress the word if, then we would be making Horatio etc etc Toad, homeless would we not? A homeless, dare I say swindled, Gentleman Toad is quite likely, nay certain, to recourse to the law. As it stands, he cannot legally remove you from what once was his abode… reason for vexation enough, one imagines…'

Montgolfiere smiled. 'I've been doing my research on Horatio Toad, and it transpires that he is a descendant of a family of, let's say, interesting characters.' He looked about the room taking in the shelves of fusty, dusty leather tomes and went on. 'Not to put it in too defamatory a way, he is a crook.'

Silas Snipe suggested that wealth of the order of Horatio Toad was invariably garnered by nefarious means. Such, wealthy types usually ensured they were untouchable, he added, and likely to know a handy barrister or two.

'Ah, but there, you've hit the nail upon the head Silas,' went on Montgolfiere, not noticing the grimace on Snipe's face at the presumptuous use of his first name. 'Barristers, good ones, cost money and to my knowledge, Horatio Toad has suffered some disastrous business deals of late. To wit, he's mortgaged his properties to the hilt.'

Snipe tightened his lips, fixed Montgolfiere with a glassy stare and twiddled his fountain pen, his instrument of torture, between his fingers. 'And you intend, Mr. Montgolfiere, to take his one remaining property, which I know for a fact not to be mortgaged, from him.'

Montgolfiere reddened at the temerity of the accusation, as he regarded it, so abruptly put. This, he considered, was a scurrilous accusation; however, he held his tongue as he processed it. Yes, there had been some misgivings at first, some qualms, but the cause, the cause was the thing and nothing, but nothing must stand in its way. Eventually he replied in measured terms.

'To begin with, I would not be the owner of the property, merely the leaseholder…'

'For one hundred years,' interrupted Snipe, keenly.

'Well, yes, beyond my lifetime, but don't you see? Why can't anybody see? If we are to restore the biodiversity from the humble dung beetle right up to the bear, we need time. If animals are to put right what we have done wrong, we need time!'

'And the span of a Gentleman Toad is brief is it not? "Out, out brief candle…"'

Snipe enjoyed engendering disquiet in his clients. He knew full well that a bung was in the offing, and he liked to provoke the precipitous, clumsy move to an offer.

'That's as may be,' stated Montgolfiere, attempting to collect himself. 'But so too is mine and I intend to live to see my vision to fruition.'

'What of the heirs?', quizzed Snipe pointedly. 'I believe there are six wives, ergo a likely abundance of heirs, all with an axe to grind, all with a good reason to hone their axes for your neck.'

'None as yet', stated Montgolfiere flatly. 'Married for years without issue, perhaps he can't, small wonder the amount he drinks and smokes.'

'Yet he is your business partner,' Snipe stated curtly. 'Ruin him and you might just ruin yourself.'

'I don't need him, and I certainly don't need his preposterous vision. I just need the full use of the Hall…and the land of course, the land is everything.'

Many a scoundrel had passed through the doors of Filch, Stripum & Tuckham and Georges Montgolfiere was just another. The company did not, could not, accede to every bribe. However, a Gentleman Toad would invariably be on the losing side in a courtroom battle. He would be demoted to a common toad in the eyes of a prejudiced judge. Only if such a gentleman could buy, with oodles of cash, top barristers, did he stand a chance. Besides, Snipe had in his drawer a final, final demand addressed to one Horatio Toad for legal services rendered. He knew now that it was unlikely to be settled.

He decided therefore to take some pity on this Gentleman Toad and release him from the charge. It would be added to the account of Montgolfiere.

'It shall be done,' Snipe announced smartly and inclined his head toward the attaché case which Montgolfiere duly opened. 'Not enough,' Snipe issued abruptly.

'But...but surely,' stammered Montgolfiere who considered five thousand to be just reward. 'It's all I have with me,' he concluded, lamely.

Snipe, now standing, ushered him toward the door.

'How much more?', pleaded Montgolfiere.

'Another two thousand, plus...' Snipe sneered in the direction of the case. 'Plus that. It will be added to your account. Payment thirty days strict,' Snipe said, relieving Montgolfiere of the cash and adding 'Good day to you.'

How many others had exited the doors of Filtch, Stripum & Tuckham,' wondered Montgolfiere, feeling that they had been royally fleeced?

Finding two parking tickets, one pinned to the horse's bridle and one to the cart, did nothing to improve Montgolfiere's humour. He tore them up and scattered them like confetti. On the long plod homeward, George was assessing the likely income of a sub-let and how long it would take to recoup his losses.

**

Back in their cubby hole, Nibbler and Gnaw carried with them a transcript of the meeting which had been prepared, verbosely, in approximated 'Yokel' by Rita.

The house and city rats had parted on excellent terms making the usual offers of mutual visit and accommodation. Both parties knew they never would. They came from different worlds and the language barrier was an impediment to what all rats love best – a good chortle.

That is not to say that Nibble and Gnaw were not impressed by life in the big city.

'Like dem garms dude, sick,' said Gnaw.

'Yo bro, like smooth as, ain't no hessian itch dere. Gonna get me some stitches like dat and cruise de strip my ends – respect.'

Talk on the way home focused on a Gentleman Toad, although considered to be a major knob, he didn't deserve to be scammed and taken to Sketchley's by Uprights, the two rats adjudged.

Chapter Nineteen

Toad in a Hole

'*Il pete plus haut que son cul,*' Taupe asserted, offhandedly, concerning one Horatio Toad. A curious French expression meaning that the animal in question, farts higher than his arse – Is a pompous snob. She wanted nothing to do with the fellow. Besides, she was still ministering to the badger who now sat wrapped in as many blankets as could be found, by the fireside.

Horatio, having arrived in a state of disrepair, had soon reverted to type. He knew badgers to be landowners and as such, a fellow might expect a decent claret to be in the offing, failing that, a nicely chilled Chablis. To be given a mug of what might best be described as bat's piss, some atrocious elderflower concoction, he considered bad form.

Outside, Brian and the water-vole were in conversation.

'I think you're being too harsh on the toad,' protested Brian. 'After all, he's been through an ordeal.'

'Harsh?', questioned the vole, incredulously. 'Tell that to the squirrels. They've had to chew holes all day in that sheet blocking out their sunlight, and has he apologised?'

'Still, I think it was harsh to call him all those names,' maintained Brian.

'Richly deserved. He is an opinionated, reckless, self-aggrandising, selfish, cruel, vain, buffoon.'

'Still.'

'Still what, Brian?' asked the vole, vexatiously.

Brian didn't care for the vole's tone, and so went on the offensive.

'And that's another thing I've been meaning to ask you, Trevor-Stan...' he said, pointedly.

'And that is?'

'No easy way to say this; you're after my bird, aren't you?', Brian declared, categorically.

'What!' got caught somewhere in the water vole's vocal cords, and he could but turn his stupefied gaze upon the mole.

'I thought so,' continued Brian, heedlessly. 'I'm never wrong about this type of thing, seen it before, many times,' he concluded casually, failing to keep the hurt from his voice. He then fixed the dumbfounded water vole, jerking his head up sharply for a response.

'Cat got your tongue, eh? – Go on, vole-up, spill the beans, vole to mole.'

'Brian, I don't know how much of this has escaped your attention,' the vole began at length, 'but I am a water vole and Taupe is a mole. Have I really got to talk about the birds and the bees?'

Love is blind it is said, and when it came to matters of the heart, few were blinder than Brian. He was digging for a categorical no, and thus far, he hadn't got one.

'Not just about shagging though, is it?', stated Brian, indubitably.

'Then what Brian?'

'Well...' he commenced uncertainly. 'She laughs at the things you say. All that clever talk. She only ever laughs at me...not with me,' he concluded dolefully.

For a moment, the water vole had to take this on board, to think it through. Had he monopolised the conversation? Had he excluded his friend? Had he revelled too much in the rapport struck up with an intellectual equal? Had he joined in laughter at Brian's expense? The sudden realisation that he had, made him sorry, made him sad for his now, best friend. Moreover, it made him abjectly ashamed of himself. Ever an emotional type, a tear welled in the corner of his eye, and he brushed it away with his paw. Brian noted it.

'Not wrong, am I?', he questioned, sadly.

The vole choked on his answer.

'Oh Brian, my darling boy, you couldn't be more wrong,' he began as he wiped away another tear. 'I'm so sorry, I would never, never do anything to hurt your feelings. I've been selfish…vain, cruel…' He faltered as he reflected on the same terms he had applied to the toad.   'I've been a buffoon not to realise.'

'So, you haven't shagged her yet then?', Brian asked, brightening.

Ever flabbergasted by his friend's ability to wrong foot him, he stated adamantly and incredulously. 'Of course not, how could I? I'm a bloody water-vole Brian!'

This seemed to do the trick. 'Just asking, and by the way, no need to get so upset,' Brian replied unaffectedly, as if immune to his friend's unease.

For good measure, the water vole let Brian in on a little confidence, He felt a slight betrayal in doing so, but he thought it for the best.

'Between you, me and the honeysuckle Brian, Taupe's got you lined up for the season.'

If ever a mole returned to spirit, it was now. Brian's eyes sparkled through his spectacles. He flexed the muscles in his powerful forearms, took a deep breath puffing out his chest and pulling in his stomach, then an impish grin spread over his muzzle.

Without a hint of self-consciousness, he peeked inside his trousers.

'I've got a boner coming on,' he stated proudly to the stupefied vole who, collecting himself, for he'd caught a nasty whiff, advised: 'I should think her decision will be contingent on...'he began, as he backed away pointing toward the offending organ, 'you doing something about that.'

With the water-vole gone, Brian secreted himself behind a tree to carry out an examination. As he lowered Taupe's knickers, several flies took to the wing. 'Healing up nicely', he told himself. 'Give it a wash this summer.' With renewed confidence in his desirability, he did a little jig and sang a little ditty:

> *Oh, for the spring when the sap will rise in birch, elder and larch,*
> *An irresistible thing she'll find Brian the king,*
> *And her knickers will be off in March!*

**

The badger sat swaddled in blankets beside a roaring fire. Although it was a fine day without, albeit with a chilly easterly, within it was dank. Nurse Taupe had declared it such and insisted upon the fire. That the badger had succumbed to all of Taupe's edicts, was a source of wonderment to the vole. Yes, it had began badly, however with incremental improvements in his condition, the still enfeebled badger seemed to know which side his bread was buttered.

She brooked no nonsense did the matronly Taupe, the badger ate when instructed, mostly fortifying nettle soups, and he took his medicinal brew at sunrise and sunset. Any rebuke was sharp and incisive, and it made the vole smile to see old Quincy start, then comply, meekly.

Horatio Toad was finding his stay too tedious for words, yet the prospect of braving the wood alone was one he did not relish. He had convinced himself that the cut-throats that lay in wait were baying for his blood. His hand went to his head and although the bleeding had ceased, it was still very sore from the rook's pecks.

'I say *mademoiselle*, take a peek at my head, would you?', asked Horatio sitting forward in full expectation of compliance. Taupe shot a glance in his direction.

'*Oui, c'est laid*' – yes, it's ugly – she snapped and turned her attentions back to the badger.

Horatio, somewhat versed in French, did not take kindly to being called ugly, but he let it ride. '*Très drole mademoiselle*' he began but faltered, as his school-toad French deserted him, allowing Taupe to intervene.

'Nothing funny about that. If I wake up with face like that, I jump in the river.'

Biting one's tongue did not come easily for an animal who was more used to employing it, and he now sat back with a thinly disguised glower. Clearly the badger was making a recovery because he found Taupe's cutting remark amusing. His massive shoulders shook up and down beneath his blankets as he stared into the flames, although his laughter brought on a cough.

'Now look what you do!', censored Taupe, scornfully, as she cast a fierce glance in Horatio's direction.

Feeling ill-used and angered at the lack of respect he was receiving, Horatio Toad determined to get even. Who did these woodland oiks think they were? Nothing but a bunch of untutored, uncivilised ruffians who still lived in holes exactly as their ancestors did.

'What progress!', he scoffed quietly. 'I'll show 'em,' he muttered. 'Set Montgolfiere's cats on 'em, see how they like those onions...bunch of inbreeds!'

Taupe may have been ignoring Horatio's utterings, for she did not react. The badger, now hard of hearing, exacerbating his tendency to shout, probably could not hear anyway, but the water vole picked up on the comments all right.

'I would like to remind you Mr Toad, that although you may find this humble dwelling basic, you are a guest of Mr Badger and as guest…'

'Guest? Is that what you call it?' stated Horatio, laughing derisorily. 'I treat my servants with more respect…'

'That I doubt,' interjected the vole sourly, but Horatio didn't hear him for he was away and although toothless, as most toads are, he nevertheless had the bit firmly clamped in gums.

'Let me tell you, guests of Horatio Toad are presented with a bouquet, they have champagne of the finest vintage, and we don't stint on quantity, not a bit, they have the bottle. They have the finest rooms and five-course dinners washed down with the best of Burgundies and Bordeaux. They are entertained, with every whim and desire catered for, in short, they are treated as kings and queens.'

Horatio looked about the room, noting with satisfaction that his chastisement was taking hold, the badger stared gloomily at the flame, Taupe was paying attention whilst Brian was staring wide-eyed. Only the water vole retained an obdurate regard.

Further work required, reckoned Horatio. 'Since my arrival, I have received nothing but ridicule and scorn. I have been expected to sleep in a worn-out, flea-infested, lumpy armchair and as for dinner,' Horatio scoffed loudly, 'snails that must have taken the trek last summer!'

The room was silent except for the crackling of the fire and the laboured rattling of the badger's chest. Clearly this admonishment had found fertile ground, Horatio considered, and so he adopted a more emollient tone.

'Of course, you woodland chappies can't be expected to offer the first class service that I render to my guests, your hovels don't allow for it, but…'

'That's enough!' shouted the water vole, stopping Horatio in his tracks. He marched over to the door and held it open. 'See what hospitality awaits you out there!'

'Don't get above yourself Rat,' rattled the badger, his gaze still fixed to the fire. 'I'll thank you to remember this is my house.'

An awkward silence ensued, which Horatio thought only proper to bring to an end.

'Well said that man, English animal's home is his castle, eh?'

'Shut up!', barked the badger.

Now, the toad was in a hole both literally and metaphorically, he was scared to leave and downright determined not to remain. Clearly, the accursed water vole was not an option and neither, he suspected, was the female mole. The male, Brian, was it? He was a possibility, but a poor one. No, thought Horatio, what I need is muscle and bulk. Badgers are greedy beggars, he knew that much and so, it could only be a matter of the price.

'Name your price...Quincy, isn't it?'

'What?', replied the badger, confused.

'Just that', said Horatio airily. 'What do you want, money? I've got oodles by-the-by. Food, is it? Larder's stocked to overflowing. Wine? A decent St Emilion perhaps or maybe a fine Montrachet, eh? No, no, I expect you fellows prefer beer...as I say, name your price.'

'Arrant bribery!', shouted the vole.

'What do you want?', asked the badger, ignoring the vole's comment and turning his gaze from the fire toward Horatio.

'Get me out of here. Off your hands if you like, just out of the wood, that's all I ask. Spot of protection needed. They must all be terrified of a hearty fellow like you.'

Had it not been for the mention of beer; it is likely that the badger would have given the toad short shrift.

'Beer, you say. How much?'

Horatio, momentarily encouraged, was just about to expand on his offer and declare there would be sufficient to fill the badger's sett twice over, when a hitherto uncharacteristically silent Taupe intervened.

'He stay here *crapaud*!', she commanded, only taking an instant for a wry smile at her own joke. The French for toad transposed well in English she thought, especially for this specimen before her. 'Quincy is ill, he not going anywhere.'

'I say old chap, you're the master under this roof…' began Horatio, discouraged by the big animal's supine acquiescence to a mole, and a Froggie one to boot. 'Are you going to allow her to have the whip hand?'

The badger mulled this one over for a moment, beer and oodles of it, Upright beer no doubt. It held a powerful attraction for him. He imagined the long winter nights by his fireside with six bottles before and an endless stock behind.

'How will you get it here?'

'Servants dear boy, they'll have it here before you can say rabbits!', a brightening Horatio exclaimed.

The badger scratched his greying muzzle. 'Rat, you and Brian get him home, take as many cudgels as you need,' he insisted.

'Shan't,' declared the water-vole and he crossed his arms in defiance. Brian had already taken up a cudgel and held it aloft however, one stern look from Taupe had it droop impotently to his side. The badger wheezed as he turned awkwardly in his winged armchair to look at them both. The vole returned a steadfast stare whilst Brian hunched his shoulders and nodded in Taupe's direction. The badger sighed, said nothing, and returned to a mournful vigil on the fire.

Horatio slumped back in his lumpy armchair with a doleful, defeated look upon his face. He entertained thoughts of making the journey alone at nightfall, but quickly dismissed them. The worst of the devils were nocturnal, he estimated, and he'd never find his way in the dark anyway.

The water vole cleared his throat. 'There are questions to answer,' he said purposefully, as he strode over and stood by the mantlepiece, resting an elbow upon it, adding 'questions we should take this opportunity of asking.'

'*Ah oui.*', joined Taupe, as she too took up position.

Not wanting to be left out, Brian took up position beside Taupe, although she made him stand a few paces from him, and determined to give him a lecture on personal hygiene. Brian had no idea what these questions pertained to, so he simply parroted 'Oh, yes, questions all right.'

With all eyes trained upon him, memories, traumatic ones, flooded back, making the erstwhile cocksure Horatio, gulp.

Pinned to notice boards and pasted to lampposts on the island of Bermuda, were fading images that bore an uncanny resemblance to one Horatio Toad.

Indeed, staring out between bars on that island were two policemen condemned to a spell of reflection for the aiding and abetting of the Toad family's escape.

As these traumatic memories clouded and muddied Horatio's mind, he shrank back into the armchair and deflated, visibly. The overbearing presence of the badger, with his grey striped head, took on every appearance of a judge. The keen-eyed fellow leaning with a cruel casualness on the mantlepiece seemed to Horatio a conniving, spiteful lawyer. The colourfully clad mole was some sort of embittered plaintiff no doubt, and the scruffy little urchin standing nearby, unquestionably a courtroom usher.

A traumatised Horatio began to relive every moment of his ordeal. Muffled, indignant, accusatory voices arraigned his ears. Court room imagery, with its dark foreboding wood, smelling of beeswax, he could see and smell. It sapped all hope from him. He saw again the pointing, vindictive fingers which now flew at him like arrows. He saw the faces of the jury, twisted, and contorted in spite and the awful, leering faces of the plaintiffs. Now loomed the gaunt, reproachful face of the judge as he passed sentence and his words echoed in Horatio's ears:

'Take him down! Fifteen years – take him down, take him down.'

Chapter Twenty

Before the Beak

Sir Edwin Preece-Moog, his wife Constance, and the cygnet flotilla were patrolling the river, by Toad Hall, when he espied an incident that, in his opinion, brought shame upon the river's fleet.

"Pon my soul, surely not...' Ever dutiful, Constance fished in the water and retrieved her husband's monocle, wiped it on her feathered breast and replaced it in its socket.

'Whatever is it dear?' asked Constance, unsettled by any impairment to her spouse's equilibrium.

'We shall have a word,' stated Sir Edwin. 'Going-about,' he commanded and with his family in tow, he set up a bow wave at the head of the flotilla and headed directly for the lawns of Toad Hall.

'I say, Canard old chap, what in the name of Pan do you think you are doing?', scolded Sir Edwin.

Rear-Admiral Canard looked up from his slice of Mother's Pride, guiltily. This did not prevent him however from gulping down another portion in short order. About him, members of his entourage were gorging themselves similarly.

'I repeat, what explanation have you for this unedifying display of vulgarity?'

Once more, Constance retrieved the monocle.

A group of Uprights, some fifteen in number, were smiling and laughing at the antics of the ducks as they threw slices of bread on the lawns. A couple now spotted Sir Edwin and family and were making their way down to the river's bank proffering slices. They were dressed in orange robes, wore sandals and their heads were shaven. Upon their faces they wore smiles of benevolence.

'Arise and hiss,' commanded Sir Edwin. 'Beat up,' he insisted and all but one of his family obeyed. The young miscreant made a lunge for the floating slice as the Uprights backed off. The wrongdoer was quickly submerged by Constance accompanied by a tirade of flapping admonishments. Amid the kerfuffle, she downed the soggy slice herself, upbraiding her charge with a strong flap to the head when he dared to complain.

'Oh, I see, it's all right for you mama!'

En-masse, the Uprights sauntered back to Toad Hall. Rear-Admiral Canard, already feeling bloated, looked toward the river and his spirits sank. Sir Edwin's monocle glinted in the sun, making him avert his eyes, and Canard knew there was no escape from the inquisition.

'One might expect this type of boorish behaviour from the common coot, Canard, but I never expected to see such vulgarity from the house of Mallard. As leader of that house, it is unseemly to engage in such an orgy of excess.'

'Hear, hear dear,'confirmed Constance approvingly, if, somewhat guiltily.

Sir Edwin fixed the Rear-Admiral with a steely glare, awaiting a response. This was not forthcoming as the duck had an irresistible urge to clear his crop, and had the swan not backed away, it would have coated him.

'Now that is perfectly disgusting!', a horrified Sir Edwin declared as he swam about in a loop of avoidance. 'What do you have to say for yourself Canard?'

A sickly Rear-Admiral Canard regurgitated the last of the excess, collected himself, then replied. 'Food in this river is not what it was Sir Edwin. My family is often hungry.'

'Nonsense duck, I've noticed no shortage.'

'With respect Sir Edwin, your neck is longer than mine, we are dabbling ducks, not divers.'

The Rear-Admiral's remark met with a raucous quack of approval. 'Silence in the ranks,' he demanded, and this at least met with Sir Edwin's approbation.

'Every season the green clouds get larger,' went on the Rear-Admiral. 'Every year some of us fall sick.'

Quacking agreement all around which, this time, Canard ignored.

'More and more we are forced on land for berries, there is less and less food in the river, fewer snails, fewer beetles and so we must risk the land...' Emotion caught in the crop of the Rear-Admiral and he raised himself and flapped his wings angrily.

'But we are river ducks!', he quacked loudly.

Sir Edwin studied the heated Canard closely.

'And yet you accept the Uprights' food. There may be poison in a green cloud, I personally steer a wide berth, but I would suggest the Uprights' food may be more poisonous still.'

Constance had rather enjoyed her slice, and she couldn't quite see how something that tasted that good could be bad for you. 'Do you think it's all that bad dear?', she ventured.

But Sir Edwin, as he so often did, ignored her.

'Uprights are to blame for all this, Canard, and now they come in their droves. You are right to be angry, but you are very wrong in accepting their vile offerings. Are we to be fed like exhibits in a park?'

'Oh, that is quite demeaning,' concurred Constance. 'Sir Edwin and I once visited one, never again.'

'We are creatures of the wild, or we are nothing Canard. Let us not accept the crumbs from their tables, let us leave that to the common house rat.'

With that, Sir Edwin Preece-Moog set sail leaving a chastened, if somewhat belligerent, Rear-Admiral to reflect.

Another group of robed Uprights took to the lawns and headed for the river; some of the mallards became excited. 'Afloat and full ahead,' insisted the Rear-Admiral, not brooking any dissent. When they reached mid-stream, he ordered them go about-

'Present arse!', he demanded, and in unison, all tails went up.

**

'Wot is it son?', asked Reg, poking his head into the holt. 'bad bream, was it?'

'Leave 'im be Reg,' said Trace who was cradling her juvenile Nipper. 'He ain't in the mood for your jokes.'

'Wasn't joking,' replied Reg. 'Make me guts grumble, them bream.'

Clamp surfaced with a small dace between his jaws and deposited it at the mouth of the holt. 'There you go Nips, nice juicy dace,' he said, impishly, taking pleasure in his brother's discomfort. Nipper groaned and turned his head away.

'Leave your brother alone! Reg tell 'im!', scolded Trace. 'Your brother's ill, he's as 'ot as the sun.'

'Leave it out son,' chided Reg, barging Clamp back into the river. 'Yer mum's right, he's well crook.'

'I reckon it's the turds,' Clamp announced, as he poked his head back up. 'He swam right through 'em chasing that bream.'

Trace and Reg exchanged worried looks. 'This river ain't fit for raising kids Reg.'

'Not in front of 'em Trace,' he asked, turning away at what had become a familiar refrain of his wife.

'I mean it Reg!', warned Trace, hotly.

Reg sighed heavily and scanned the skies, another heavy downpour loomed, meaning another tide of shit no doubt. 'Wot can I do about it Trace?',' he replied, impotently.

Trace studied her mate coldly, evaluating his use as protector of her young. Where had that feisty young otter gone? Where had the cheeky chappie gone who had won her heart? For the briefest of moments, the memory of the chalk stream and the dappled shade beneath the willows played over in her mind, of how they had sat in the shallows as the crystal-clear waters swelled about their chests, of how they made love for the first time. She fell pregnant and then, oh then, her face hardened, at the memory of their trapping and *translocation*, that's what the Uprights had called it-

'Fucking Uprights!' she cried aloud.

'Mum!', shouted Clamp mischievously. 'And you tell me!'

But Trace was in no mood for levity, her vomiting, sickly child had been ill for two sunsets now.

'You'd better think of something Reginald Otter because I ain't 'avin my babies die in this sewer!'

'I ain't no baby,' complained Clamp.

'Shut-up son!', snapped Reg.

**

The *common* house rat was not averse to crumbs from the Upright table; indeed, it was relished. This influx of newcomers was the softest touch yet. Below boards, the assembly were being regaled with a barely credible tale.

'Like I'm in the larder taxin' the bites when dis Upright in the weird garms shakes up…'

The assembly nodded in unison; they'd all been there. Three escape routes had been gnawed for quick getaways.

'Hold up,' continued the house rat, raising a paw. 'I'm limberin' for the dash when the Upright starts verbin' on, like squeaky stuff and shit, he's like literally offerin' up the bites…'

'Yeah, like we all dumbass,' stated an elder. 'Ain't no way fallin' for that bro.'

'Nah, dude, I'm verifyin' his other hand, he ain't got no stick nor nuffin.'

Some of the younger's eyes were wide in disbelief as the tale unfolded. However, the elders were quick to caution that Uprights were the most duplicitous of creatures. If an Upright is throwing food in your direction, then it usually means it's been laced. They also recounted stories of dumb rats who accepted offerings, only to be clubbed with timber.

That the new incumbents had removed the ancient traps, all of which had been sprung before anyone could remember, was nevertheless curious. The testimony of another rat lent weight to the notion that these Uprights were cut from different cloth.

'I'm flirtin' the skirtin' in the back room when dis Upright clocks me. Ain't no biggy, I got de legs, but he's crackin' the grin and pointin'. I'm like, burn it round de corner dude and hang de back end out, don't spare de pins, but I's hangin' up coz, de other Upright checks it an' he's like smiling. Den I'm doin' a double-take coz, he literally puts his hands together and bows!'

Now, all of this muddied the waters at the rodeo where all the resident house rodents were present. The testimony provided by Nibble and Gnaw, as transcribed by the interpreter Rita the city rat, had been read out amidst gales of laughter. Expressions from antiquity such as – "You dig?" – "Far out"- "Bummer"- "Out of sight"- Were interspersed with idioms no one could easily understand. And so, it was left to the intrepid Nibble and Gnaw to fill in the gaps, as best they could...

Horatio Toad had been taken to Sketchley's, on that there was concurrence. It was also the opinion of all, that Montgolfiere displayed cuntish tendencies, even for an Upright.

A vote was carried (rodents were the only animal with such a system – Rodocracy – brought by ship-rats from Greece in antiquity) to the effect that a shrew be sent to inform the toad.

But a discussion, on action to reinstate the toad, ended in no clear resolution. There were those who argued that Uprights had no right to displace an animal from his abode and that it was they who should be evicted. Quite how they could achieve this had not been thought through, and it weakened their case.

There were those who maintained the Hall to be sufficiently large to accommodate the new influx as well as the toad family. These were rats of a liberal persuasion and were usually dismissed as wishy-washy fence-sitters.

Then there were those, considerable in number, who thought the new influx had got off to a promising start, food was plentiful, traps obsolete and they didn't want a return to the status quo. 'Like deese Uppies feed you bro, ain't no more wearin' down de pads searchin' for nuts outside, is it?'

Finally, such had been the squabbling that a second vote had been adjourned. They would see how things panned-out and wait on the toad's response.

**

Horatio was waiting for sentence to be passed. The jury was out, out in the kitchen. The process of interrogating the toad had a beneficial effect upon the badger's health. Yes, he still wheezed and coughed, but there was less blood, and he felt his strength returning. He had enjoyed the spectacle of watching the gentleman toad squirm.

'Well done, Rat,' he said hoarsely, clumping the vole on the back and making him spray a mouthful of chestnut. 'Hooked him, played him, and got him on the bank.'

Taking his cue from the fishing analogy, Brian began to recount his triumph with the giant perch-

'What that got to do with the toad Brian?', quizzed Taupe shaking her head at him in dismay.

'Oh. Err nothing I suppose,' he spluttered.

'*Alors, tais-toi*' – shut up then.

As he sat alone, awaiting he knew not what, Horatio's sagging ego began to reinflate. He knew it of old, here it came. First the outrage at being handled like a common oik by his inferiors. Next the conceit, and he puffed out his chest, as if those simple creatures think they could ever get the better of me. Then the *amour-propre*, me Horatio, the greatest escapologist that ever lived! He likened himself to a balloon – perhaps not a well-chosen analogy, he mused, but let it stand – You might squeeze me at one end, but I'll only pop up at the other, and I shall never burst!

During the vole's interrogation, Horatio's first recourse had been to lie. His dynasty had been founded on the sound principle of being parsimonious with the *veritas*. He and his ancestors had often found that it allowed you time to get out of a scrape. Besides, any fool can tell the truth, it takes imagination to fib.

And didn't I do well?, he now reflected; I had them on the run for a goodly time what with my lines about Montgolfiere being a lettuce-munching, hippy farmer only here to till the land. The zip wires and balloons? Just for the amusement of my wives, nothing more. But then his face clouded once more. 'How was I to know the sneaky buggers were behind the tapestry?' he cursed. 'Who wouldn't pay to see that?' Horatio mouthed, mimicking the vole's damning evidence. Blasted fellow!

Perhaps it wasn't my best line, he now reflected, but as I told them, it was only meant for dramatic effect. Anyway, I put them in their place – *defraudat numquam prosperatur* – Cheats never prosper – I told em, just to baffle the rustic fools.

Horatio halted in his deliberations as, once more, imagery of the Barbudan judge's face hove into view, and his heart rate quickened.

'For a moment there I thought I might crack, what with all that talk of the old pecuniary – "what exactly is your fiscal arrangement with this Montgolfiere?" – must have spluttered something. Damned unnerving that vole, nasty little piercing eyes. None of your blasted business!, Horatio muttered defiantly, as he settled back in his chair awaiting the return of his tormentors. 'What's more, not a blind thing you inbreeds can do about it,' he concluded.

With an acuity of hearing that bordered on the supernatural, Taupe picked up on Horatio's remarks from the adjacent room and she jerked a thumb in his direction.

'He puffed-up again – hopeless case.'

The first of the evening shrews arriving at the badger's door brought news destined to puncture Horatio's balloon, the second sent Taupe into a spin as she swept herbs from the table into a pelt bag.

'*Allez* Brian, come.' She bundled the bemused mole out through the door and tugged him along by the paw.

Slow on the uptake, Brian hadn't anticipated that his long-dreamed of liaison would be as peremptory as this. He'd imagined a romantic wormguini with a bottle of hooch and certainly some canoodling as a prelude. To be tugged along with such urgency had him wondering if tommy-todger, as he affectionately termed him, would turn up to the dance.

'It's that way', Brian indicated, pointing his arm toward his love nest. 'What is?', snapped Taupe, who stopped in her tracks. She searched his eyes for a second.

'I don't believe it, *merde*! Can't you think of any bloody-fucking thing else Brian!', she exclaimed, and then stormed off.

'Yes, Brian, can't you think of anything else?' came a squeaky, chuckling rejoinder from a weasel's hole.

With a petulant kick of his foot, Brian sent a shower of soil down the hole then hurried to catch up with his intended.

Chapter Twenty-One

A Mounting Fever

'Come on,' ordered the badger. 'Let's get you home.'

'Home?' replied Horatio, forlornly, for he was still reeling from the news the shrews had brought. 'I'm not sure I have one to go to.'

The badger and the vole exchanged glances. What a transformation in this poor animal. Gone was the conceit and his every utterance was dripping with pathos. Neither conceit nor abject misery were edifying conditions.

'Nonsense animal, we shall have none of this, that swindling Upright won't get away with it,' promised the badger as he wielded his cudgel, coughing as he did so.

'I'll go alone,' said Horatio, pathetically. 'Or, perhaps if the water vole would accompany me...I don't think you ought to be out,' he concluded with a sorry regard toward the badger.

'Stuff and nonsense! Old Quincy's made of sterner stuff', insisted the badger, not altogether believing it to be the case. 'You'll never get through these woods without me.'

Shrews don't just make for excellent messengers, they are accomplished editors and translators, albeit if a message at source becomes a little scrambled at terminus due to the relay system they operate. Any message deemed by the recipient as fanciful, can be verified by running the relay again and Horatio requested this service, twice.

He took the news very badly. He had been undone. Such a conniving, cunning stunt, he would not have thought possible of Montgolfiere. That he had practiced similar malfeasance in his own business practices, was of no import to Horatio now. He castigated himself for being a grade A, top-drawer, first-class chump in not reading through that damned contract. Would he have understood it if he had? Perhaps not. Yet, had he at least given the semblance of having done so, it might not have propelled Montgolfiere on to further fraud.

Exposed as a crook, what now was a gentleman toad to do? He could hardly drag the bounder through the courts. An awful realisation took hold; he was a penniless, homeless animal with six wives to provide for, (hopefully now only four) and destined to live out his days in a dank hovel. He was too sad for anger, maybe that would come, but for now he had to suffer the ignominy of taunts from wretched, spiteful creatures, as he cowered between the cudgel-brandishing badger and vole. A once proud animal, the gentleman toad, the king among animals, was now laid low.

As the faded grandeur of Toad Hall hove into view, the badger and vole halted. They noted several Uprights busy at work on the roof.

'They seem to be dismantling the contraption,' remarked the water vole looking toward Horatio who could barely muster the enthusiasm to look up.

'Oh, are they?' he replied weakly. 'I'm tired of it,' he added, disingenuously.

The badger shot a disbelieving look at the vole who simply looked to his feet with a sorry shake of the head. Not right to kick a toad when he's down, he considered.

Atop the roof, some of the Upright workmen had spotted Horatio.

'There he is the bastard, surprised he's got the gall to show his face,' said one worker, fiercely.

'Not our problem John. It's Henry I feel sorry for, he's lost big time on this.'

The workmen returned to their labour, dismantling the zip wires.

'One rule for those gentlemen and another for us,' an older workman said, sagely, adding 'He'll come up smelling of roses, you mark my words. His type always does.'

Horatio was forewarned of the animosity that lay in wait for him. He had not sent just two shrews, but many and they had returned with increasingly grave news.

He tried to avoid eye contact with the disgruntled workforce. He had banked everything on the fund-raising dinner and all he had was a vague offer of jam tomorrow. He had engaged the workmen with Montgolfiere's initial payment, which was nowhere near enough to complete the zip-wire project. The contractor had not been paid and Horatio was out of cash.

With his villas sequestrated by the Bermudian courts and his other houses mortgaged to their hilts, Horatio Toad was broke. All he had, or did have, was the great Hall before him.

Whilst news of his financial collapse had proven enervating, thoughts of an injustice done now sowed its seed in his breast. He grew angrier with each step as he considered the ignominy of being the last toad, in a long line of illustrious ancestors, to occupy Toad Hall. It wouldn't stand. Somehow, he knew not how, he would wrest control from that lettuce-munching slug, Montgolfiere.

As he straightened his back and marched onward, leaving the badger and vole behind him, Horatio's long, sticky tongue shot in and out in viperish fashion. He could feel the anger welling and he began issuing vituperative remarks aimed at the slug, to sustain his ire.

When your hackles are raised and you're spoiling for a fight – a rumpus, a melee, a fracas, a ruck – a lawn full of monks bowing and smiling at you serenely, is not conducive to a punch-up. In fact, rather the reverse, it has a mollifying effect, it appeases you, placates you, soothes and ends up by pacifying you.

'Drat!' grumbled Horatio as he weaved his way among them. They were seated cross-legged, beneath shrubs and trees. All were smiling benignly.

'Well, at least they show some deference,' Horatio thought.

So kindly were the beaming faces that his anger began to dissipate and with it, his resolve. His memories strayed back to his Eton days and the antique Upright bard he had been compelled to parrot:

'"What to ourselves in passion we propose...the passion ending, the purpose lose."' Horatio sighed and came to a stop. 'Oh, bollocks!' he muttered, softly, as the last vestiges of his ire seeped away.

He sat himself beneath a weeping willow to assess his next move. As he sat, a chant went up among the monks. Horatio cottoned on eventually that the tune was called: *Om Mani Padme Hum.* Seemingly, there was no second verse so he assumed that to be the title.

To his amazement, he found himself chanting along, it soothed him greatly and he felt the tension in his neck ease. It wasn't difficult for a toad to sit cross-legged, in fact it came quite naturally and when the chanting stopped, he found himself bowing reverentially to others in the group.

'I just wonder...' he whispered in a low voice. 'I wonder...he who laughs last, laughs the loudest.' Horatio lifted his eyes to a blackbird singing melodiously in the upper reaches of the willow; why had he never taken the time to listen before? He then looked toward the monks, so much in tune with nature. 'Decent enough fellows' he mouthed. 'Don't go a bundle on the sandals though...'

A plan was formulating in Horatio's mind, and he narrowly avoided congratulating himself.

**

'Brian fetch this, Brian get that...not those you idiot...I not say those!' A scowling Brian repeated Taupe's words moodily as he tramped the length of the river and scoured a nearby copse to fetch all manner of herb and medicinal plants. 'Lot of work for a shag,' he muttered, testily.

Matters did not improve when he returned to the otters' holt, this time with armfuls of what he hoped were the correct herbs.

'Is no good Brian,' Taupe declared. 'He can't stay here, make *civière*.'

First, Brian didn't know what a *civière* was and secondly, when Taupe drew a picture with a stick in the earth of a stretcher, he didn't know what that was either.

'Come on mate, I reckon I can make it over to that copse wiv yer,' declared Reg, leading Brian away by the arm before Taupe could launch another tirade in his direction.

'Can't be that 'ard, can it?' said Reg, encouragingly.

The two animals, with only the sketchiest of plans of how to make the article, made tracks.

'Mate, she don't 'alf give you an earful, don't she?' said Reg as he lumbered along beside a taciturn Brian. He looked over at his brooding companion and added 'probably because she loves you mate.'

Young Nipper's fever still raged despite Taupe's attempts to subdue it. Trace was beside herself with worry and young

Clamp had long ceased his habitual teasing of his brother, in fact, he was trying to invoke Pan, as he feared he would die.

Trace had done all she knew how and in desperation, sent a shrew to fetch Taupe. She had heard snippets that the badger was under her care and making progress.

'Get fish. Do something useful!' Taupe snapped abruptly at Clamp; she had little time for deities. As a scientist, she placed her faith in medicines.

Naturally, Trace did not wish to be parted from her sickly Nipper, but she had Clamp to consider. She was not about to entrust Clamp to an ineffectual Reg, with whom she was still furious. If, Pan forbid, she were to lose one baby, then she was not about to lose sight of the other.

Next time, when the rains fall and the shit-tide begins, then, Trace decided, they would stay out of the river – even if that meant starving.

'We gotta make a bed Brian, that's all it is,' stated Reg with a bemused look at his co-worker. Reg had heard that moles, stout dependable animals though they be, were slow on the uptake.

'Nah, it don't need a bleedin' 'eadboard Brian!' exclaimed an increasingly exasperated Reg as he stripped bark with his teeth from the willow trunks.

'Sorry mate…it's just I'm under a bit of stress,' he said apologetically noting the hurt on Brian's face.

On the way back, Brian was once more in a laconic mood and his replies were sparse. The stretcher poles, made from two coppiced saplings, had been gnawed by Reg.

'Hey Brian, look at me mate, I'm becoming a bleeding beaver!' Reg had shouted to cheer his companion, to no avail, as he felled the saplings.

As they walked back, Reg offered 'Lucky you was 'ere mate, wouldn't 'ave 'ad a clue on me tod.'

Brian sighed heavily. 'You made it all.'

'Not true though, is it? I mean, you did the weaving.'

'And you did most of that as well.'

'Ah, but she don't know that does she?'

Reg allowed for the idea to filter through, it took a while, but he then noticed Brian brighten.

'Exactly Brian, old Reg was bleeding clueless, weren't he?'

Taupe had no time to listen to Brian's detailed plan of construction, for Nipper was loaded post-haste onto the stretcher. His mother showered him in teary kisses and tucked a childhood toy, a shiny freshwater mussel shell, in beside him.

The journey back uphill to Brian's abode was arduous for the two moles and they did not go unnoticed by concerned onlookers. 'If anyone can, she can,' said a rabbit to his mate. 'I saw the badger this morning, we all thought he was for the trek. No animal gave him a hope.'

Brian was happy to be back home, he knew where all the pots and pans were, so when Taupe fired her orders, and these were terse and many, he at least knew where everything was. He made frequent excursions to fetch a plethora of grasses, herbs, berries, and leaves and returned in quick order.

As Nipper fell into a sound sleep, Taupe looked over at Brian, who was by the bedside of the sickly otter, and smiled. She reached out her hand and placed it on his arm gently. '*Merci*, Brian,' she said softly. Had she been able to see clearly through his bottle-bottomed spectacles, she might have detected a tear.

**

Having bowed to each and all of the monks, and some by mistake twice, for they all looked the same to Horatio, he scurried off for the wild wood. Clad in full orange regalia and in the guise of a monk, he assured himself 'won't recognise me in this get-up.'

Horatio's germ of an idea had grown into a green shoot: Those chanting-chappies are paying through the nose for something I can offer for free. That they must be short of the old pecuniary is self-evident, Horatio estimated. After all, they've got their arse in the grass all day and don't do a blind stroke. Can't butter many scones like that – I reckon they'll jump at the chance of rent-free. Mind you – Horatio's mind clouded a little – they don't look like they'll cut the mustard in a ruck.

There was a fresh spring in the steps of Horatio as he made his way up to the wood, the larks were twittering high and the hedgerows were bustling with birds. Strewn along the banks were wildflowers, stichwort, red and white campion, flowering wild garlic, Oxeye Daisy, and brilliant yellow gorse. As he entered the wood, he threaded his way through, yellow celandine, herb-robert and a carpeted mass of bluebell. Horatio stopped to take it all in.

Vague memories of his school days, of the holidays spent with an old dowager aunt, seeped back. Had she taught him the names of these plants? If so, he couldn't recall, for if taxed on the enforced time spent with the Old Redoubtable, as he had named her, all he could remember was being bored out of his tree.

He did, however, recall being banished to his room for having stolen a policeman's bicycle to cycle to a neighbouring village and public house. Three days had the old dowager locked him in with only the thinnest of gruel. Had it been intended to force him on the straight and narrow? If so, then it had failed. Regret, a most infrequent imposter in Horatio's breast, now paid a fleeting visit, but was summarily banished. 'Paf!'

Marching onward, incognito, Horatio began to wonder if those bald-headed, chanting chappies hadn't imbued him with a touch of percipience. Must be something to do with the mumbo-jumbo chanting, he reasoned. Drum the fellow in enough and some will stick. And so, he checked his gait as he approached the badger's neck of the woods-

'Now, those fellows prefer to see a chap contrite,' he muttered. 'A supine, pliant sort of cove.' Horatio promptly adopted a gait to reflect his new condition. Gone was the resurrected, ebullient spring, to be replaced with a humble shuffle.

**

Fergal Fenian's suggestion fell on stony ground. 'I know what I saw Fergal,' Molly insisted as she licked her paw and swept back an errant hair from one eye.

'Spectacles, my arse, you'll not catch me dead wearing them!' Molly turned back to re-enter the den with a parting shot.

'And don't drink any more of that,' she said, crossly, as she snatched Fergal's bottle of potcheen.

'You can save it for later when the Peels are here, I'll not have you cooted before they arrive this time.'

Fergal sighed, as he thought on the Peels. If ever a couple of foxes had a ridiculous name, it was the Peels. And it wasn't just the name of the impending visitors that irritated Fergal, it was his being compelled to mind his p's and q's. Molly had lain down the law following their last visit.

'Twill be the wonder if they ever come again,' she had complained, visibly upset. 'You with your old, feck this and feck that, and to use the c-word five times, I was ashamed, so I was.'

All this nagging just because I suggested the mole make her a pair of spectacles, thought Fergal, who had also caught a glimpse of Molly's vision, albeit a fleeting one. He laughed as he took a surreptitious swig at a bottle he had hidden from Molly.

'What in the name of all that's holy was it anyway?' he asked himself aloud. ''Twas no fox, Molly's wrong there, 'twas too orange, but 'twas no Upright neither.' He took another swig. 'And the walk, mooching along as if it had shat itself or something, no self-respecting animal walks like that.'

Fergal decided he'd better stay off the hooch until that most dismal of couples, the Peels arrived. 'Linda has had me hard at it all week,' mocked Fergal derisorily, imitating Peter Peel's very English accent with its accompanying, affected laugh. 'She had me excavate four new cupboards. We're doing-up the kitchen,' he mouthed with a mocking sneer.

Letting the feckin' side down you English prat, that's what you're doing, sneered Fergal.

Since their last visit, Fergal hadn't heard the end of it. Molly wanted him to dig a new kitchen extension.

Still, he lay back now to enjoy the dappled sun. He'd been to the farm shop that morning and brought back a nice, plump hen and for good measure, picked up a pheasant on the way home. He'd done his bit. He'd even found time to pay his respects at the pheasant's Coronach.

Chapter Twenty-Two

You Say You Want A Revolution

Horatio's return to the badger's sett had come at an opportune moment and curtailed a morbid conversation that centred on life's great inevitability. '…and then shall darkness prevail…'

The water vole had been citing from the Book of Pan that foretold of extinction and the subsequent loss of knowledge. The badger had sat, nodding sagely, indeed he had instigated the conversation. The walk down to the Hall and back had taken it out of him and, his own demise, he now no longer considered fanciful.

A water vole may seem to many an indolent chap who sculls his way carefree through life, but in fact, he is the font of animal knowledge and the keeper of the Book of Pan. In a mournful tone, he recited 'When the last of the swimming-rats leave the rivers, then shall darkness prevail.'

The pair had sat in sombre silence and even if the badger thought his end was at paw, it would not have the significance of the water vole's demise. There remained a strong population of badgers in neighbouring woods whereas for the water vole, none now knew of others within the bounds of the known world.

An impartial observer might conclude that neither badger nor vole had contributed toward the prolongation of their respective species.

And so, a 'rat-tat-tat' on the door brought the dismal conversation to a close. The apparition before, clad from head to toe in orange robe with only two copper-coloured eyes, peering through slits made in the fabric, made both animals start.

'What in the name of Pan is it Rat?' cried the badger hoarsely as he reached for his cudgel. 'Not more ruddy foreigners, is it?'

'Wait!' cried the vole, staying the arm of the badger, as the apparition began to disrobe. Muffled sounds emanated from beneath as Horatio, fearful of a crack to the cranium, struggled to present himself.

Raised eyebrows were exchanged between badger and vole as they listened to Horatio. Gone was the miserable self-pitying and, more refreshingly still, gone was the hubris. In its stead was a calmer, more measured animal, that accepted a jug of the badger's vile homebrew with equanimity, and even gave every semblance of being capable of stomaching it.

Horatio did not really have a plan, it was more of an amorphous concept, and yet as he rambled on, he noted the water vole scratching his chin in thought. It all sounded a lot of tosh to the badger who wanted to know why Horatio had not simply marched into his hall, taken the execrable, miscreant Upright by the neck, and thrown him in the river. But he held his tongue.

'Why, Horatio, you clever old stick...' began the vole.

A keen student of the gentleman toad might have detected the faintest sign of puffing up, but this was held in check by the new, self-aware animal.

'It might very well work Horatio...you said you sent a shrew? What exactly did you get in return?' asked the vole.

During a pause in chants, Horatio had happened upon a shrew going about her daily routine. He had asked her what the current mood was in the Hall and to what extent everyone was missing him. She said she would go and ask the first she bumped into.

Just as she was scurrying off, Horatio called her back.

'Whilst you're at it, you'd better ask the *memsahibs* how they're faring without me.' The shrew looked evasive, so Horatio clarified. 'You know, the wives, six at the last count.'

Horatio then bent his head for snout-to-ear insertion.

'What? All of 'em?' Horatio replied, stunned.

This had been part of Horatio's comeuppance; the news that only one wife remained and one that was at the wrong end of the batting order, as far he was concerned. He frowned, his first wife, Cornelia, wasn't it? Seemingly, she had not deserted his sinking ship.

The returning news that a house-rat was more than happy with his absence, but particularly delighted with the influx of chanting-chappies had spawned Horatio's idea. One rat doth not a summer make, Horatio warned himself, but then, the cads were prone to groupthink, so it might just work.

'But wouldn't all that chanting get on your wick?' quizzed the vole, as a precaution, before launching upon his battle plan.

'*Mani Padme Hum, Mani Padme Hum, Mani Padme Hum,*' Horatio chanted, puffing out his poly-chinned throat in a preposterous bubble.

'Shut up!' barked the badger.

'And you say...' began the vole, ignoring his gruff companion, 'that you could cut along fine with these fellows?'

'Hall is plenty big enough, I'd have the top floor, chanting-bods the second, and the rats can have the ground floor. Near the kitchens you see, they prefer that.'

'Then Horatio, I'll hoist this one up the mast and see if we're on a broad reach,' concluded the vole.

The water vole's plan was predicated upon a hitherto unknown type of Upright having taken up occupancy in

Toad Hall. Reports to date were not just those of Horatio, but of woodland, field, and river. Seemingly, this new species goes out of its way to live in harmony with all that crawls, slithers, and slinks. Indeed, it even offers up its food.

Now, the provision of food between Upright and animal is a contentious issue: The house rat has a trade to ply, and the surreptitious taxing of food needs to run a recognised gauntlet, or else what is the point of the covert operator, where is the dignity? Indeed, where's the fun? For the haughty and proud river dweller, Sir Edwin, and his ilk, food provision is tantamount to the soup kitchen. For the field rabbit, well if they are not sourcing their own, then they will only spend the time shagging, for they have no other diversions.

Earlier that day, the vole chanced upon Fergal Fenian and talk turned to the new orange apparitions. Happy to be vindicated that it was his vixen whose eyesight was failing and not his, he was less happy with the name the vole had suggested for them – Orangemen. Fergal insisted that name, would not be heard in his den. And so, a suitable name had to be devised for the sandal-wearing monks; they batted it back and forth. Finally: 'Orangedals' Fergal allowed, he could live with.

The vole's scheme spread wider, much wider and could only have been encompassed within that most erudite of craniums. How to return the woods, fields, and riverbanks back to a bygone age, one that is detailed in the Book of Pan, without Upright intervention? As the vole saw it, their known world was circumscribed by the range of each animal, and the range of most lay within the boundaries of the Toad estate.

Many a sleepless night had the vole tossed and turned in consideration of Georges Montgolfiere's high-blown vision. So much of what he had said made eminent sense. So much of what he termed biodiversity was the quintessence, a veritable distillation of the Book of Pan. But what troubled the water vole was the precipitative nature of an Upright's wild imaginings and his haste to restore a new, old order, within his own limited span. This impetuosity considered the vole, was a major failing in the Upright.

His thoughts bent on Brian, which was always problematic when in cerebral mid-hypotheses, and on how his pelt would be passed down and worn by his ancestors, smelly though it be. The wearers of those pelts know that their span is short, and that change is gradual.

Silent spring may be real to Uprights, but so too was a fractious spring to animals, and change, which the vole allowed for as being inevitable, could wait; it would happen, in its own sweet time.

Impatience and self-aggrandisement were Upright faults and not those of animals, the vole believed, although one exception had to be allowed for – the gentleman toad.

The water vole decided to call for, what had not been called in generations. Most probably he alone, as keeper of the sacred text, knew what a Conanimum was. The meeting would call every animal to a place and for the inclusion of all, this would have to be the riverbank. But it would also have to be held hard by trees, for the ceremony would invoke Pan and the jack-in-the-green. Would they come? Could they be summoned? Only if the water vole, the last keeper of the Book, got it right.

'You're meddling with powers none of us can comprehend,' warned the badger, sternly, and to a degree, the vole thought him right.

'Get 'em all singing the same tune, eh?' ventured Horatio, greatly encouraged, adding 'strength in numbers and all that sort of caper?' he quizzed the vole, breezily.

'This is not a caper!' the badger admonished, severely.

'Oh, er...didn't mean to suggest...quite right Quincy old chap, quite right, just so.'

All that remained was to disseminate the news to every corner of the known world and every shrew would play a part, yet it would not be sufficient. Birds would play their part too, setting up calls and flying to the outer reaches. Perhaps most importantly, that most ingenious of moles, Taupe, might be persuaded to make a broadcast…

The vole's idea? To work together, each and every animal in common cause to oust the Uprights (and one in particular). The Orangedals could remain.

**

'How you bloody-fucking know I can do that?' shouted Taupe angrily at the water vole who, inadvertently, glanced at Brian. She then turned on the hapless mole.

'Why you never keep trap shut?'

Taupe's initial vitriol soon abated, for she too had been wrestling with Montgolfiere's vision. She now regarded it as an unworkable dream which did not stand the scrutiny of day. It was a zoo, she considered, only worse, and not the initial vision Montgolfiere had espoused.

Yes, she had been drawn in at the outset, had agreed to spy for him, to report back on every occurrence however minor, however inconsequential. But now, having lived and gotten to know so many, she could no longer place herself at one remove – she had gone native.

Science had always been her driver, and it was to that which she owed her allegiance, not to Montgolfiere. In her spare moments, she had begun to formulate a plan to improve the river's health, perhaps it was pure fantasy, but worth a try…after all, she owed it to little Nipper, who was only making the slowest of recoveries.

Alors, this is bloody-fucking first, Taupe thought, as she settled by her *mycelia* soundbox. I am first mole to make call to arms to occupied land. Just like old Upright general. Taupe then began her broadcast. She made the precaution to write it down first and delete *gros mots* – swear words.

'I call to all animals who want to remain free to listen to my voice and follow my instruction, meet at Esox Island in full moon tonight. Conanimum, repeat Conanimum – water-vole to invoke Pan...bring packed lunch...*Et oh oui, – vive la France!*'

For good measure, Taupe repeated the call several times, but at Brian's request, dropped the *vive la* part as he thought it would only antagonise the badgers and stoats – attendance was key.

Chapter Twenty-Three

A Tangled Web

If any animal knew of another not present, then it would have stretched incredulity to its limits, for there, gathered in multitude, was every known creature from beetle to stag. From the distant woods and fields, they had come and from furthest stretches of the river, including the mink.

Upon Esox island, the old holy isle, the water-vole had constructed a makeshift lectern and, upon that lectern, the Book of Pan.

On the riverbank, in pride of place and facing the island lay Nipper on his stretcher, Trace was stroking his head and to her overwhelming delight, her baby had returned a smile.

Next to the stretcher stood the badger in his great coat and beside him, Horatio.

Taupe stood some way off. As was her wont, she had selected a white and black pelt which allowed her to move among the darkened tree trunks and moon shadow, barely seen. The superstitions of these poor simple creatures, she found risible. Still, as an ethnographic study, it might prove of some worth, she reasoned.

Yes, she had broadcast the call to assembly, but it had been all she could do not to laugh. It was science that held the solutions, not the string of abracadabra the vole was now chanting to a hushed, reverent, assembly. To boot, it was taking an age and so she thanked her prescience in bringing her pelt because, invisible, she could bob-down to pee.

Taupe was in mid-flow when a gasp went up. She quickly straightened, a little too quickly and felt the damp on her leg.

'Smell like Brian soon,' she muttered crossly, adding 'where is he anyway?'

She then took off her bottle-bottomed spectacles and wiped them on her pelt-

'Bloody-fucking superstitious fools,' she muttered. 'It just... *brume '*– mist.

She screwed up her face in annoyance, why did that word always evade her? The elusive word, *mist*, sprang to mind at the very moment she realised it had form. '*Curieuse*', she whispered. With countless awe-inspired gasps about her, she may have well shouted the word; none would have heard.

Upon Esox island, the water vole had incanted himself hoarse. If the wretched animal takes any longer, he thought, then I shall cut all ties with him. He felt a multitude of eyes boring into his back.

Beneath the water vole's feet, and boring into the earth was Brian, and he had been doing so for an eternity. He could sense the water vole's frustration and intermittently, hear it.'Canst work in the earth SO SLOW old mole!' The water vole interspersed these admonishments within his incantations, with each repetition being angrier than the last.

'Not as if I'm making normal holes, is it vole?' griped Brian, as he screwed his way downward on his seventh, and final tunnel. In a state of exhaustion, he collapsed in the central chamber from which seven narrow, spiralled tunnels led up to the surface. He studied the pile of old clothing heaped in the centre, which included several of Taupe's dyed pelts. 'Serve you right for being a spy,' he said. Yet his hand, holding a candle, trembled.

'She'll kill me,' he said, weakly.

'CANST WORK IN THE EARTH...'resonated once more and Brian threw the candle onto the mass, which ignited so quickly that he had to make a spinning dash for the surface.

Brian then hid among bushes to admire his handiwork. Whatever else the cunning water vole had stuffed the pockets of all those old clothes with, Brian had no idea, but the effect was magical. A veritable kaleidoscope of colours twisted and entwined as the smoke rose skyward. He could hear the gasps of astonishment and a broad smile spread over his face.

'Who's the dimwit now?' he muttered. 'Twisty tunnels? Yes, me Brian, all my idea! ...I thank you!'

'THEN, SHALL JACK BE IN THE GREEN...'

The water vole's prompt was more of a sharp poke than a cue, spurring Brian into action again.

With his prop prepared beforehand, Brian now brought the green man to life. To all intents, it looked like a giant lollipop, but when, after much conspicuous undergrowth rustling, Jack's face sprang from the high bushes on the island, turning this way and that, the reaction was deafening. The water vole's artwork was sublime and Jack's face, fashioned from many shades of green foliage, was illuminated in the moonlight.

Then did the one true mystical event of the night occur- The water boiled, the river boiled, and those who could not, due to their physiology, display their wonderment on land, now did so in the water. A silver sheen of fish flanks covered the surface, reflected the moonlight, glinting and flashing. Shimmering, the flanks formed into an orb, an aquatic orb, to mirror and rival the moon.

Brian, ever fearful of being spotted, almost fell into the river agape as he craned his head to look. He was happy for it, delighted, if not overjoyed, for there was a large part of him that felt the ingenious workings of the night to be a cruel deception.

'DO YOU HAVE WORD FOR US JACK FROM WHENCE YOU CAME?

Brian then gulped, not once but several times, and with a tremoring paw, he activated the lever working the puppet's mouth. Would he, could he, remember his lines?

'Animals all, hear my voice...' began Brian, adopting a rehearsed, ethereal voice. He waited, as the vole had instructed so that the assembly's brouhaha might be quelled. 'I bring a message from the roots of the earth...'

'The very roots of the earth!' the water-vole mouthed, crossly.

'...this land, this river is yours. We grow tired of the Upright defiling it...'

'Good, good, well done!' mouthed the vole, scarcely daring to hope that Brian be capable of remembering the whole text.

'Now must you resist!' At this entreaty, a roar of approval went up.

'But...' At this point, Brian, with eyes screwed tight in concentration, remembered that he was supposed to be acting upon the lever that worked the puppet's mouth in synch with his words. As he now began to do so, he forgot his lines. Jack was struck dumb, his mouth was working, but sound, came there none. Restless voices all about permitted the vole to hiss 'BUT!'

Brian picked up on his cue. 'But there is to be no violence. Change will come, but slowly...' Brian was now pulling his lever frantically up and down giving the impression that Jack was speaking ten to the dozen.

'Listen to Trev...I mean...The Swimming Rat! All heed the keeper, the Swimming Rat.'

'Idiot!' mouthed the vole at the mention of his name, however as he glanced over his shoulder, all eyes were still turned upon him in hushed adulation.

With nerves shredded and and limbs exhausted, Brian slumped to the ground, his work complete.

The water vole was still speaking; something along the lines of establishing shrew contact and the woodland web of roots, but Brian was done in. He lay down in a briar and stared at the remnants of mist-like smoke drifting upward. He was dimly aware of departing animals, of distant voices and when he awoke, it was the water vole's voice he heard.

The bleary-eyed mole found his co-deceiver to be oddly downcast, for hadn't they just escaped the ignominy of discovery? Hadn't their plan been a triumph?

'We missed it, Brian,' the vole said, sadly, as he slumped down beside his companion.

'Missed what?'

'We missed it, and all my life I have been waiting.'

Brian was puzzled. 'The fish? Oh, don't tell me you missed the fish, they put on a real show.'

But his friend sat staring disconsolately at his feet. 'So you didn't see it either then?'

'See what?' replied Brian, tetchily, as he extricated his rump from a tangle of spiky bramble.

'Pan, he was here, he came!' exclaimed the vole, adding flatly. 'Everyone saw him, except us. It all happened behind my back.'

Accounts varied, there were those who contended that the great deity, half Upright-half goat, bestrode the river. Others claimed he was on the opposing bank and still more who said he had glided toward the island in a ghostly vessel. Many claimed to have heard him play the pipes, others said he never did. There were plenty who maintained that the instant he put the pipes to his lips, the waters boiled with fish. Perhaps, every animal saw and heard their god in their own way, that at least was the water vole's doleful conclusion. What seemed beyond question, however, was that Pan had appeared.

'Ballbags!' declared Brian, and the vole shot him an incredulous glance.

'Is that all you have to say, Brian? The very god of everything, of all we are, of all we ever were, and all we ever will be, walks among us, and you say "ballbags!",' concluded the vole, hotly.

'What?', responded Brian, distractedly, as he fidgeted about. 'Oh, no, no it wasn't that...' he went on, 'it's just that I've got a thorn stuck in my arse.'

The water vole rowed homeward in a moody silence as his companion, still fidgeting with his aft end, left him wondering what, if anything, other than food and sex, passes through the mole's mind.

**

Taupe sat looking at the wild-flower bouquet, gifted by Trace and Reg, and tried to summon a smile. *'C'etait Pan, c'etait Pan...'*she mimicked in a grumble.

Not that she wasn't happy that little Nipper had got up from his stretcher and walked. She was. But for his whole recovery to be attributed to willowing wisps of mist, she found galling. What of her herbal remedies, what of her scientific rigour? Did none of that count? How could she ever gain recognition when her contemporaries were no more than superstitious fools who only see what they want to see? Nevertheless, she was troubled by the fish. What inspired them to behave in that way? There had to be a reason and one that had nothing to do with deities.

More irksome still, was that she found herself missing Brian. There was no logic to this. Apart from her desire to breed next year, what earthly benefit could his presence bring?

She shook her head crossly and moved over to her *mycelia* soundbox, the roots were buzzing, and every other word, was Pan.

She sighed and decided to go to bed. Quite what inspired her to rake through Brian's drawers and don one of his old, scavenged hessian vests, made from potato sacking, she couldn't say, but when she awoke at dawn with a pungent, musty, perfume affronting her senses, she tore it off in alarm.

**

Cornelia Toad cast a sideways glance at her corpulent husband who was walking beside her as if in a trance. She was discomfited to be holding his hand, he had simply taken it, seized it. What did he think he was doing? Had they ever held hands when walking? If so, she couldn't recall. Wife number two had come along so quickly that she had then been relegated to the second division in short order, forgotten about, a has-been. Fed and watered yes, but of no more importance to Horatio than a stick of furniture.

They were walking back to Toad Hall after the Conanimum, a strange and mystical event indeed, when the inexplicable occurred, Horatio took Mrs. Toad's hand. Clearly, it was a night for preternatural events because, as far as Cornelia was concerned, this was the most extraordinary happening of all.

Alongside them, the badger walked, in a world of his own. As they approached Toad Hall he pared off. 'Goodnight', he said softly and trudged away.

Cornelia dug Horatio in the side-

'Your friend is leaving, say goodnight,' she insisted.

'What? Oh, err…yes. Goodnight, Quincy,' hailed Horatio, but the badger seemed to take no heed. 'More things in heaven and earth, eh?' Horatio shouted, brightly, hoping to engender a response, yet the badger did not turn, nor did he acknowledge.

Horatio and Cornelia watched him in silence for a few moments as he disappeared into the gloom. A cloud then occluded the moon.

**

The water vole and Brian sat together on the landing watching the river's flow. The moon was fading and sinking in the west. The remnants of its light reached along the river as a silver lane, it beckoned to be taken, soon it would be gone.

'Oh…oh dear me,' whispered Brian, as he looked over to his friend whose eyes were fixed upon the argentine lane. Gently, he placed his paw upon the vole's shoulder and held it there for a moment. 'Badger is dead,' he whispered.

'Yes, yes he is,' replied the vole, softly.

They sat in silence, each with their memories of the badger playing over, until the dawn's monochromatic light chased shadows from the earth.

As the eastern sky grew red, any lingering wisps of mist evaporated, and the first fish rose to the mayfly. Soon the ripple of fish rising; dace, rudd, and roach were to be seen along the river. Opposite the two friends, a sudden spray of fry leaped in panic and a swirl beneath signified a large perch hunting for breakfast.

They watched on as the air became busy with hatching mayflies who would live but for a day. Damselflies of iridescent blue alighted on the reeds and outshone their dragonfly cousins. Birdsong filled the air; chiffchaffs sang their melodies and reed and sedge warblers darted in and about. It was a glorious spring morning, that morning the badger took the last trek to – only he knew where.

The friends breakfasted well.

'Will you miss him?' asked Brian, frankly, as he tipped back a large snail fried up in slug lard and garlic – a recipe he'd gleaned from Taupe.

'Be a good fellow and wash the pan out in the river before you go, won't you?' requested the water vole who found sharing a breakfast table with Brian difficult.

'But will you? I think I shall,' said Brian, his jaws working on his rubbery snail.

The vole pushed back his chair, as much to distance himself as to stretch his legs.

'Will I miss that old curmudgeon? That irascible, acerbic, bigoted, bullying brute?' began the vole.

'You won't then,' declared Brian, hastily, as he tipped back another snail. He was yet to get the swing of rhetoric.

'I was about to say,' continued the water vole, with a look designed to brook no interference, 'he may have been all of that and more, but at heart, he was a goodly animal, and I shall miss our winter evenings by the fire.'

Brian stopped chewing for a moment to consider, as the vole went on.

'We go back a long way and not only us – our ancestors too. He wasn't one for company, was old Quincy, and I think he suffered for it. I don't know how he sat staring at his fire all winter long, with only beer for company.'

'Like us all,' answered Brian simply. 'Like us all. From the fall of the leaves until the first shoots, I rarely see another animal.'

'How do you manage that?' the vole asked, perplexed.

'Just the way it is,' shrugged Brian as he attacked another snail, adding, 'spring comes around again, always does.'

The understanding of the badger's demise came to all wakening animals, an innate sense that he was gone. A simple look was exchanged and then the new day was underway. There was only one ritual, if it could be deemed such, and this was observed by a fleeting pause – an animal would look up briefly, and then carry on. A bird pecking at the ground would lift its head, look sharply left and right, then recommence its search for food.

As if to erase his presence, the badger's sett would be emptied of food and all his chattels. First come, first served, meant for a disorderly scramble, yet it was the accepted way. Those who took were then obliged to close the sett. Earth would then be heaped about the doorways and the windows. An animal, new to the woods, would find no trace of him.

But in the items taken, and these might be as significant as a chair or as negligible as an eggcup, the memory of the badger lived on.

Nothing remained in the deserted sett, now entombed in permanent darkness, save for the badger's beer. No animal, but no animal, wanted his beer.

Chapter Twenty-Four

Controlling Pests

Two seasons earlier, the Upright hunters and their dogs had chased dear old Rosie Renard to exhaustion. Fergal Fenian had vowed to avenge her death, for this was persecution dressed in the guise of sport and anathema to right-thinking animals. However, Fergal knew not how to go about it. Time had passed and as is the way with animals, life went on.

Two sunsets earlier, just as music had once penetrated the Fenian's abode now had the voice of the water vole with a call to unity. To say that the vole's *mycelia* broadcast had sparked a flame in Fergal's breast would have been an exaggeration. As a Fenian, he was all for direct action.

'Listen to the swimming rat,' Molly insisted. 'You're no use to me dead…not much use alive, come to think of it.'

It was just before nightfall when Taupe despatched Brian to carry out a sound check. She'd told him that it had to be a good distance away, and so, with warnings to look up for hawks, she'd pecked him, gently, on the cheek.

Brian bounced along with all the lightness of foot and giddiness of head as is afflicted upon those infatuated and driven to verse. The dog roses were just coming into bloom, and he crowded his mind with a mental note to return with an armful.

Rosie Renard's den had been closed in the customary manner and yet, it was easy work for a mole to dig his way through. Deep inside he settled back and awaited the water vole's speech. As he waited, he fished in his pockets for some snacks. Two juicy lobworms saw him through the boredom of the lengthy wait.

Not having slept the previous night, Brian's eyes began to close and in the still, pitch dark, he fell asleep.

'Come in Brian, come in Brian,' had been repeated so many times without response that Taupe feared the worst. Her malodorous little tyke had become food for ravenous chicks.

'Come in Brian!' shouted the water-vole. 'Brian, do you read? Repeat, Brian do you read?'

Brian awoke with a start at the vole's shouts, but only cottoned on to 'Do you read?' At once affronted by the vole's impertinent question, Brian leaped to his feet, ready to remonstrate. Was the water vole trying to belittle him again in front of his bird? He addressed the white roots poking through the ceiling; conscious that the whole neighbourhood was listening in, he shouted disdainfully.

'Of course, I do! I've probably read more books than you have... actually.'

Muddled in the ensuing brouhaha, Brian thought he detected his name, certainly there was laughter, whether this was at his expense or not, he couldn't tell. And so, he slumped back down to listen, grudgingly, to the broadcast – except he fell asleep again.

'That it?' questioned Taupe. 'You think you start a revolution like that?'

'I'm not trying to start a revolution...' began the water-vole, but he was summarily dismissed by Taupe who paid no heed.

'To start revolution, you must get blood boiling, you must get heart running, you must make barricade, you must bring six-course packed lunch, if no lunch, *révolutionnaires* go home for lunch. End of revolution.'

'As I was saying…'

'Your *discours* just send me to sleep,' continued an oblivious Taupe. 'Even Brian say things more interesting. "Oh Taupe, sky is bit bluer than yesterday…" Bravo, you beat Brian – not easy. Revolution need leader Trevor-Stan, if you leave decisions to others, nothing happen.'

'That's the whole id…'

'Idea? Is not idea! "Make self… disagreeable."' Taupe mimicked the vole's speech. 'What bloody-fuck that mean?'

As the water vole made his way homeward, he could not but notice that Taupe's assessment of his speech seemed to be shared. The community had been gripped by a fervour, following the Conanimum, some by a revolutionary zeal, and had waited on his speech in keen anticipation of a call to action. Although he was greeted with respect, as the animal who could summon Pan, his reception was lukewarm. Polite nods from the confused and disillusioned were all he received.

The idea was to sow a seed, to create an atmosphere wherein animal would liaise with animal and formulate their own plans. The water vole did not want to be a leader, he only wanted to be part of a movement. He placed his faith in others to decide on their own course of action. There was only one caveat, that resistance be peaceful, just as the Jack-in-the-green had decreed. That this supposed sacred message had come from the lips of the mole-in-the-hole was a secret burden he and Brian would have to carry all their days.

**

'Horatio...Horatio, when are we...?' Cornelia picked up a pine cone and lanced it at her husband. 'Horatio, are you listening to me?'

'What's that? Oh yes, my cherished one, I'm all ears,' replied the toad, distractedly.

'This caravan is all very well, but I need my bath, I want my clothes, I haven't changed in...' – Cornelia stopped to calculate – 'not since the bluebells went, and now the foxgloves are here,' she moaned. 'Horatio!' she then exclaimed. 'You're not listening!'

Peering through a pair of binoculars at the windows of Toad Hall from the back of a decrepit gypsy caravan, Horatio responded, inattentively. 'All ears Cynthia...all ears.'

'Cornelia!' yelled Cornelia. 'Cynthia was number three!'

A large pine cone collided with Horatio's ear. 'Oh, um yes, quite so...quite so.'

Horatio maintained his vigil from the corner of the field, noting the comings and goings of Montgolfiere's staff.

'More of the blighters by the day,' he grumbled.

Cornelia sighed and picked up her novel, a clandestine affair between a Lady toad and her dashing, diamond-smuggling gentleman. She tried to concentrate, but her mind wandered and, not for the first time, she wondered if she had made the right decision to stay. To be brought down to this; a squalid, gypsy caravan with a broken axle, overgrown with briar and left to rot out its days in the corner of a field as a squirrel's nut store. A caravan that last moved in the days of her husband's illustrious ancestor.

It was not that Cornelia missed the trappings of wealth, just a bath and a change of clothing. Her diamonds and pearls she held out no hope for. Doubtless, they would have been purloined by Tamara who, in the short time she had been a wife, had demonstrated kleptomaniacal tendencies.

Had she herself been younger, Cornelia thought, she might have bolted too, however, she had reached an age where romantic possibility seemed doomed to fiction. She looked over at her reality, Horatio, and estimated that he had grown yet another chin, his belly sagged low, and his head was more knobbly than a pine cone. He has brought every misfortune upon himself, estimated Cornelia, and all due to his cavalier attitude and carelessness. Still, she realised, she too had benefited from his ill-gotten gains, she hadn't asked where the money was coming from, she had harboured suspicions, but had turned a blind eye. He cast a sorry figure now, staring up at the only possession left to him, swindled as he was by Uprights – they always proved his undoing.

**

May was as good a month as any to foment revolution and if acorns can grow to mighty oaks, then so too can a mouse instigate a great upheaval. One little act, repeated at intervals in the night, drove Georges Montgolfiere's staff to the traps.

In the still of night, with only the lonely cries of owls to break the silence, a mouse gnawing on half a walnut shell, close by your ear, will wake you. For that same mouse to wait until you have settled back to sleep only to recommence, will annoy you, for him to repeat the process all night, will drive you to distraction.

One member of Montgolfiere's staff was dead-eyed the next morning as he tipped cup after cup of coffee down. His protests were met with howls of laughter from the other members, some eight in number – although this wouldn't last long.

The instigator, of what would become known as the Fur Revolution, was subsequently feted and named Fidel. The youngest of eleven, he was feisty, mischievous, and a royal pain in the arse. His short suffering parents knew him only as Bastard. That his young, aggravating life was brought to a swift conclusion, martyred in a peanut-buttered, baited trap, came as a relief to his parents, but as a tragedy to his fellow revolutionaries.

The talk now was of direct action, some advocated violence and these separatists were led by a red squirrel who had taken up occupancy in the lofts – grey squirrels were easily incited.

'Make yourselves disagreeable' – if the water vole's plea barely kindled a flame, then the death of little Bastard did. Traps were disagreeable, most disagreeable, and the naive young were taken in by them.

Efforts were stepped up and gnawing teams worked in relay.

Discord was sown within the Montgolfiere camp, there were those who sided with Georges and were virulently opposed to traps, despite having undergone sleepless nights themselves. Then there were those who, at the ends of their tethers, would have willingly stamped to death any rodent they chanced upon.

Sleep deprivation, the rodent's tool, was proving efficacious.

Shrews carried the news of minor triumphs throughout the Toad estate.

As the days fly by and mid-June, the start of the angling season arrives, when the dog-roses are in full bloom and the lark is in full cry, many an Upright takes up his rod and heads for the banks. With the prospect of a peaceful day ahead, he casts his line, sits back in bliss, and waits.

Otters are not the fisherman's friend. Oh yes, one may be charmed momentarily by their little labrador-esque faces, yet to have them appear time after time, to have them circle your float, scaring away fish, only then to dive, and come up with a decent roach clamped between their teeth, is taking the piss.

Ducks in search of titbits can prove irksome, and when they crowd in noisily upon your swim, the clapping of hands will normally shoo them away. Rarely will they linger if no food is on offer. So, what inspired this flotilla to persist to the point of distraction, the fisherman couldn't fathom.

Swans with cygnets then maintained the harassment. With the Upright fishermen standing to shoo them off, Sir Edwin Preece Moog hissed at his loudest and rose himself up to his full grandeur and flapped his wings. This had the effect of sending the fisherman scurrying back up the bank and provided Constance her cue to pinch the Uprights' bait, loaves of bread. The cygnets, usually adept at not getting their feet snagged in the fishermen's lines, then deliberately did so.

Grass snakes, swimming, always prove a diversion with their small heads held above the water like a crooked finger. Like a submarine's periscope, they now patrolled up and down the river. Whilst fishermen were distracted by this spectacle, mink chewed through their lines as a team of land rats pilfered their bait.

The result of this activity was to see fishermen huddle in groups shaking their heads in disbelief. Even hardy souls who persisted, eventually threw in the towel.

**

News of these early victories, minor as they were, brought a grin to the face of the water vole. 'And so it begins,' he muttered in self-satisfaction.

Brian, fixated not on the revolution, but on his love life, was perplexed and less light-hearted.

'I mean, the way she said it, it wasn't harsh, she wasn't in one of her strops. Are you sure that's what it means?,' he asked, searching the vole's eyes for clarification. He found his friend smiling sympathetically.

'She probably just meant it in jest Brian,' placated the vole, who had to explain that moron wasn't a term of endearment. 'Moron is not the same as *mon-amour* Brian, I think that's where you are getting confused.'

Brian shrugged his shoulders in dismissal, he had been called worse.

He had been regaling the vole with the story of the missing pelts. Naturally, their absence had been lain at his door and as a precaution, he had edged onto the threshold of his own, in case a quick get-away be called for.

Taupe's reaction to the news baffled him. He had expected her to hit the roof and then hit him. As his apologetic explanation of their burning went on, he grew anxious as she approached him with an ever-widening smile. This could be the prelude to a slap, he thought, as he shifted uneasily on his feet. When she clapped her paws together smartly, he jumped out of his pelt and made a bolt for the exit. The sound of hysterical laughter enticed him to poke his head back in.

Taupe was rolling on the floor with tears in her eyes, pointing at him and then doubling up once more.

'Oh, *mon petit con...c'est trop*' – my little twerp – that's too much.

More laughter. '...*l'homme vert – une poupée!*' – the green man – a puppet!

Laughter with gulps for air. '*Mon petit moron, vraiment, tu es la limite!*' – my little moron, really, you are the limit!

Taupe believed her day just couldn't get any better, what with her belief in science having been vindicated. However,

Brian's further disclosure concerning the miracle of the fishes, proved her wrong.

It was a snippet he had picked up from young Clamp the otter. Following the stunning spectacle of silver-flanked fish – a wonder to behold certainly – Clamp had dived down for a look. There had he discovered the great Esox alongside a pack of his ilk – some of whom were still circling.

"Eard about it before, ain't I Brian? Them pike drives 'em up. I reckon that's what they did. Mind you, weren't no scales nor nuffink so they didn't touch 'em.'

Taupe assessed this new information with studied satisfaction and nodded slowly.

'So, what make *le brochet*...what you call it – Pike?' Taupe asked, and Brian nodded. 'What make them do this if they do not eat?'

Brian hadn't stopped to consider this one. 'Pan,' he replied, hopefully.

Taupe shook her head with a sigh, and then clasped Brian's muzzle between her paws. 'No hope for you my *petit moron*.' Then she kissed him.

'Well, she snogged me anyway,' said Brian, semi-contentedly, as he paddled his feet in the river.

'Trevor-Stan?' he then asked turning to his companion.

'Yes, Brian?' the vole replied wearily, for there were days when his friend's questioning became tiresome.

'Do you reckon my legs are getting longer?' he quizzed, sincerely, turning to look at the vole's disbelieving face.

'It's just that a few days ago the water was just above my ankles, now it's up to my knees.'

Chapter Twenty-Five

From Tiny Acorns

'What do you think Moira?' asked Jock McTavish the beaver as he straightened his back with a grimace. 'Is it feasible hen?' Moira bent to study Taupe's plan of the river system. 'Does your back in, this type of work,' mentioned Jock with a meaningful glance at Taupe, to emphasise the toil of a beaver's daily grind.

'As I see it,' began Moira McTavish, 'if we dam this inlet here,' – she prodded the large map, intricately drawn by Taupe on the inside of a pelt – 'It'll only back-up, run down through that culvert there and back out by our place. Ach, we'll no' achieve anything.'

Moira looked to her husband for inspiration. Finding none, she then added 'but, if we block the inlet right up here...' – she prodded the map again – 'it'll run down that wee valley there...look.'

Jock studied the plan, squinting as the bright June sunlight reflected off Taupe's winter disguise pelt. 'It's dazzling my eyes. Let's away under the trees *madame*.'

'*Mademoiselle*' corrected Taupe, firmly, a little miffed to be taken for older than she felt.

All three, now seated beneath the cool of an elder, bent to the task.

'I just don't see it Moira, it'll no be enough to do the job, a wee dam there... no, I don't see it.'

Moira had always been chief engineer in the McTavish set-up. Jock was the brawn. That said, Moira knew that she had to get her husband on board, he had to believe in the plan otherwise he'd only become irritated and give up half-way through. This had been the cause of many an abandoned dam and much marital disharmony in the past.

'You're right my dear, quite right...but, if we dam the main river again here...'she indicated a spot and looked toward her husband who was bent to the plan and who still hadn't twigged. 'Look here,' persisted Moira, prodding the map with her paw.

'What with the land being lower here, than there. Don't you see?' Moira bent her head to search her husband's vacant eyes, adding- 'Then what will happen to all that water up there?' she quizzed, her patience ebbing.

'Ah! Of course, yes that could work...the land up there is higher, is it?' spluttered Jock, unconvincingly, attempting to justify himself.

Moira looked at Taupe and they exchanged a knowing smile. Both then cast a quick glance at the higher land, which was plain as the muzzle on your face, but they made no comment. Antagonise Jock and the whole plan was scuppered.

'Will it take long time?' ventured Taupe.

Jock sucked in air through his teeth, began to walk in circles, and expelled it slowly with a whistle.

'One moon,' Moira stated, earning her a sharp look from her husband. 'Wouldn't you say Jock?'

Jock's expression spoke volumes and Moira stole herself for the backlash that would surely follow when Taupe departed.

'Beavers put big stick in wheel of Upright,' Taupe encouraged.

'We can do it Jock,' coerced Moira coquettishly, as she rubbed her shoulder against his. 'We'll make a lovely big pond for the bairns.'

Jock wasn't so easily swayed.

'I cannae see this working; I mean, we get the Sassenach Upright out only to put the gentleman toad back in, ach, I cannae see the point. He's no better than the Upright.'

'He changed. New toad,' Taupe asserted, as convincingly as she was able.

'Changed? A gentleman toad?' exclaimed Jock, laughing in derision. 'They're all the same. Fatheads the lot of them, and that one is one of the worst.'

Jock stomped away leaving Moira and Taupe together.

'He'll come around; I'll work on him,' Moira assured.

'Withdraw benefits,' Taupe suggested.

'Oh no dear, that won't work with Jock, it's all I can do to get him interested. No, if I work from sun to moon, he'll work harder. It's all about appearance with Jock, he won't have the other animals think he's not up to it.'

'You are lucky. I have sex-crazy boyfriend,' Taupe replied wearily. 'Even steal my knicker.'

'Oh, aren't you the lucky one dear,' returned Moira, wistfully.

**

Georges Montgolfiere's smiles were wearing thin. For five nights in a row, his sleep had been disturbed. Not normally one for daytime naps, being full of nervous energy, he had today succumbed. However, even this had been disturbed when a red squirrel, normally a positive joy to behold, had repeatedly thrown nuts at him from the window ledge. A hazelnut had caught him on the temple, possibly more than once, he was so dog-tired he couldn't tell. He awoke with a start, and then smiled benevolently upon the charming creature, who promptly hurled another. 'It's feeding me,' he muttered in wonderment as he noticed the floor strewn with nuts. 'Plucky little chap,' he remarked, as he approached the open widow slowly, holding out one of the hazelnuts in return. The squirrel, known to the other rodents as Red-Ted, stood his ground and did not flinch as Georges proffered it. Gently, oh so gently, the squirrel closed his claws about the nut and then sunk his teeth into Georges' finger.

Standing now in his recycled organic cotton pyjamas, embroidered with animal motifs, he cast a wary eye at his bed. What ought to be a place of repose, had become a place of torment. But all was silent save for the mournful hooting of owls. Through the open widows, he couldn't sleep with them shut, a gentle early summer breeze billowed at the curtain. Tonight, he would sleep.

Five hours – Georges never slept for more. From midnight to dawn was his never wavering routine. Invariably, he slept soundly and sprang from his bed with all the alacrity of a man purposed to rewild the planet.

Georges was the architect, although he never considered himself as such, the man with a plan who one day would make everyone realise that it had been their want, their need and desire all along. If pressed, he might avow to being a catalyst, but the architect? Too grandiose, that would be akin to a deity. 'Let nature put right' – he was fond of saying and it had become his catchphrase – 'what we have done wrong.'

And so, Georges closed eyes, bloodshot through lack of sleep, on another day and drifted off.

Beneath boards, Toad Hall's oldest resident rat was unlike any other. Rodin was a black rat, an artist, and a recluse. How long he had lived in Toad Hall was a mystery to all. The brown house rats only knew that he had been there since their arrival, and given that they had been present for generations, it was assumed that Rodin was eternal.

Young rats were taught to bow their heads if he happened to chance by. Should any young scamp dare to speak, then he was certain to earn a cuff about the ear from an elder. In living memory, Rodin had only ever spoken once; he had stopped and fixed a chastising parent with his dark, reddish-brown eyes and muttered something in an archaic language that no brown rat could comprehend.

Rodin sculpted at night. His work could be seen on floor joists all over Toad Hall. Strange sculptures of no discernible form, mesmerising to some, but dismissed by most. He would begin work at sunset and then disappear, no rat knew where, at sunrise. The house rats would absent themselves from any section of the Hall he was working on. They were unnerved by him.

His current *oeuvre* was taking shape directly beneath boards above which, Georges Montgolfiere slept. Rodin's sculptures were reputed, by some, to exert mystical powers. Others attributed this belief to be the result of eating fermented windfalls.

The more adventurous house rat would, during daylight hours, venture into Rodin's section to check on work in progress. The more open-minded would tilt their heads and nod slowly feigning comprehension, whereas others would squeak furtively, in derision. Concerning the current work, all had to agree that it was Rodin's most ambitious so far. From head to tail, it had to be nine rats long. The oak chippings were now two rats deep.

Given that Rodin was busy on his section, the house rats took up the cause of Upright pestering beneath other bedroom floors. The Montgolfiere staff numbered eight, six men and two women: all were sleep-deprived. A desperate few had ordered in traps. This was expressly forbidden by Georges, who was becoming unpopular with his staff. Such high principles were to be lauded, yet a few members of staff thought there were limits. One hour's fitful sleep could drive anyone to murder.

A team of specialised trap-springers, much feted for their bravery, was employed by the chief rat. Traps were sprung during the night, the noise of which caused momentary jubilation above boards, even by those who had not thought it right to set them, it was their guilty secret. The gnawing would then begin again in earnest causing Uprights to clamp the pillow about their ears in tormented despair and wish for daylight.

Alas, a few younger, inexperienced rats led by the nose to the peanut butter met their ends in the traps. Had they but obeyed their parents, and waited for the disposal team's return, there would have been butter enough for all.

**

Fergal Fenian was under strict orders from Molly to remain sober during their visit to Linda and Peter Peel's den to witness the improvements. He was, Molly warned him, to make appreciative noises.

''Tis a grand job and there's no getting away from it Pete,' Fergal enthused as a disbelieving Molly narrowed her eyes. 'Would you look at the depth of that cupboard Molly? Sure, you've worn your paws down to the bone on this one right enough Pete.'

Peter Peel, inordinately house proud, nevertheless feigned fatigue at his wife's desires for home improvement. He tutted, laughed, and nodded toward Linda.

'She wants a spare bedroom next.'

'Ah, but you'll be wanting that sure enough, what with the litter you'll be having next season,' Fergal replied, brightly.

Molly, who was in deep conversation with Linda about the soak-away in the latrine, the latest fad in den design, pricked up her ears at her husband's comment. Fergal had made every excuse under the sun as to why now, was not a good time to start a family. 'They're keeping the hens inside more and more Moll', 'They've shot all the pheasants,' etc etc.

'And the rabbits are not laying.' This had been Molly's riposte as she stood, paws on hips, demanding that Fergal come clean. 'You don't want cubs, do you?'

Dinner passed away peacefully enough, and Fergal used the excuse of smoking his clay pipe outside to partake of a small bottle he'd secreted in his jacket pocket. Emboldened, he went back down to put his revolutionary plan forward.

''Tis sheer madness!' Molly exclaimed as she rocked back in her chair. Then, with a sudden lunge forward, she grabbed Fergal by the snout and took a sniff of his breath.

'I might have known it. 'Tis the feckin' drink talking again!'

Agitated to distraction, Molly had broken her own edict. there was to be no language at the Peel's, and yet, what else could she say? Fergal's big idea to end the persecution of foxes was to set the hounds free. Only an eejit of the first order could come up with a plan like that, she considered.

'Wouldn't the hounds then chase us every day?' posited Linda, reasonably.

'Ah Linda, don't humour the eejit, forget it, he's been at the drink…again!' replied an exasperated Molly.

'They would not,' declared Fergal, adding 'they might a bit, at first, but they'll soon learn that there are plenty of others, tastier and easier to catch than us.'

Peter Peel didn't quite know where to put himself. Fergal had requested his assistance in what he considered to be a hare-brained scheme. He searched for his wife's eyes and was alarmed to find that they were glued on Fergal.

'Might we not have more competition for food then?' Linda quizzed further. 'I mean the hounds will feast on the pheasants.'

'Ah, but that's just it Lindy,' replied Fergal, warming to the task and earning him a pointed glare from Molly, who bridled at the use of the familiar. Lindy? Since when was she Lindy?

Fergal went on. 'We'll chase the Uprights off the land, off the farms until the whole of the estate is ours!'

Molly Fenian had heard enough, her husband, the mad fecker that he was, had now taken leave of the bit of sense left to him.

'Home! Before you cause any more trouble,' Molly shouted, pushing back her chair.

But Linda Peel requested calm, advised that they all take a drink and ordered her husband to fetch the glasses.

'But we don't have any...drink,' Peter said, with confusion writ large.

'Just get the glasses,' Linda commanded as she reached into a cubby hole she herself had dug. 'I need this,' she whispered to Molly. 'He's the most boring fart going!'

Never judge a fox by her den, that was Molly's conclusion. Never had she seen this side of her sensible friend.

Finally, a still reluctant Peter was roped in; only on the proviso that he be given time to finish his home improvements first and that the wild boar would be included in the mission. He insisted on minders.

A sceptical Molly put her doubts aside. Being Fenians, it would be remiss, indeed shameful, not to join the revolution. Her proviso was to extract a devout promise from Fergal to impregnate her next season.

Linda's antipathy toward the foxhunting Upright found full venom in drink. Rosie Renard's death would not go unavenged. As the customarily polite vixen so eloquently put it, 'we'll show the cunts!'

'Atta girl Lindy!' Fergal enthused, and the remark earned him a sharp nip in his arse on the way out.

Chapter Twenty-Six

His Master's Voice

Georges Montgolfiere was awakened by shafts of brilliant June sunshine streaming in upon his face. As he came to, he realised that he had slept his five hours, he must have done because the glass of water on his bedside table remained untouched. So why did he feel so exhausted, so unrefreshed? He knew that he would never regain sleep, it was pointless, he never could.

He lay staring up at the large ceiling rose, the face of a toad depicted in plaster stared down upon him, doubtless one of the great gentleman toad ancestors. It appeared to be gurning at him.

Strands of a dream were drifting from him, certainly, the dream involved rats, and Georges was none too keen on rats. This is an admission that he would never make, but it was a fact. And yet, in his dream he had no horror of them, in his dream, fading fast, he had spoken with them.

At the wash basin Georges studied himself in the mirror, his bleary eyes were red-rimmed, and it looked as if he hadn't slept in days. Another element of his dream drifted back. There had been an owl perched on the heavy oak foot of his bed, a barn owl with its moon face ringed in brown, its black, inscrutable eyes had fixed his.

Georges had reached an age whereby he had lost most of the hair upon his shins and so, as he pulled on his cotton socks he frowned, his spindly, white legs needed a wipe with the flannel. Curious, he thought, as he rubbed to no avail. Pinpricks of black, rather like blackheads, stood stark against the brilliant white of his skin. How odd, he thought as his brows knotted, he rubbed his hand along a shin, it was smooth-ish. Could it be a rash? he wondered. Certainly, the green hemp suit, he habitually wore, was rough. He shrugged his shoulders, dressed and made his way down to breakfast.

None of his staff was yet abroad and this was the way he liked it. To be seen up before them, and last to bed, set an example. His muesli contained what looked suspiciously like droppings and yet, instead of picking them out, as he had of late, he found himself tucking in.

Later, as Georges sipped at his nettle tea, a member of his staff recoiled in horror when he filled his bowl. 'It's full of rat crap!' he hollered, pushing his bowl away in disgust. A female member of staff then put an ultimatum to Georges.

'If you don't get pest control in, then I'm out of here!' She went on to say that she'd barely slept a wink. 'This bloody house is infested!'

Montgolfiere had never been quick to anger and yet, mention of 'pest control' had his hackles raised. He stood and glared at his team.

'We are here to live with nature, to embrace it, to become part of it. We are NOT HERE TO KILL IT!'

'Suits me,' said Susan, throwing down her spoon upon the floor. 'I'm already gone!'

She was followed by two sleep-deprived others.

'Sorry Georges, I can't work like this,' said one apologetically. 'I've had enough.'

Five members of staff now remained and as a collective, they made a request that they travel to the nearest town where they might procure a tent. Georges shrugged his shoulders, he thought it unnecessary, but if that's what they wanted, then OK.

I don't need them, thought Georges, as he sat in his study attempting to draft a letter to a Monsieur Loup in Belgium. I can do all of this on my own.

Try as he might to concentrate, Georges' mind would not fix itself to the task. He laughed, as he looked at his hand, it was as if he's never held a pen before. It was as if he had lost all dexterity. He picked up his fountain pen with his left hand and placed it in his right, but all he succeeded in doing was to hold it as might an infant, grabbed in a fist. Stranger still, he didn't care one iota.

Then his mind clouded. What was the letter about? He began to pace about the room, he had moments of lucidity in which the answer came. It was a letter about the wolves Monsieur… what was his name again? And then the thought evaporated.

He slumped back into his chair and was soon asleep. His body twitched as he began to dream. When he awoke, he felt hungry and thirsty. He looked at the clock, he was aware of it being an instrument for telling the time, but that was all. He stared at it blankly, it made no sense to him. A childhood memory returned. The big hand is on the…. what was it? The small…Once more he laughed, then left the study and headed outdoors.

Upon the front lawns, the orange-clad monks were seated in silence facing the river. The river water was rising and now covered the steps. In fact, it was halfway up the lawn with only thirty metres of incline before it reached the steps to the house.

Georges got down upon his knees, and then drank from the river. One or two of the monks exchanged glances and said nothing. Georges then picked the blossom from a lime tree and ate it; next, he spotted pineapple weed – wild chamomile – and ate the seed heads. He then wandered off, he knew not whither and stopped intermittently to listen to the songs of birds. His face was expressive, his ears attuned, and he picked up on every rustle, every movement in the undergrowth. Nature was a cacophony of sound and as the day wore on, this dissonance became less discordant, he could isolate individual animals, although he could not understand.

**

An advance party of field rats was sent in, a type of expeditionary force, to soften up the tenant farmers and their families. A farmer needs to be abroad early in June and rarely gets to bed before eleven pm. Ingress proved easy enough into the draughty old farmhouses particularly as a team of badgers from a nearby wood terrorised the farm cats and kept them at bay. Once under boards, they felt safe. These were experienced rats for the most part and they took with them a small party of expert trap-springers from Toad Hall. Mounds of turquoise-coloured poison corn abounded, and this was pointed out to some of the lesser experienced field rats, who might have succumbed. Their mission was to lie low during the day and then make as much kerfuffle as possible as night fell.

Under the cover of dark, the hounds began to bark. This brought the pyjama-clad farmer to his door with his shotgun. Fergal, Linda, Molly, and Peter scarpered back to the woods. They would wait until they heard five short screeches from a barn owl and then, they would repeat the process- all night. In his raging anger, the farmer loosed off both barrels although, he had no idea what he was shooting at. If his family managed any sleep at all, then they certainly couldn't sleep through that.

The very next day, the pest control man came, however, a relay team of shrews brought the news in good time and the rats all made it out. Once he had lain more poison with a promise that, it would do the trick, the rats moved back in again.

Night after night this kept up until the farmer was spotted looking into the end of his gun, he was nearing the end of his tether.

**

It was never going to be easy to reason with a pack of hounds, even though Fergal dragooned a team of squirrels to throw several hens he'd culled into their pen from overhanging trees as bribes. No easy task for squirrels as they are mostly vegetarian, so lancing dead hens was unpalatable for them. Sacrifices had to be made for the Fur-revolution.

'But don't you see now boys…' began Fergal, but he didn't get far.

'We're not boys,' came the voice, muffled through feathers, of one hound as she competed for a hen. 'We're all bitches.'

'You're not wrong there,' said Linda, acidly.

'I heard that!'came the venomous response from a hound with murder in her eyes.

'Will you leave it to me Lindy, please?' Fergal insisted, keeping a weather eye on the farmer's door.

'Now girls…will you pipe down and let me speak?'

Fergal looked up to the tree and gave the nod for the final two hens to be thrown in. 'There goes my feckin' supper,' he grumbled under his breath.

The ravenous hounds went at the hens as if famished. Finally satiated, they calmed. They looked at the four foxes with tilted heads.

'Ah, now that's better girls.'

'Ladies,' insisted one bitch, pedantically.

'Now then, ladies,' Fergal, mustering patience, began again. 'I expect you're wondering what we're doing here…'

All eyes within the pen turned to one hound, evidently the leader of the pack who maintained a sullen silence, she jerked her head upward and bade Fergal continue.

'All animals on this estate are joining in the revolution,' Fergal looked down on the feather-strewn floor of the pen adding 'apart from some of the hens that is.'

The head bitch made no reply.

'Get to the point Fergal,' hissed Molly.

'The point is, we're driving the Uprights off our land. We the animals will be in charge from now on, and we thought it fair play to let you join in, so.'

'What's a revolution?' asked the head hound. Fergal turned his head away in disbelief. 'Honest to Pan, Molly, thick or what?' he muttered.

'What's that?' growled another hound, menacingly.

''Tis when you take control of your own life, tis when you get rid of your masters.'

'It's when you bastards stop chasing us,' Linda said (she assumed quietly), but it had several of the hounds circling and growling.

'You can't get rid of masters,' spoke the head hound, silencing the pack. 'There will always be masters, masters have the food, masters feed us. We want masters.'

Howls of agreement went up allowing for Fergal's 'Feckin' arse licking eejits' to go unheeded.

'You don't bite the hand that feeds you,' declared another hound adamantly, winning the consensus of the pack.

'What's that?' Fergal retorted, indicating the carnage at the bottom of the cage. 'Wasn't the master that gave you that now, was it?'

'If you feed us, you'll be the master,' declared a younger bitch, resulting in howls of derision.

'I don't want to be your feckin' master!' shouted Fergal. 'You'll be your own masters; can't you see that? What's difficult to understand about that?'

By raising his voice, Fergal noted, sadly, that the hounds quietened down. He hadn't realised to what extent they were conditioned to obey. He tried another tack.

'Look, how many hens do you have – did you have, there?' he pointed with his paw.

The hounds looked dumbly at the ground. 'Some,' responded one.

'But how many?' persisted Fergal. 'Look, four here and how many over there?'

'Some more,' answered a bitch unsurely.

'Give me strength, muttered Fergal, losing his patience. He made a quick head count. 'Look, you've had seven hens between twenty-one of yis, so that's… er… er…'

'One hen for every three of you,' piped up Peter Peel.

The hounds began to bark in unison – if there was one thing they did understand, it was portions.

'Shut up!' yelled Fergal, and miraculously the hounds fell silent, all apart from the leader.

'The master gives us more,' the head hound asserted.

'Does he, does he now?' mouthed Fergal, at a loss of how to proceed.

'But is it any good? Is it fresh?' interjected Molly. 'Does he give you enough?'

The hounds looked to each other; the consensus was 'no'.

'I'm always hungry,' declared one hound and the others bayed in agreement.

'Over there,' Fergal shouted, pointing a paw, 'is a chicken farm with thousands of hens'. He was met by blank expressions, and he faltered. 'Lots of some hens, enough some hens to fill this pen some more, and more some!'

'And why can't you eat them?' Molly shouted.

'Because the Uprights keep you in here!' Fergal hurled. 'Because the Uprights keep all the food to themselves!'

The notion of more food took hold and the head hound had difficulty in quelling the unrest. She barked loudly and bit a few to bring the pack to order. 'Get us some hens then.'

'I will not!' Fergal retorted angrily. 'Get them yourselves.'

Once more, blank expressions were returned and Fergal turned to the other foxes. 'They just don't get it, 'twas a bad idea, a mad idea, I never realised they were this stupid.'

'What does the Upright feed you every day?' Molly asked pointedly.

'Meat,' answered one blankly.

'What kind?' pressed Molly only to be met with blank faces. 'I thought so, he gives you the same old shite every day. Out here you can have hen one day, pheasant the next, you can have rabbit, even deer, you…'

'And fox?' chipped in the ever-hungry hound, starting the hounds barking again.

'No, no, no not fox!' shouted Peter Peel, backing away.

'Out here,' continued Molly, raising her voice over the baying for blood. 'You can have anything you want, as much as you need – except for fox!'

'How?' asked the head hound bringing the pack to order. 'Who's going to get it for us?'

'I'm off,' said Fergal turning sharply on his paws. 'You might just as well be talking to hedgehogs. Small wonder they're the Uprights best friend, they haven't a brain between them. They've no notion of who the oppressor is, no idea where they sit in the hierarchy, poor, sycophantic bastards!'

'I have,' piped up a voice from the back of the pack.

Fergal and company stopped in their tracks and turned about. A slender young bitch weaved her way through the others to the front of the pen.

'They make us chase you. They keep us hungry so that we must chase you. If we didn't, they wouldn't feed us. I know the Uprights give us just enough, keep us locked up so that we can't find food for ourselves. We are conditioned by them, until we cannot think for ourselves.'

Fergal's mouth fell open as the hound went on.

'Your idea is to set us free, but would we really be free? Every day we would have to search for food, we would have to go further and further until perhaps, the Uprights would hunt us.'

'But you would have your freedom,' said Peter Peel, stepping forward. 'You could make your own decisions.'

'I should like that,' continued the slender hound, looking toward the others. 'But we hounds must hunt in packs, we are not independent like you foxes, and if I go, we all must go.'

The lead hound began to growl, but the others ignored her.

'You must be the leader,' said Linda. 'Tonight, two wild boar will come and set you all free.'

'Chicken farm is that way,' indicated Fergal with his paw. ''Twill be tough at first, but an empty belly will soon teach you.'

That night, Gunter, and his partner Helga let the dogs out.

Chapter Twenty-Seven

A Feral Call

'Isn't the boat supposed to be lower than the house Trevor-Stan?' shouted Brian from over the river at the slumbering vole. 'Sleeps more than a dormouse these days,' he muttered and repeated his question in a louder voice.

In the catalogue of Brian's irritating habits, his dogged persistence in not being ignored, ranked high. The water vole was pretending to be asleep having seen the mole's approach. On his back on the landing stage with the water rippling and flowing mellifluously beneath him, he had been listening to a sky-lark chittering on high, interspersed by the lilting tones of reed warblers hard by. Mid-summer, the longest day of the year was nearing, and the sun was close to its zenith.

'Trevor-Stan, I say hello, isn't the boat…'

'Oh, for the sake of Pan!',' grumbled the vole, sitting up- 'What do you want Brian?' cried the vole, failing to keep the agitation from his voice.

'Dunno,' returned Brian, shrugging his shoulders and furrowing his brow, what did he want? He'd forgotten. And so, he simply stood staring. The water vole laid back down.

'Oh yes, isn't the boat supposed to be lower than the house?'

Knowing full well that peace was now irretrievably shattered, the vole, in some bad grace, rowed over to fetch his irksome chum. It was, in any case, hot in the sun and time to move inside, even if that meant swapping sunstroke for Brian's company, the effects of which were similar.

As the vole was preparing one of his infusions, Brian was regaling him with the latest gossip, most of which he already knew. Yes, he knew that Clamp and Nipper had terrified a couple of Upright canoeists by jumping up on to their craft and bearing teeth. Yes he knew that Reg had been tugging on the fisherman's line below water and giving him false bites. And yes, the mink had chewed through his line so that when he yanked his rod up to connect with the fish there was nothing there. No, he didn't know that Constance Preece-Moog had knocked an angler from his seat when she came into land.

'You've heard about the Upright as well I suppose then?' quizzed Brian, dejectedly.

It was the preamble to Brian's gossip that aggravated the most. Any event began with the onset of his day and all his non-consequential actions leading up to it. A discursion into the depth of lobworm, given the current dry conditions, was hardly germane to an otter jumping on a boat.

'What Upright exactly Brian? If you don't mind,' issued the water vole wearily.

'The one in Horatio's place, you know, the one with the flying bubble...things.'

The water vole sat back in his armchair, sighed, closed his eyes, and bade Brian begin.

'Well, it was a rabbit that told me…or was it Taupe? No, it couldn't have been Taupe because she wasn't there this morning…actually, I don't know where she was last night…anyway, I took a short-cut through the wood, those stoats are asking for a sharp one up the muzzle, they were taking the piss again…hold up, no it couldn't have been a rabbit because….'

By the time the punchline arrived, the vole was drifting off.

'....and then he climbed a tree and spoke to a squirrel – in animal.'

The water vole sat up. 'In animal? That's not possible.'

'That's what Sid said...or was it, Cindy? Whoever...they said they nearly fell out of the tree.'

The vole sat reflecting on this revelation, two revelations really – an Upright speaking in animal and Brian having said something interesting.

'Brian, would you mind awfully leaving old chap?' asked the vole, deep in thought.

Noting his friend's dismay, he added quickly 'I have to consult the Pananimal.' He said it abstractedly, then noticed Brian's vacant expression. 'You know, the Book of Pan.'

**

Brian mooched along the river with his hands in his pelt pockets. Where was Taupe last night, he wondered. Probably found another boyfriend I bet, wouldn't put it past her, he thought. Then he gladdened, not the mating season so he can't shag her at least.

He came upon a bend in the river. 'That's odd, wasn't there before,' he muttered. Something is amiss, he thought, and he racked his brain to think of what.

It came to Brian in one of his flashes – a flash for Brian equated to the time it took to cook an egg – often the water-vole would put Brian's duck egg in the pan and ask him a question, when he answered, he knew the egg to be cooked. On cue, his eureka moment arrived.

'The bullrushes are usually on the end of stalks,' he declared in triumph. 'Not halfway under the water like fishing floats.'

He shrugged his shoulders and wandered on and then, quickly took cover. Uprights were approaching. They were running. That's odd too, he thought, why have they got their pelts over their heads?

The answer was airborne in the form of a squadron of greylag geese who were circling and then coming in to dive-bomb the fleeing Uprights. Those that could muster a deposit, and they were many, coated the Uprights in splats.

In a happy little niche, having chortled himself into merriment, Brian spent an amiable time in conversation with a dormouse who, being nocturnal, was too polite to tell Brian to f-off. Waxing lyrical on the merits of this caterpillar over that caterpillar, Brian's circumlocution had the effect the little fellow desired – he simply couldn't keep his eyes open.

Meandering onward, he chanced upon Sir Edwin Preece-Moog and family at whom he waved. 'Ignore him children,' Sir Edwin cautioned as he paddled faster, pushing up a bow wave. 'That, I'm afraid, is the common oik.'

'Bloody snob!' hurled Brian, affronted, but no response came. 'Typical,' he mouthed sourly. 'One revolution for you and another for me. Nothing ever changes.'

**

For seven nights, Rodin gnawed, tore, nibbled and chewed the joist beneath Montgolfiere's bed. In the pitch darkness, the black rat toiled. He looked at his work, scurried up and down its entire length inspecting every detail with his beady, red eyes, then on the eighth morning, with chinks of light filtering through gaps in the floorboards above, he walked slowly away, his work complete.

Through all these nights had Georges slept. On the third night, he had attempted to undress before bed, however, his clothing clung to his skin as if by static electricity and so thereafter, he slept fully clothed.

In Georges' dreams, which were vivid and kaleidoscopic, he felt himself swirling and falling. He allowed himself to be taken and it was a joyous acceptance. Everything made sense, it was a unification, not a departure.

Outwardly, his appearance changed. Coarse, black hair began to permeate his green hemp suit and his stature decreased as his back became curved. Facially, he was more hirsute, but not in the manner as would be expected for a man who had not shaven for a week. His cheekbones and forehead now displayed a blackish, soft down. The form of his face grew more acute as if taking a cue from his aquiline snout.

Day by day, Georges was changing. He dispensed with his shoes, wrenching them off as if his feet had always been prisoners yearning for escape. His toenails now resembled claws and his feet were matted with a darkish down.

Days were now spent outside and on the ninth day, he no longer slept in the hall. Instead, he fashioned a shelter deep within thick briar, he seemed impervious to the sharp, tangled mass. His gait, once loping and purposeful, now took on every appearance of a scurrying creature, flitting from one food source to another. His diet changed, no longer was he vegan, he became an omnivore and would catch insects, pillage nests for eggs, and even scavenge carrion where he could.

As time passed, he began to make sense of the commotion about him, and it was loud, for now, his ears, which attained the ability to prick up, seized upon every sound. He began to differentiate and decipher the language of the tiniest to the largest of animals. In short order, he ventured to speak, and eventually did he come to converse.

The needs, wants, fears, and thoughts of animals came to be understood by Georges Montgolfiere as he now shared the very same needs and emotions. The zoologist's greatest aspiration, the grail, was his alone among men. But Georges, the man, no longer existed.

**

'Any use with a hammer Brian?' asked the water vole, more in hope than expectation.

'What's a hammer?'

The vole evaluated the time required to appraise the mole of its purpose, even considered using it on his head, but decided a practical demonstration would be the most economical, timewise.

Time was indeed short, for the river water was now above the landing and the vole's boat was soon to enter his abode. Was the water vole disconcerted? Not a bit of it, indeed, that afternoon, he had sculled down to Toad Hall where a great lake was forming, it now lapped at the very steps of Horatio's palace. Here, on this lake, thought the vole, will I have the latitude to hoist sail.

The vole had already emptied his abode of his possessions, and these were piled high on the bank way above. Only once in his lifetime had the water attained such a height, and this was in winter after a month of heavy rain. He estimated that his reconstructed abode needs be a third of a willow higher.

Brian proved useful, to the vole's utter astonishment. The little fellow took to carpentry like a duck to water. Once acquainted with the correct end of a pencil to use, he had it lodged behind an ear, and nails, similarly, the pointed end went in first, he discovered.

He took on a builder's swagger and whistled cheerfully. A catcall and a whistle to Constance Preece-Moog with the remark 'look at the arse-end on that!' as she went tail-up for food, outraged her husband and forever categorised Brian, in Moog eyes, as an irredeemable oik.

They worked tirelessly for two sunsets and late at night, they put their feet up in the water vole's newly positioned old house. The reconstruction of the stonework chimney, which now stood alone as a testament to the former existence of ancestors, would wait until autumn.

With a special bottle of hooch, lain down by the great ancestor himself, they celebrated their achievement. The vole skinned-up and as always, Brian feigned indifference, until it was passed to him, and he then went at it like a mole possessed.

'So, what did you find in that Book of Pan then?' enquired Brian, distractedly, with all his attention on the joint, held by his friend.

The vole blew a cloud toward the ceiling and, not for the first time, pondered the inequity of being alone among animals to keep the Book of Pan, of being the only animal to be able to read and understand it. What use the Fur Revolution, he thought, if this inequity prevailed? He decided to go against all edicts passed down and allow Brian a glance. In any case, if he were to be the last of the swimming-rats, then other animals would surely see it, when the day comes to take the long-scull.

'What is it?' declared Brian, in wonderment, as his bulging eyes beheld a line-drawing in the ancient, illuminated tome. 'Is it animal?'

The vole snapped closed the tome and stowed it in a waterproof chest beneath his bed. He felt a sense of betrayal in having shown the book, all very well to hypothecate on the fairness of it all, but the deed itself had shaken him. He resumed his seat and sat in silence, leaving Brian perplexed.

'I wasn't supposed to have seen that, was I?' Brian said apologetically. 'I shan't tell anyone Trevor-Stan.'

Was it the mention of his now hyphenated name that underscored the vole's realisation of his impending end? Would he be the last of the swimming-rats to scuttle his boat, as ritual dictated, and go down, lest another swimming-rat be found? It was all too likely. The vole drew a deep breath.

'What you saw was the image of a creature, half Upright, half animal. A feral Upright some say, but it is so much more than that. The Book of Pan says that certain animals have the power to enter the spirit of other animals and maybe even Uprights.'

Brian's face was a picture of puzzlement and so the vole went on.

'These special animals then take dominance.'

'What types of animals?' asked Brian sitting forward.

'Oh, hares, but maybe only one in generations, owls, but the same applies.'

'Not rats then?' asked Brian, resignedly, slumping back.

The vole studied his friend's face closely. 'Why do you ask that?'

'Oh, just something I heard…you know, special animals…probably bollocks.'

'Only the black rat, the ship-rat, and they disappeared longer ago than anyone can remember. The great ancestor met one once, a foreign rat, but he was only passing through.'

Brian then did what Brian always did, he wore a smug expression and remained silent. It infuriated his friend to see him sitting with his paws joined on his bulbous stomach in possession of, what he esteemed to be, precious information. This was usually in relation to a cache of nuts hidden by a squirrel, or some other inconsequential matter.

'Yes, Brian, what is it? I give up,' said the vole tersely and then sighed wearily as Brian kept stum. 'Oh, for Pan's sake. Please?' followed up the vole, quickly tiring of the game and knowing this to be the only way to end it.

'There's a black rat in Toad Hall.'

'What?'- Exclaimed the vole, sitting forward.

'Been there since the place was built,' he added, casually.

'Impossible,' declared the vole, and Brian simply shrugged.

'That's what the house rats say. Never eats, never drinks...just is. Always chewing things, maybe he eats the wood.'

'I don't believe it,' maintained the vole.

'Ask them. They call him...I've forgotten what they call him.'

Chapter Twenty-Eight

Up, Up and Away

'He's lost the plot.' This was the verdict of Georges Montgolfiere's staff. 'Not the only one,' said a staff member, with a nod toward a colleague who suspected the orange-clad monks to be orchestrating the pandemonium.

The staff's mental health was at breaking point. Sleep-deprived and now with an aversion to rats that bordered on the hysterical, they had tried sleeping in tents, but nowhere were they immune from the persecution of animals.

The last sighting of Montgolfiere, albeit at a distance, had distressed them all. 'What malign force is at work in this place?' posed one staff member who was suffering daytime hallucinations.

Georges Montgolfiere had suffered some form of mental breakdown, that was the consensus. Doubtless, he needed medical attention, yet as only fleeting glimpses had been made of the boss, and none in weeks, they felt powerless to act.

Without pay for two months, a vote was taken on whether to remain or leave.

Only one member voted to remain, the hardiest of all, yet she had no wish to remain alone, not with the weird Montgolfiere at large.

River water was now spurting up between the ground floor floorboards in Toad Hall and at night, the eerie howling of wolves could be heard.

Staff members were at a loss. How was any of this possible? The fencing work was far from complete, and wolves were yet to be brought in.

Now owed many thousands, the remaining staff voted to sequestrate all Montgolfiere's possessions, chief among which were the three remaining hot-air balloons.

Thus, it was at dawn, on a still summer's morning, from within the crenulated surrounds of the roof of Toad Hall, that the balloons arose.

Their relief to be leaving what had become a house of torture was palpable. As the balloons rose higher, their astonishment at seeing the flooding wrought by beavers was immeasurable.

'You're telling me that one pair of beavers caused all that? No way.'

'Just like the wolves, Georges was lying to us about them as well.'

Sarah, the hardy one who would have stayed, looked back at Toad Hall and sighed. A dream was at an end when so much could have been achieved.

'You know, those rats, they knew this flood was coming. Poor things, they were only anxious to get off the ground floor.'

Her two colleagues, sharing the basket, exchanged glances of disbelief. Rats? They'd had enough of them for one lifetime.

As the balloons picked up a stiffening westerly, they passed over farmland.

'Look at that,' said the pilot, pointing downward. 'Wasn't that the chicken farm?'

He picked up his binoculars, looked, and handed them over.

'They're everywhere,' declared Sarah gleefully. 'Yay! They've escaped.'

They drifted on and passed over another farm, seemingly deserted, and then another.

'What's been happening here?' asked the pilot, perplexed, adding 'it's not the end of the world, is it? I mean, I haven't heard the news in months.'

'Maybe it's just the beginning,' replied Sarah enigmatically. 'The start of this little world.'

**

The departure of the balloons was witnessed by all the inhabitants of wood, river and field and greeted with elation. Now could they return to their homes and resume the natural rhythm of their lives.

No animal was more delighted than Horatio Toad, apart from Cordelia perhaps, as conditions in the old gypsy caravan, which was now afloat, hadn't been ideal.

Not ideal conditions either for the meditating Orangedals, some of whom were chanting in treetops to the annoyance of nesting birds and squirrels. Many had fashioned makeshift floats from old doors they had scavenged from the stables. Some were basket-weaving, making coracles. At night, afloat, with their candles alight, they made a picturesque sight from the rooftops of Toad Hall.

It was from this lofty location that Cordelia reminded Horatio that he owed a debt of thanks to all animals. She mooted a party, such a party that Toad Hall had not seen in generations. At the outset, Horatio had poo-pooed the notion on the basis that below, and all around, lay the common 'oikery.'

'My dear, you don't understand these...these...' He waved a dismissive hand and noting Cordelia's frown, chose his next words carefully. 'These simple animals, they have no idea how to behave. No decorum, don't know a flute from a goblet.'

'Then I shall hold one of my own,' Cordelia replied, steadfastly.

'Ah, um, wait a moment...I...' spluttered Horatio.

Massaging a gentleman toad's ego was a simple affair, deflating one equally so, and Cordelia was adept at it. She may have been once relegated to division six, but she was now back in the first.

'You could make a speech...a very important speech. You could make it from the balcony.'

At once enthused to be seen as lord of all he surveyed, there did appear however to be one fly in the ointment. – 'But we are surrounded by water, my pearl, my everything.'

'For now,' came Cordelia's cryptic response.

**

Blessed silence fell within the walls of Toad Hall in the following days. The house rodents were exhausted from their gnawing, and many had dental problems. They had now taken up residence beneath boards on the second floor, and as the ground floor larders were flooded, they had taken to swimming to fetch food in.

Horatio practiced forging the Montgolfiere signature. He was a dab hand and had it off to a tee in short order. He had discovered, locked in a desk drawer which he picked easily, a bank book and a statement. It seemed as if a good deal of money was to be had from a London bank, more than enough for a lavish party. And with the remainder? A motor car perhaps – providing the statement was correct. He sat down and composed a letter to the bank and enclosed a cheque, made payable to one Cordelia Verity Toad.

Montogolfiere's bank paid the money, some eight thousand pounds, over to Cordelia's account. Cordelia's account was, however, frozen with a sequestration order upon it. The cheque was returned to Montgolfiere's bank with a large question mark upon it. Montgolfiere's bank re-examined the cheque. A handwriting expert declared the writing and signature as a forgery. Numerous letters from the bank to Montgolfiere had gone unanswered. The bank then contacted Montgolfiere's lawyers, Filtch, Stripum & Tuckham to alert them of a fraud attempt on their client's account. The communication landed on the desk of Silas Snipe.

Curious, thought Silas, so he delved deeper. He requested a copy of the fraudulent cheque and with aid of his own handwriting expert, matching the cheque against the leasehold documents, determined that the signatory was Horatio Toad. Delving deeper still into Toad affairs, he discovered that a reward of fifty thousand pounds was in vigour for the whereabouts of Horatio Calidus Superbus Dimidium-Nelson Toad, and furthermore a warrant for his extradition to Bermuda.

Rubbing his bony, white hands together in satisfaction, he picked up the telephone-

'I believe I know where you might find case number HCSD-NT-11...'

**

Back in control of his affairs, Horatio spent much time trawling through the estate's accounts. He brightened enormously when he discovered that three tenant farmers last paid rent decades earlier. 'Blighters have got away with it Scot-free!' he exclaimed. 'Well, we shall see about that.'

Cordelia cautioned that he needed to look the part of an estate owner, he needed a tweed jacket, a checked Tattersall shirt, plus-fours, and a riding crop if he was to go on his rounds collecting rents. 'Just like your ancestor, look,' she advised, pointing to a heavy oil painting on the stairway.

'Snag is old girl, until I…we, have got a spot of cash, the gents' outfitter is beyond reach. Couldn't touch you for a few quid, could I?'

Cordelia took Horatio by the shoulders. 'Look into my eyes,' she commanded. 'NO!'

Horatio thought she was becoming more brazen by the day; he was unused to being bossed about by females. 'Only asking,' he muttered, sullenly.

'Anyway, how could I,' continued Cordelia. 'The little bit I did have has gone to pay off your debts. My account was frozen a long time ago.'

'Really?' replied a stunned Horatio, weakly, as a lead ball dropped into the pit of his stomach.

'I told you!' rebuked an exasperated Cordelia. 'You never listen. Of course, they froze my account, I am your wife!'

The slough of despond was not a bog in which Horatio intended to wallow for long. A toe had been dipped in with the mention of his debts, a foot with news of the frozen account, and a whole leg when Cordelia reminded him that she was his wife.

Weighed down by his past sins? Not at all. Horatio looked on the bright side; he was on the up. Never mind the eight thousand measly pounds, he calculated the farmer johnnies to owe him ten times that sum.

Paddled to firm ground on an old door by a chanting chappie, as he termed him, it occurred to Horatio that these types were living at his expense too. Had he made some off-hand suggestion that they might share Toad Hall gratis? If so, he erased it from memory now. No, no, if he were to regain his dignity, he considered, then he needed a spot of the old spondoolica with which to do it.

Resplendent in ill-fitting, moth-eaten country tweed he had discovered in a trunk in the attic, he strode across field and lea carrying a cello bow, which had to serve as a crop. His purposeful gait faltered however as he approached the first farm; it appeared deserted. The door was open, and he ventured inside. Daubed on the kitchen wall in red paint was the word 'RATS'. Horatio's brow furrowed as he looked about him, the place had the appearance of a deserted ship. He called out. 'Hello, I say hello there.' Silence. He walked upstairs to find more graffiti. 'THE DEVIL'S HOUSE!' and 'GET OUT!' and 'RUN'.

How odd, thought Horatio, as he wandered away, rats? What's wrong with rats? Amusing little coves.

It surprised Horatio to discover just how large the old ancestral estate was, his feet were sore in the stiff, leather boots, a size too small, and so he sat down upon a fallen ash. He realised he was peckish. Old habits die hard and from the corner of his prominent, copper-eye he noticed several woodlice and a few beetles. Out shot his sticky tongue and he lapped them up. This was not the comportment of a gentleman toad and so he cast about to check that he was unseen.

'Ah, now, there they are,' he said aloud as he spotted members of the peasantry. 'Young Uprights and scallywags all, I'll be bound.'

Horatio made his way across a meadow to a group of Upright boys.

'Not at work, eh? Lunch time I suppose. Shouldn't you be helping your fathers mow the hay and…wot not?'

'What?' replied the first boy.

Horatio's brow knitted, no sense of propriety these sons of toil, he thought.

'Helping your family on the farm young fellow-me-lad, not gallivanting about.'

The boys looked at each other and smirked.

'We haven't got a farm; my dad goes to work on a train.'

'Train driver, eh?' replied Horatio dismissively, 'I suppose we need those too.'

'Are you a gentleman toad?' asked another.

'Indeed, I am, and you, young fellow, are on my land.'

'My dad's a policeman,' said the third boy, haughtily.

'Oh, err is he indeed…' faltered Horatio. 'Good egg, is he?'

'What?' replied the boy.

News of deserted farms took the wind from Horatio's sails.

'All because of a few rats?' Horatio questioned, incredulously, adding 'Farms always have rats, that's their home.'

'Not thousands of them,' stated one boy.

'And the crows attacked the farmers.'

'Crows? Weren't rooks, were they?' replied Horatio, anxiously, as he looked skyward.

'And the pigs!' joined the third boy, whose dad was a policeman. 'My dad says pigs are more dangerous than dogs.'

'He should know…' muttered Horatio.

It was a disconsolate toad who tramped homeward, his mind troubled with images of policemen and their infernal handcuffs. 'All too close to home,' he muttered as he went. There was no prospect of rent save for whatever the chanting chappies could muster.

'Probably haven't got a bean between them,' he grumbled. 'Sitting about on your arse all day isn't going to boil any bacon.'

Still, I'll have to fleece them for all they've got, he considered, they must have been paying that old swindler Montgolfiere something. Odd to go off your chump like that, he thought, whatever did happen to him anyway?

As he walked on, the issue of the forged cheque played on his mind.

'Never find me here,' he mumbled.

But try as he might, he could not expunge imagery of the long arm of the law. He shuddered at the memory of the Barbudan judge's spindly finger wavering at him. 'Take him down.' The very notion of spending the rest of his natural life embroidering beach towels, the Bermudian version of mailbags, filled him with dread.

Now did Cordelia's enthusiasm for a party to celebrate the Fur Revolution, or whatever preposterous name the water vole had come up with, seem hollow indeed to Horatio. For what is a gentleman toad, he ruminated morosely, without oodles of the old necessary? Without an aeroplane, a yacht, and a sports car, all of which he had once owned. He would be nothing but a common toad!

Chapter Twenty-Nine

A Rising Tide

'When I pull the kingpin, she'll go. Are you ready hen?'

'Aye, quite ready Jock McTavish,' replied Moira, excitedly.

'Yippee!' cried the two beavers in concert as they broke the inlet dam and body-surfed on a surge of backed-up water. As they rode the crest, they looked at one another and smiled. 'It's great to be a beaver, is it no'?' shouted Moira.

Aching backs, necks, and teeth were all forgotten now, no more gripes from Jock (and there had been many), and Moira, having coaxed Jock into lodge action, even believed she might be pregnant.

With the inlet waters broken, the flood about Toad Hall began to recede gradually. The lake at the front of the Hall would remain, however, due to the second main river dam. The two dams were acting as sediment traps and already the clarity of the water was improving, was almost limpid, away from the main current.

**

In Horatio's absence, Cordelia had sent out a drove of shrews with party invitations and recruited the Orangedals to assist in the mopping-up of the ground floor.

'They really are most accommodating Horatio; they go about their work in silence and then they sit down again.'

'Is that so?' replied Horatio moodily as he sat staring at his feet.

'And when I offered them something to eat,' added Cordelia, 'they just smiled, put their hands together and bowed, wouldn't touch a crumb….what in the name of Pan is the matter with you now? You've got a face like a squashed avocado.'

Her buoyancy was beginning to grate on Horatio's nerves, he now remembered why he had taken wife number two. Number two had been less apt to organise him.

'Fat chance of getting a bean out of those chanting-chappies, can't get a word out of them…*Om mani padme*…Paf! Pad me pockets, that's what I need. All that bowing, scraping, and smiling, I've worn my jaws out. Don't believe they've got a spondool between them.'

Cordelia rounded on her husband with hands on hips.
'Are you telling me you asked them for money?',' she snapped.

'Why not?' protested Horatio. 'Blighters are living at my expense, food and board and all that.'

'What food? What board? They sit outside all day and for all I know, most of the night. As for food? Well, they must eat berries and nuts because they never touch the larder…not that there's much left…what with the rats…I can't believe you've asked them for money. After all they've done for you!'

'What, exactly, have they done for me Cynthia?' retorted Horatio hotly.

'Cordelia! Cynthia was number three…or was it four?

Anyway, another thing, what is the Rat-Tax-Bite rate these days?'

'What's the R.T.B. got to do with anything?'

'Because I need to know, someone has to run this house.'

'About five per cent, I suppose,' Horatio answered, disinterestedly.

'Well, they're taking closer to ten, I'll have a word,' stated Cordelia, crossly. 'No point asking you!'

Horatio was left to sit and mope with an earful of fleas. He was, according to Cordelia, a selfish, avaricious, vain, bloated, arrogant...the full list Horatio preferred not to recall. Cordelia had departed citing an old refrain he'd not heard for a long while.

'I should have listened to my mother, she always said I was a fool for not marrying Captain Temerity-Toad. But oh no, I believed in all your big talk, didn't I? Poor naive slip-of-a-toad that I was. Well, see where it's got me!'

Horatio scoffed at the memory of his first love rival. 'Captain Temerity, indeed! Nothing more than a jumped-up boating-lake attendant,' he muttered derisorily.

Before him was a blank sheet of paper and a pen. Soon the grounds would be inundated with animals. They had all been promised a speech.

He looked over to the second-floor balcony that gave off the master bedroom, it was to have been a triumphant speech safe in the knowledge that he was, once more, lord of all he surveyed. Now, he couldn't even afford new clothes.

'I suppose they won't notice from a distance,' he muttered as he looked upon his moth-eaten, tattered, apparel. 'Have to give them something,' he grumbled, as he put ink to paper.

**

'It's a westerly Brian,' exclaimed the water vole excitedly, as he stripped the bedding. 'We'll be able to sail in.'

'What's sailin'?' replied a distracted mole who was busy putting the finishing touch to his round party hat, which unknown to him, was formerly an Upright fisherman's maggot tub. 'What do you make of that?' he asked, displaying the black tub resplendent with its red lid. But the vole was too busy attaching sails to a willow mast to notice.

'Reckon Taupe will go for me in this?'

The vole continued knotting and rigging and did not look up.

'I said, do you think Taupe will go for me in this?'-Brian persisted.

With a sigh, the vole looked over, it was the only way to shut his friend up, he then had to turn promptly away to disguise a snigger. Brian looked patently ridiculous with a bait box strapped to his head, beneath which his barbed wired framed, bottle-bottomed spectacles glinted in the evening sun. Brian was smiling, which had the unfortunate effect of making two front teeth protrude, lending nothing to the air of sophistication and intrigue he had hoped to engender.

'Perfect Brian, she won't be able to resist.'

'Thought as much,' replied Brian, as he picked up a chair and practiced a dance.

Off they set, rowing at first and when they approached the great lake, which now fronted Toad Hall, they would head into wind, hoist sails, come about, and with a steady westerly aft, gull-wing all the way up to the front steps.

The water-vole had selected white jacket and trousers and a blue peaked cap to top it off, as his attire.

'Look a bit of a prat dressed like that, if you don't mind me saying, Trevor-Stan,' commented Brian, off-handedly.
Coming from anyone else, the water-vole might have taken this to heart, but from Brian?

**

Excitement was building in the wood. Jack and Jill Stoat were gathering all the hooch they could lay their paws on, and weasels were practicing airs on their fiddles. Tonight, was going to be the biggest, most drunken, loudest party of their lives.

Fergal and Molly Fenian were making their way to the party along with Peter and Linda Peel. As Peter noted the stoats, ferrets, and weasels with armfuls of hooch, he advised 'We should make it an early one dear; this lot don't know when to stop.' Linda shot a glance at Molly and rolled her eyes.

As they passed the badger's old sett, they paused.

'Ah, it's the shame the old bastard is no longer with us,' Fergal stated.

'Probably wouldn't have come anyway,' Molly added, wistfully.

'Never one for parties old badger, said Peter, casually. 'He never really knew how to let his hair down.'

Again, Linda and Molly exchanged glances – incredulity writ large.

**

Horatio's shoulders slumped as Cordelia entered the room briskly. 'The chief rat says it's officially fifteen percent and that they're only taking eight, that can't be right, can it? You'll have to have a word. Oh, and while you're at it, tell them to pipe down. Pan only knows what they're doing up there.' Cordelia pointed upward. 'They're making a horrible racket.'

'I'm trying to write my speech,' complained Horatio.

'Well let me see,' snapped Cordelia, whisking it up from the desk. She then began to read aloud.

"…Blah de blah de blah…Did we allow Uprights to control our lives? No, we did not. Did we let them fence us in like Upright zoo prisoners? No, we did not. Will we ever let them try again? No, we will not. I tell you friends, not if Horatio Toad has anything to do with it….'

Cordelia fixed her husband in the eye; her expression was one of disbelief. She batted the paper with her free hand.

'But you were everything to do with it, you fool! They know that,' she cried with a wave of her hand toward the grounds.

'What they want from you Horatio is humility, what they want from you is sincerity and thanks. What they want from you, above all, is an apology!' Cordelia waved the paper in the air and continued. 'If you read this out, then they'll be a second revolution. And then, we'll be the ones turfed out!'

'They wouldn't dare. This is Toad Hall, not some ruddy burrow. The estate they dig their holes in belongs to me!' declared Horatio, raising himself to his full *hauteur*, which wasn't very high. 'Oh no, if they try that little game, I'll. I'll…'

'Have the law on them?' mocked Cordelia, hands on hips.

Horatio slumped back down as the weakness of his position sunk in 'Certainly know how to take the wind from a fellow's sails,' he muttered, balefully.

'I'll leave you to it, but you'd better hurry, animals are already arriving…remember, contrition, and none of your puffed-up nonsense. You've been warned.' Cordelia gave Horatio one of her looks. 'If I hear any of that then… well, you'll have to do without me!'

With that Cordelia whisked from the room, but not before pointing upward and adding briskly 'and do something about that racket up there!'

'Is that a promise?' muttered Horatio when she'd gone. He thought he could very well do-without. Images of number six, his lovely exotic Tamara, paraded before his eyes.

'Suppose I shouldn't have tried to chuck the other two out of the balloon', he concluded, dolefully. His face clouded.

'Fancy Tamara taking it like that...would have thought she'd have been pleased.'

With a heavy sigh, Horatio put pen to paper. 'If they want contrition, I'll give them ruddy contrition, I'll give it to 'em until they're sick.' He began to write, muttering as he did so. 'Can always keep the old fingers crossed behind me back I suppose...'

**

'Like Rodin's gonna squeal extra when he sees what they done bro,' exclaimed Gnaw as he gazed down at a gaping hole in the floor above which Montgolfiere's bed had formerly stood, adding 'not like he ever done anything good before innit?'

'Totes old chap, dey messed up big style. Like he must 'ave worn down the chews on dis job innit, old bean?' added Nibble, who had begun to affect city-rat speech to the chagrin of the elder rats.

**

Cordelia was passed on the stair by four Orangedals carrying a heavy section of timber on their shoulders. They stopped, smiled, bowed their heads, and continued on their way. Cordelia frowned, she wasn't an expert, but what they were carrying looked suspiciously like a piece of house. She decided to investigate. When she looked in third-floor bedroom seven, she discovered a pile of floorboards and a gap where, she surmised, the timber ought to have been. Nibble whipped a sizeable chunk of cake behind his back when she entered and Gnaw gulped his portion of taxed-bite down quickly.

'Why have the Orangedals taken a bit of house?' a puzzled Cordelia asked, knowing full well the futility of the question. Obfuscation was a house rat's stock-in-trade.

'Like, I'm supposin' dey gone outside to gnaw it down a bit. Probs don't fit innit?' answered Nibble.

'Yeah, like gettin' it right first time ain't no cinch Mrs T,' joined Gnaw, spraying crumbs.

'Tell me, that's not my cake, is it?' demanded Cordelia, sternly.

'Five per cent totes, Mrs T. Like I'm pluggin' back the tax hole with de icin'. Bad for the chews that icin'.'

'Yo blood sets mine well on edge – simply ghastly,' agreed Nibble.

Cordelia shook her head, she could waste a season of moons trying to get any sense out of this pair, she decided. As she was leaving, Gnaw called out 'Mrs T, you shiftin' shapes later?'

'I haven't the faintest idea what you're talking about,' Cordelia returned, as she swept from the room.

'Like dose toads dude, got all da bling and no zingzing,' Gnaw remarked through a mouthful of cheddar, adding 'anyways,'– as he examined his taxed bite – 'where's dat little bit of pineapple on dis stick? You gleanin' what I'm verbin'? You gotta have de cube – dey got no style bro – no class.'

Chapter Thirty

Cometh the Mole

Standing aloof against a backdrop of flowering peonies, Taupe's party-pelt of pink flowers on a green background rendered her invisible. It was wrong of her to laugh, she knew that, but the incident with the water vole's boat had her in stitches. As her laughter subsided, she surprised herself by her concern for Brian, was he really hurt? She came close to running down to the water's edge; however, she stayed her ground.

It was a triumphant arrival for the water vole. Animals gathered at the water's edge and stared in wonder. Approaching was, what seemed to them, a billowing, white cloud scudding over the wavelets.

With the boom carrying the mainsail set at right angles on the port side, and the genoa pregnant and billowing off the starboard bow, the vole was at the tiller ensuring the westerly wind stayed directly aft. Brian sat next to him on the port side.

'Did I ever mention, Brian, that boats are the thing – the only thing.'

'I think you might have done, once or twice,' replied Brian, kindly. The vole's familiar refrain had today some merit, Brian thought, for he was enjoying it too.

'Whoa, what a gust!' exclaimed the vole in raptures as the stiff westerly sped them toward shore- The shore being a fragment of non-submerged lawn.

Had Brian, in his haste to disembark not hampered the vole's movement of the tiller, then all would have been fine. They would have beached bow first and got out in an orderly fashion. However, at the last moment, the boat turned through ninety degrees, broadside to the shore, and the vole, seeing which way the wind was blowing, hopped out as only an experienced helmsman might.

'Boom Brian – duck! Look out for the...'

Now, all this nautical terminology was lost on Brian and as for ducks, well he didn't care for them one iota. So, he dithered – too late. The wind got on the other side of the mainsail and the boom gybed! It swung across at a ferocious pace and connected with the back of the unwitting Brian's head.

This was not the entry to the party Brian had planned; entering the water head-first, gulping down a copious quantity of river water, and having to be helped ashore in a dazed and spluttering condition by a tittering Reg Otter. It was demeaning.

'Brian, I love yer mate! Ain't no animal who can give us such a laugh. Pan bless yer,' Reg declared, wiping tears from his eyes.

'He might be hurt Reg!' chastised a concerned Trace as she studied the mole's glazed eyes. 'Brian, how many fingers am I holding up?'

'You ain't got any fingers love,' reminded Reg. Trace then gave him a hard look, as Clamp and Nipper dissolved into fits of the giggles.

'Well then, that's the answer innit!' retorted Trace, hotly.

Aside from his pride, Brian was not too badly injured.

The ridicule of ducks – and Rear Admiral Canard and flotilla were quacking hysterically – was water off a mole's pelt. What did concern Brian was that Taupe had witnessed this ignominious entry. He cast about but could not see her.

Taupe looked on. Whatever has he got on his head, she wondered. She watched in growing sympathy as he threaded his way between animals, evidently searching for her. She saw him ask Fergal and Molly who craned about and shrugged their shoulders. He looked crestfallen. Taupe was on the point of stepping out from hiding when the music stopped abruptly. Ferrets and weasels put down their fiddles, tutting as they did so.

'The toad's going to make a speech,' declared the chief weasel. 'What a treat for us all,' he added, sarcastically.

Horatio was standing on the second-floor balcony overlooking the assembly. He chimed a spoon on a champagne flute, which was empty, there being no champagne. It took some time for the gathering to come to order. Cordelia sat in the bedroom looking at her husband's back. She was ready to intervene, if necessary, should Horatio revert to type.

The light was beginning to fade on this midsummer's eve and as Horatio looked over the expectant crowd below, even the Orangedals, floating on what seemed to be coracles, were in rapt attention.

For once in his life, Horatio's hubris left him. He looked down at his script and noted that despite his efforts at humility, he had defaulted to vanity. What's more, he found it pedestrian, lacking in...well, everything. What use now to play the feudal lord? Those below had just as much as he – nothing. The Orangedals were smiling at him, and it seemed to Horatio that their smiles were broader than ever.

'Oh, yes, smile at an animal when he's down,' he muttered, despite himself.

'What's the matter Horatio?' called Cordelia impatiently, her voice tinged with a hint of concern. Animals below had begun to chatter, and a few weasels had started a slow-paw clap.

'Get on with it dear, for Pan's sake.'

Dear? It's been a long time since I heard that, thought Horatio, softening. He turned to look at Cordelia as if for the first time in seasons – and smiled.

'Are you quite well Horatio?' she asked, mildly astonished.

'Never better, dear,' he replied and turned to face the crowd.

'Friends, river bankers, wood dwellers, and country…sorts. Lend me your money!'

An instant clamour of disapproval was quickly quelled as Horatio continued-

'Just my little school-toad joke, fact of the matter is, I'm broke.'

As if to illustrate the point, he tipped up his empty champagne flute and then threw it over his shoulder. He then turned out the linings of his pockets.

'Haven't got a bean. Truth of the matter is, Cordelia and I had to run away from the Uprights. They claimed we diddled them. We had to run for our lives.'

A ripple of sympathy ran through some in the crowd and yet there were others, arms crossed, whose faces remained obdurate.

'And so, we had to take refuge here. Now, I know some of you blame me for getting into bed with the oddball Upright but believe me when I tell you that I had no idea what his plans were.'

A stony silence pervaded and nervously, Horatio scanned faces. Even though darkness was descending, he noted that the Orangedals had dropped their smiles – he had never seen that happen before.

'Apologise and then thank them Horatio!' yelled Cordelia.

"I mean to say…' spluttered Horatio, 'I never thought he meant them. Thought he was a nut short of a vegan sandwich if truth be told.'

'Sure, you wouldn't know the truth if it bit you in the arse!' hurled Molly Fenian sending up a chorus of remarks – 'You're not wrong there Molly'– 'Same as ever was'– 'All cut from the same cloth those gentleman toads.'

Horatio was all at sea; the clamour of discontent was growing. Cordelia decided it was time to intervene and she pushed in front of her husband.

'My husband and I would like to thank you from the bottom of our hearts,' declared Cordelia in high voice. 'Wouldn't we Horatio?'

'Oh, quite so, yes indeed right from the jolly bottom,' enjoined Horatio, craning his head around his plump wife. 'Moreover, we want to thank you for your parts in the Fur Revolution, it was magnificent, it was glorious, it was remarkable, it was...oh dear, I've quite run out of superlatives...'

'I haven't,' insisted Horatio, pushing to the fore. 'It was first-rate, top-drawer, tremendous, amazing, splendiferous, sensational, incredible, it was phenom...'

'They're not listening Horatio,' Cordelia advised, as she craned her neck to see around the corner of the building. 'What's going on? Why are they all scattering?'

Dog barks and whistles had an instant sobering effect on Horatio. His five chins deflated at the sound of his name: 'Horatio Calidus Superbus Dimidium-Nelson Toad; we have a warrant for your arrest!'

They swept around the corner of the house. Salivating German Shepherds, straining at the leash, barked and growled when Fergal called out from the bushes 'You're nothing but lickspittles to the Uprights, so you are.' Then Silas Snipe, at the head of the group, pointed up to the balcony.

'There he is. That's Horatio Toad, there's your criminal.' The dogs bared their teeth and snarled. The chief of police singled out Horatio with a pointed finger and then pointed theatrically downward to his own feet, demanding Horatio present himself.

'The Uprights have got him; we must do something,' declared Brian.

'There's nothing we can do now Brian,' replied the water vole, sadly, resignedly.

The next few moments would etch Brian's place forever in animal lore. His actions, that night, would be passed down from father to pup for generations to come.

Brian picked up the vole's cricket bat (they intended a moonlit game against the weasels) and he charged. He charged with a ferocious battle cry that belied his size, about his head he wielded the bat, whirling it this way and that until it became a blur, and he headed straight for the dogs. Immediately, the dogs turned on him – snarling beasts that their handlers had difficulty in restraining. The mole connected and dealt one of the beasts a blow to the snout making him howl, only enraging the wild dog more.

'*Lache-moi! Lache-moi!*'– let me go – Taupe cried tearfully as she struggled in the grip of Linda and Peter Peel. 'They kill him – *NON!*'

Brian couldn't hear hundreds of animals imploring him to back off, he was beside himself as he kept up his relentless attack. Nor could he hear what every other animal heard, the mystical, ethereal chanting that arose from the lake. It grew in rhythm and volume and gradually, all the animals, not knowing the reason why, joined in. Brian's windmilling slowed. What was happening? Then he stopped.

The rabid dogs sat before him. The dog with the smarting snout, offered him his paw. Brian took it and bowed and the two dogs, now passive, reciprocated.

More than anything else, his next action transformed a mole, so often ridiculed, into a figure of legend. He released the dogs from their leads, and they lay, the male and female, submissively before him, at his feet.

The chanting, at once melodious and other-worldly continued. Animals gathered at the edge of the lake, chanting themselves and they stared, at the mysterious Orangedals, whose smiles seemed broader than ever.

The policeman, their leads hanging limply by their sides, looked about in confusion. 'What are we doing here?' 'Where is this place?' 'How did we get here?' They and Silas Snipe wandered about in circles bewildered for a while before they sauntered away, as if in a trance, as if sleepwalking, as if enrobed in a dream.

The chanting subsided, and became fainter as the coracles, in which the Orangedals floated, drifted out to the centre of the lake.

Then did happen what no animal present would ever forget. The Orangedals began to glow, began to change hue to a yellowish green which grew in luminosity, and they started to ascend. Slowly at first, did they lift from the lake, hover, and then, one by one, take to the night sky.

A collective gasp of wonderment resounded as animals all, raised their eyes upward to watch, what for all the world looked like fireflies, drift high and above Toad Hall, and float away in the direction of the wild wood and into the night.

Animal searched animals' eyes for explanation. There was none. All were stunned.

The answer, if indeed it was one, came quite suddenly. A large cumulus cloud, its fringes tinged with silvery light, drifted aside and a shaft of moonlight pierced downward. No ordinary beam this, for it radiated, it pinpointed, and it focussed upon a totem pole, hitherto unseen within a thicket.

Simultaneously, far, far away, far from the wild wood, howls went up, a ghostly and eerie sound. The two German Shepherd dogs reciprocated. With their heads stretched back they howled at the moon. Then, in tandem, they trotted away.

Animals moved, instinctively, toward the light. They crowded into the thicket. They caught their breath. For towering above them stood an oak-carved effigy of Georges Montgolfiere, as he formerly was, perfect in every detail, illuminated by the moon.

Animal looked to animal, for they knew instinctively as they always did, that at that moment, this very particular Upright, this very strange animal, was no more. A fleeting silence – a coronach – was observed, and then they drifted away.

The water vole's eyes were drawn upward, and their eyes met. From beneath the roof tiles of Toad Hall, two intensely bright, red eyes looked down. Rodin fixed the vole's eyes for a moment; he then turned and was gone.

And so, are myths and legends born.

There was talk of the Green Man – talk of the green-suited Montgolfiere as having been the Green Man. 'He was always animal,' the water vole overheard time-over and many such other reverential utterances.

But, tonight of all nights, was a night for a party.

The weasels, stoats, and ferrets struck up and played mad, wild jigs and reels. Amid the frenzy, Taupe clung to her Brian.

'The clue is in the name, Taupe,' said Brian, basking in the adulation. 'Brian – it means king… actually.'

Taupe planted the biggest, most passionate kiss upon his muzzle. 'You my king Brian,' she replied holding his paws in hers. 'You my brave king. You bloody-fucking amazing!'

As he clamped her to his breast, Brian wasn't certain which organ was swelling the most, but he believed that his heart wasn't far behind.

Chapter Thirty-One

Just Desserts

It was dawn when the animals staggered home. Those heading for the woods held each other up and the distance covered was twice that of their arrival.

Horatio, who had been included in the dance, sat pondering the meaning of wealth. Yes, he still hankered for motorcars, aeroplanes, and yachts – a gentleman toad can never cure himself of that. And yet, these not so simple animals had demonstrated something far greater – friendship.

'That little fellow the mole...name eludes me, Cynthia.'

'CORDELIA!'

'Just so, just so my dear,' Horatio spluttered quickly, examining an empty bottle he was holding. 'Whatever do those stoats put in that hooch of theirs? No, I mean to say, he's got a lot of spunk for such a small chappie, wouldn't you say?'

Cordelia, seated next to her husband on the steps of the Hall, stared directly ahead. She was in a more pragmatic mood. How would they ever heat this cavernous house when winter came, she wondered. They were boracic and would need to live off their wits. She only wished she had a little more faith in the wit of the toad seated next to her.

'You know that chanting business...' went on an oblivious Horatio – 'being able to take off like that, what do they call it? Levitate, that's the fellow. Deuced if I've ever seen the like before. Might give it a bash, you know? Could be fun. Wouldn't you say old thing?'

But Horatio was talking to himself. Cordelia had walked away, eyes rolling.

**

The water-vole and Brian were sculling leisurely homeward when they passed Sir Edwin Preece-Moog and family.

'Well done that mole, always said you had it in you,' declared Sir Edwin.

'Oh yes, quite the hero. Cometh the fracas, cometh the mole,' replied Constance haughtily, as she followed Sir Edwin into an inlet.

Brian raised a middle digit and made no reply. What did he care? Taupe had returned home to prepare a *Wormguini a la Surprise* and his fervent wish was that the surprise element was extra to the dish.

'Do you think we'll ever have another spring like this one, Trevor-Stan?'

The vole sculled on, lost in a world of his own.

'I said, do you think…'

'I hope not Brian,' came the curt response.

'Oh.'

They were nearing the final bend in the now meandering river. The river had taken on a more sinuous aspect since the McTaggart's' arrival. It was more alive – kingfishers darted past in turquoise sprints and the air was buzzing with new life. Lily pads bloomed yellow in the margins and frogs abounded.

'Trevor-Stan,' whispered Brian, and getting no response kicked at the heels of his friend who seemed annoyed to be broken from his reverie.

'What is it, Brian?' he asked, testily.

Brian put his paw to his lips, leaned forward, and whispered in the vole's ear. The water vole let go a weary sigh, then with the merest hint of a smile, shipped the oars and let the boat glide.

Up ahead, in raucous cackle, swam Rear-Admiral Canard and his fleet.

The Mole stood at the crease, cricket bat in hand and when the object ball, the rear end of Canard, came within range, he swung the bat behind one shoulder and hit an exemplary cover drive. Canard took to the air along with a mighty whoosh of water and was propelled, wings and legs flailing, into the reeds – knocked for six.

'Not such an admirable rear now!' stated Brian gleefully, rubbing his paws together and resuming his seat.

'That was cruel Brian,' said the vole, giggling, despite himself. What ever would he be without this amusing little fellow, he asked himself – and he didn't like the answer.

'Oh, if you only knew,' replied Brian unapologetically. 'He's had that coming, since half-past April.'

**

Brian saw it first through a heat haze, for it promised a glorious summer's day. The water vole could not see, for he was rowing with his back to the vision. Brian took off his bottle-bottomed spectacles and rubbed them on his pelt. He then popped them back on and squinted. That was the colour, he recollected, wasn't it? With uncustomary tact, he remained silent.

'What is it, Brian?' enquired the vole.

'Oh, er nothing, just thinking,' replied Brian, casually.

The water vole smiled inwardly. Of course, thinking always did tend to work his friend's features; beginning at bafflement, through the fog of bemusement and puzzlement, finally arriving at vague comprehension. He sculled onward.

A broad smile came over Brian's muzzle.

'Are you going to let me in on the joke?' asked the vole, wearily.

'What? Oh, no…just thinking of old Canard, that's all. Pull in and drop me off here Trevor,' he requested.

That's a relief, thought the vole, as he did as bid because he was not in the mood for company today. Was it the party that had brought on this malaise, he wondered? Odd, how one can feel quite alone among so many.

'I'll er…drop in soon. In a few sunsets,' promised Brian as he alighted, adding 'bit more of a dignified exit this time.'

'Oh, don't worry about me Brian, make the most of your time with Taupe,' replied the vole, wistfully. 'Oh yes!' returned his friend, gleefully.

The water vole watched him depart and emptied his lungs with a weary sigh, he sat for a moment and then, in resignation, picked up the oars again.

Meanwhile, Brian raced along the bank until he was opposite the water-vole's abode. Brian peeked between the reeds. Sure enough, an orange rowing boat was moored on the landing, and there, gazing upstream, stood a water vole. 'Hello Stan,' whispered Brian. 'Where have you been?'

Dressed in a striped blue naval top, with knee length ragged-bottomed trousers, just as Trevor had described him, he began to pace up and down, as if waiting. Suddenly, he stood stock still and stared, shielding his eyes from the glare of the river, and then began brushing back his fur to ready himself.

Brian smiled broadly and thought he should move on, however, he wanted to see this moment. His friend's deep well of sadness, which he tried but failed to conceal, had tempered his own elation that morning. He watched his friend's weary strokes at the oar and could sense his sorrow, his resignation, at being the last of the swimming-rats.

But no more Trevor-Stan. From now on, it would be Trevor and Stan.

Trevor's eyes widened, he let go of the oars and gaped. Midstream he froze and stared in disbelief. Was this a mirage? Was it a heat haze? Was this a cruel figment of a wishful imagination? He was tongue-tied.

'Hello Trevor,' said a smiling vole. 'I thought we might have breakfast together.'

**

Brian sauntered onward feeling happier than ever he could remember. Just about everything was right with the world that early summer morning. Foxgloves were in bloom, dogroses too, and the bright, yellow, water lily flowers- Brian had taken a shine to.

He made two decisions in rapid succession, no mean feat, but then, no longer was he that mole of ridicule, now was he the quick thinker. The mole to act in a crisis, the fearless mole whose disregard for his own pelt had changed the known world. Replete with valour and carefree recklessness, Brian acted on the first of his decisions, an enormous decision. He would take a bath.

Defying the convention to undress, Brian jumped straight in. His goal was twofold, to freshen himself up and to collect a few of the flowers from the lily pads.

Alas, the water was deeper than he imagined and his old pelt coat took on water. Now, he could swim, he'd bathed once or twice before, yet he wasn't an accomplished swimmer, and drowning wasn't a possibility he had entertained.

It came as a shock, as it always does, that moment of stunned recognition, the terrible realisation of events being beyond one's control. He went under, floundered, re-surfaced, took a huge gulp of air and water, went under again, and came up again with his powerful arms flailing and thrashing the surface. He tried to shout – 'HELP'– but water simply gargled in his throat. He saw the yellow lilies, blurred, through water-filled eyes and he watched them disappear again. His life swept before him and his mind raced – 'NO, NO, NO, NOT TODAY!' as his sodden pelt-coat pulled him down through a sinewy tangle of green to the riverbed.

He came close, very close to drowning. Then, suddenly, he felt himself surge upward through the bubbles, the murk, and the green tangled-weed mass and into the light. He found himself rushing forward, pushing up a bow wave before his chest, and through the blur of water-filled eyes he made out the green bank of reeds.

There was an animal, that much he knew, but with his lungs full of water, he was at death's door. Did he hear one voice, or was it two? Did he hear one shout in panic?

'GET DAD!'

All came to him as a far off, dissonant, muddled echo.

Then came the heat of breath close to his face, the panting and pulling as he felt himself being tugged through the reeds on his front.

'For the love of Pan, no!' A female voice, was it?

Another animal was shouting, he felt something clamp his shoulder, hot breath again, and then was he hauled up the bank.

'JUMP!' The word filtered through, and then he felt heavy thuds on his back, again and again.

He felt a rush of water spew from his snout and mouth, and he coughed and choked, he felt his arms being wrenched from their sockets and continual thuds as more water spewed, and at last he took the deepest breath of his life. It whistled and wheezed in through his snout and mouth as if it would never end.

Then came more coughing and spluttering and he felt himself being lifted, the world was still here, yet it was upside down, as he coughed the last of the river water from his lungs.

'You stupid bugger!' The first words to enter the ears of the born again pup. 'You stupid, stupid bugger Brian,' Reg's voice cracked and broke. 'We thought we was gonna lose yer.'

Nipper and Clamp turned their heads to their feet, they had never seen their father break down before.

'If Nipper hadn't 'ave seen yer, mate,' continued Reg, emotionally, 'you'd be in old Esox's belly now. Ain't that right son?'

Nipper, embarrassed by his father's emotion, nodded. 'S'pose so, there was a pike watching,' he affirmed in a mumble, shuffling his feet.

It was some while before Brian could collect himself to speak, but when he did, suitably chastened, he thanked young Nipper profusely for saving his life.

'I'd 'ave been dead an all, if it wasn't for Taupe,' Nipper stated, reservedly, still shuffling his feet and winning him warm hugs from his parents and a grudging smile from his brother, Clamp.

Moments passed during which they all reflected on recent, events and traumas. But the sun shone, and the day was bright. Trace broke the silence.

'How did you fall in anyway?'

'I didn't.'

'Do what?' replied Reg, with a note of concern in his voice.

'I thought I'd take a bath and collect some flowers for Taupe,' Brian responded, sheepishly.

Reg, relieved, threw back his head and laughed-

'Brian, you bleedin' idiot, you've got yer coat on mate!'

'What flowers?' asked Trace, softly.

'What flowers?' questioned Reg, incredulously. 'The point is luv, he finks he can swim with his bleedin' coat on, fuck the flowers!'

The two boys giggled, relieved at their father's return to form.

Trace, ignoring Reg, jerked her chin upward and bid Brian answer.

'The yellow ones, lilies, are they?'

'Hop in boys and get him the flowers,' insisted Trace.

Clamp pulled a face. 'Some animal might be looking mum.'

'Do as yer muvver tells yer,' Reg warned. Turning to Brian he added 'Anyway mate, I've been meanin' to say, 'bout time you took a bleedin' bath, smell yer comin', I can.'

'Reg!' chided Trace.

'Well, I ain't wrong, am I?'

The otter family found Brian a safe inlet in which to bathe.

'I'll keep an eye on the silly bugger.' assured Reg. 'And I'll make sure he washes his todger an all,' he joked, with an advisory look directed at his boys.

**

The fractious spring was at an end. Peace and tranquillity returned to riverbank, field, and wood. The long, hot summer days drifted by gently like the puffed-white cumulus above.

There were picnics by the river for the now, firm friends, Trevor, Taupe, Stan, and Brian and they were often joined by Reg and his family too. They would lay on the bank, looking up at the infinite blue in mutual silence, lost in their own thoughts.

The water vole was seldom without a smile playing at the corner of his mouth now. If it ever faded, then it was when he thought of friends departed, notably Quincy. In these moments, as if by instinct, his friend Stan would squeeze his paw. The vole's smile would broaden when he thought of the small family of water voles who had taken up residence nearby. No longer would he and Stan be the last of the swimming-rats.

Taupe would allow Brian to take her hand when no animal was looking, and she would think on the season to come, the young would have her brains and beauty, she considered, and they would have their father's bravery and strength. *'Fort dans le bras, et épais dans la tête.'* She smiled, she liked this idiom – strong in the arm and thick in the head. Perhaps, she further considered, what was more important, was her luck in finding her – *petit cretin* – as she affectionately termed him, for after all, he was a kindly soul.

On very hot days, they would all doze in the dappled shade beneath the willows. They would listen to the wind rustle the leaves on high. 'Listen,' Stan would whisper. 'Listen. That is the sound of the ocean pulling at the shingle.'

Where had he been? Perhaps, one day, he would say.

Of Georges Montgolfiere, he remained only as a statue. A visionary perhaps, a catalyst, certainly. Nature had put right what had been done wrong, and he had been subsumed by it. Perhaps that is what he would have wanted.

THE END

Printed in Great Britain
by Amazon